Books by Carol Lea Benjamin

FALL GUY
THE LONG GOOD BOY
THIS DOG FOR HIRE
THE DOG WHO KNEW TOO MUCH
A HELL OF A DOG
THE WRONG DOG
LADY VANISHES

And coming soon in hardcover

WITHOUT A WORD

FALL GUY

A RACHEL ALEXANDER MYSTERY

CAROL LEA BENJAMIN

AVON BOOKS
An Imprint of HarperCollinsPublishers

This is a work of fiction. Names, characters, places, and incidents are products of the author's imagination or are used fictitiously and are not to be construed as real. Any resemblance to actual events, locales, organizations, or persons, living or dead, is entirely coincidental.

AVON BOOKS
An Imprint of HarperCollins*Publishers*
10 East 53rd Street
New York, New York 10022-5299

Copyright © 2004 by Carol Lea Benjamin
Excerpt from *Without a Word* copyright © 2005 by Carol Lea Benjamin
ISBN: 0-06-053900-3
www.avonmystery.com

First Avon Books paperback printing: July 2005
First William Morrow hardcover printing: September 2004

Avon Trademark Reg. U.S. Pat. Off. and in Other Countries, Marca Registrada, Hecho en U.S.A.
HarperCollins® is a trademark of HarperCollins Publishers Inc.

Printed in the U.S.A.

10 9 8 7 6 5 4 3 2 1

For Mary Divya Joubert,
no one was ever lost on a straight road

The first stroke is the final stroke; there are no touch-ups.

—MICHAEL GREEN

FALL
GUY

CHAPTER 1

When I was little, my father once told me that during the war, the one after the one they said would end all wars, he used to kneel at the window in the dark and scan the night sky for enemy planes. You knew who the enemy was back then. You knew where he lived, too. Even so, and even though the war was fought on enemy soil, as their countries were called, it was still awfully scary. So if something woke you in the middle of the night, or if you just couldn't sleep, you couldn't help it, you'd find yourself at the window, watching the sky and wondering *what if*.

When I began to cry, he put his arm around me and pressed me close. I could smell his aftershave and feel the smoothness of his white shirt against my skin. "Just listen to your mother," he said, "and you'll be safe."

Like my father so many years ago in what now seems like a simpler time, in what now seems like another world altogether, I, too, can't help watching the sky and wondering *what if*. Only now, you watch in broad daylight. And now I know for sure that the terrible things you worry about are almost never the ones that happen.

As it turned out, I never did worry about the possible death of Timothy O'Fallon. Had it made the news, it might have been on one of those days when I never bothered to pick up the paper from where it landed when the delivery person shoved it through an opening in the wrought-iron gate that leads to my cottage. If not for the phone call, late the following day, I might never have heard about it at all. And even then, even when the call came, somehow, I am sorry to say, I didn't recall the name. But now everything's different. Now I know something else for sure, that no matter what happens, no matter how much time passes, I won't forget it a second time.

"This is the part of the job I hate most," the detective said, "giving people bad news."

The moment that followed seemed eons long as I held my breath, waiting.

"Timothy O'Fallon is dead," he said. And then, "I'm sorry for your loss," his voice full of grief, as if it were his loss, too.

"Who?" I asked, feeling nothing at first but relief. Not someone I loved, not a death that would crush my heart, not even anyone I knew.

So why was I being notified?

"Timothy O'Fallon," he repeated. "He was found dead early yesterday."

"I don't know any Timothy O'Fallon," I said into the phone. "I don't understand."

He asked my name again, repeated my address.

I told him yes to both, that was me.

"You're right across the street then?"

"Yes," I said, "I am."

"If it's not too late for you, Ms. Alexander, would you mind walking over?"

I looked at my watch, the hands glowing an eerie green in the dark. It was ten-thirty. "Sure," I said, "that's okay." Not so sure that it was.

"I can show you the will," he said. "We have a copy here."

"His will?" I asked, slipping one foot into the sandal I'd kicked off near the front door.

But even then, even after I'd been told that a Timothy O'Fallon had designated me as executor of his will, I drew a blank. It wasn't until ten minutes later, when I was walking up the pea-soup-green back staircase to the detectives' squad room at the precinct across the street and up the block from where I live that it came back to me. I'd paused a moment at the top of the stairs to collect my thoughts. Dashiell, the pit bull I'd "liberated" from a contemptible slime who'd planned to raise him to be a fighting dog, stopping, too, looking up at me to see if there was something that needed his attention, something I wanted him to do. Gently placing my hand on the top of his boxy head, I found it wet from a dripping air conditioner we'd passed under on the way. That's when I remembered the man who'd only said a single sentence to me, and that a world of time ago.

Detective Michael Brody got up when I walked into the squad room, but stayed where he was. There was a chair at the side of his desk and I sat, Dashiell sliding to a down right next to me without being asked. Brody glanced at him, then looked back at me, thanking me for coming so quickly. He picked up his ashtray, a Mount Saint Helens full of crushed butts, dumped it into his wastebasket and then put it on the far side of the desk to make room for the will. He placed that in front of me, taking a cigarette out of the rumpled pack in front of him, pulling the book of matches out from under the cellophane.

"You were never given a copy of this?"

I shook my head.

"And you don't remember meeting him?"

"Actually I do. I remembered on the way here."

I looked down, to where his finger pointed, page three, paragraph four.

"I appoint my dear friend Rachel Kaminsky Alexander"—my address followed—"to be my Executor under this Last Will and Testament."

"I don't get it. I hardly knew him." Wondering how he knew my full name, while Brody watched me, waiting, his cop's face not giving anything away.

"I did some pet therapy, after 9/11. That's how I met him."

"Crisis response, down at Ground Zero?" His face screwed up, what I'd said not making any sense to him.

"It was right here in the neighborhood, a post-traumatic stress men's group, on West Eleventh Street at the church. Maybe you saw the signs? The psychologist leading the group called me in because the men weren't talking."

I waited a moment to see if he'd react. He didn't. He wasn't talking either.

"Once Dashiell was there, the men began to speak, about how they couldn't get by what had happened, not even enough to fake it, how they were having trouble sleeping, how they couldn't think of a reason to go to work, call a friend, get out of bed." Thinking of the simplicity of it, the change that happens when a dog is there, puts his head in your lap, lets you know whatever it is you have to say, it's okay with him.

"That's where you met Tim? In this group?"

Tim?

Timothy, the shrink had called him, trying to get him to talk about why he was there, first names only in the group, including me. But even though I was a volunteer, I'd been given the professional courtesy of getting the list of names, last names on the list, the list somewhere with my pet-therapy files.

I nodded. "We figured he'd lost someone in the attack, but he never said so. He never said a word. And he surely never asked me to do *this*"— now my finger pointing to the will.

The phone rang and Brody picked it up, turning his back. I picked up the will and turned it back to the first page, to the beginning. "I, Timothy William O'Fallon . . ."

How had this come to pass, a man I didn't know asking this of me? He'd show up early every week and take the same seat in the circle, facing the courtyard. Hands in his lap, back straight, he'd listen but not contribute. There'd been only one time O'Fallon had spoken. It was on the last day. When nothing else had worked, not direct questions, not encouragement from the other men, not the stories they told, stories that could tear your heart to pieces, the room so full of grief and tears, I'd tried the last thing I knew to do, asking an unresponsive person for help with the dog. Doing this work, I'd told him during the break, a dog picked up a heavy burden of stress. I asked if he'd take Dashiell out for a minute or two, let him just be a dog. He'd taken the leash and gone out into the courtyard, Dashiell following along behind him. He went to the other side of the planters that divided the yard and he must have crouched down because when I looked, all I could see was Dashiell's tail, slowly stirring the wind. When they came back in, I'd thanked him and taken Dashiell back to my seat. Then I reached down to touch Dashiell and he was wet, his head and neck soaked with O'Fallon's tears. It was at the end of that last meeting that he'd spoken to me, just a sentence, but not in the group. We were outside then, where no one else could hear him. "You seem like a very kind person," he'd said. It seemed too trivial to repeat to the detective now that O'Fallon was dead, just a lonely man's way of saying thank you, nothing more.

What if, in fact, he *had* asked for this favor back then? How could I have said no? If he'd asked a perfect stranger to do something so intimate for him, didn't that mean he had no one else?

Brody hung up the phone and turned back to me. "You were saying Tim never asked you to be the executor of his estate."

"That's right."

"And that you met him because he attended

this group where you and the dog did pet-assisted therapy?"

I nodded.

"That's what you do, for a living?" he asked.

"No, it's volunteer work. It's just something I do."

He was waiting for more.

"I'm a researcher," I told him, the way I always explained what I did for a living, unless I knew that the person asking was looking for what I really did. Saying I earned my living as a private investigator made civilians paranoid and cops contemptuous. It was way more information than I wanted Detective Brody to have. "Freelance," I added.

He was still waiting.

"And before that, I was a dog trainer." I left it at that. He was a detective. He could figure out the connection himself.

"And Tim was there in a professional capacity as well, to answer questions, offer . . . ?"

"No, Detective. He was there as a participant."

"You're saying Tim went to a *civilian* group?"

"You mean he was . . . ?" Stopping mid-sentence, the air in the squad room suddenly feeling very cold.

"Twenty-one years on the job, detective for the last sixteen."

He sat back, putting more space between us.

I touched my left leg. Dashiell sat. I reached for his collar, the small brass tag in my fingers now, my last name and phone number on it, some people thinking it was his name, calling him Alexander. No trick at all, Detective O'Fallon digging up my full name and address, not after being alone with Dashiell that last day.

"How did he die, Detective? Was it in the line of duty?" There'd been nothing in the paper. Unless, of course, there had and I'd missed it.

"An accident, Ms. Alexander. A very tragic accident."

"A car accident?"

"No, ma'am, an accident in the home."

I nodded. "And what sort of accident are we talking about?" Like a lawyer, knowing the answer before I asked the question.

Brody looked away for just a moment. When he looked back at me, for just a flicker, I saw the man, not the cop, in his eyes. He held up his left hand, the thumb pointing to the wall behind him, the pointer directed toward the ceiling, the other fingers curled into his palm.

"An accident while cleaning his service revolver?"

This time *he* nodded.

Reputation protected, department protected, insurance and benefits protected. Or was I being too cynical?

Brody was looking at Dashiell. "Just having him there, is that how it works? Or does he have to actually do something?"

But before I got the chance to answer him, Dashiell stood and put his head in Brody's lap. Brody let his hand rest on top of Dashiell's neck for a moment, then he finally lit that cigarette. We sat there for what seemed like a very long time, the smoke curling slowly upward, thinning out and spreading wide as it rose, neither of us saying a word.

CHAPTER 2

Walking back down the stairs from the detectives' squad room, I had something I didn't have an hour and ten minutes earlier. I had a job I didn't want and the document to go along with it. I had turned down Brody's offer to "see me home," a quaint way to put it, I thought, but I had been unable to turn down O'Fallon's postmortem request that I see to his estate, perhaps because he was no longer around to make an alternate choice. I knew that most wills had a second choice, in case the first person named could not, or would not, do the job. O'Fallon's will didn't. There was only me.

Carrying a manila envelope containing the Last Will and Testament of Timothy O'Fallon, his wallet, address book and a set of keys to his apartment, I walked Dashiell through the lonely streets of Greenwich Village. While I thought my own thoughts, silently, he read the evening news found on trees, mailboxes, hydrants, radial tires and garbage bags left at the curb to be collected in the morning, and filed his own report in each place. The hum of air conditioners was our music, an occasional dog walker our only company.

When we got back to West Tenth Street, I looked up at the grimy windows of the precinct. Though the lights were still on, the place looked deserted. I unlocked the wrought-iron gate that kept the back cottage where I lived safe from the rest of the world—or so I liked to think—walking down the tunnel into the dark garden, then sitting on the steps that led to the door of the small brick cottage where I'd been living for five years.

Brody said he could meet me at O'Fallon's apartment the following afternoon at four for a quick look. Then he'd have to reseal it until it was officially released. I'd helped settle my mother's affairs after she'd died, but that was different. In that case, my sister and I had wanted all the things that had sentimental value, my sister more than me. She was more of a saver, a collector. And she had a bigger house, and children who might one day want to have some of their grandparents' possessions. I mostly wanted odd things, some of little worth. I'd taken the small wooden box my mother had kept on top of her dresser which held the costume jewelry she let me play with when I was a child, a pair of candlesticks, in case of a blackout, some books of poetry, a silver bracelet with a heart dangling from it, a gift to her from my father the year before he'd died, and photographs, lots and lots of photographs.

What would I do with O'Fallon's possessions with no family or friends to want them? What do you do with pictures of generations of O'Fallons, with army dog tags, assuming he'd been in the army, with the lamp he kept near his bed, his favorite books, his music? Would I know what his intentions were, since it was now my job to carry them out? The most obvious things would be spelled out in the will, how and where he'd chosen to be buried, who would be the recipient of his money and his valuables. But beyond that, what would I find, how much would I come to understand, deconstructing the life of a person I barely knew? And after I tossed the milk and butter, the mayonnaise and the mustard from his refrigerator, packed up his clothes and took them to Housing Works, donated his books to the library, then what? When nothing was left of the things he'd owned and the life he'd lived, who would remember Detective Timothy William O'Fallon? Would that be my job, too?

"You don't have to do this," Brody had told me. "The law doesn't require—"

I'd raised a hand to stop him. He seemed to be doing more than letting me off the hook. He seemed anxious for me to turn it down, to turn it over, perhaps, to his colleagues at the precinct. But I'd made up my mind at the top of those stairs. I don't know if it was stubborn resolve or curiosity. Whatever it was, I was not to be moved.

I went inside and opened the envelope, slipping out O'Fallon's wallet first. It was years old and worn. I held it in my hand before opening it, feeling the softness of the leather and the weight in my hand, as he would have felt it in his pocket. There was no money in it. I dumped the contents of the envelope onto my coffee table, spread it out and picked up the property clerk's invoice, a list of what had been removed from the deceased's apartment along with the body. Item number one: one-dollar bills U.S. currency; quantity, one; cash value, one dollar. Item number two: five-dollar bills U.S. currency; quantity, one; cash value, five dollars. And so on. It turned out that according to the property clerk's invoice, there'd been fifty-six dollars in O'Fallon's wallet. The wallet was listed as number seven. There'd been sixteen items vouchered for safekeeping. The money would be released to me upon written request. Everything else seemed to be in the envelope—his credit cards, no longer in the wallet but in a separate small manila envelope, all neatly slashed from the bottom left corner to near the upper right one. I flipped through them—Amex, Visa, Discover, a Chase bankcard. No shield in the envelope. Nor was it on the list. No mention of a gun, or handcuffs, either, or anything else that would revert to the Department. I left the list where I could see it, going back to the wallet. The credit cards had all been removed but the photos had not. They were old and faded, the colors no longer true, the haircuts and clothes from decades earlier. Five young boys, one young girl. In some of the snapshots they were together. In others, they were in smaller groupings, or alone. O'Fallon's driver's license was in the envelope with the credit cards. I took that and held it next to the photos, looking at them for a long time.

On his driver's license, renewed a month earlier, the forty-four-year-old O'Fallon's face was unanimated, the way it was in the group where I'd met him. Stony. If he was one of those kids in the pictures he carried with him, he'd not only aged, he'd changed. But didn't we all do that?

There was a picture of me, at two, propped on the mantel of my fireplace, taken when my family had moved to the apartment where I grew up. I had the same unruly brown hair, the same fair skin, but the eyes had changed. When I became a dog trainer, years before, I often stood between a dog and death, his last stop before a one-way trip to the pound. I almost always succeeded in saving the dog's life. But now that I am a PI, in almost every case, by the time I am hired it's too late for heroes. Someone is already dead and all I can achieve is the cold comfort of justice. It holds me fast, this work, sometimes I'm not sure why, but there's a price. If anyone looks carefully, the cost is visible, the way it had been with Timothy O'Fallon—the evidence of the weight he carried in his eyes, too.

I looked at the pictures again—teenaged kids, hair all slicked down, dressed up and looking uncomfortable but grinning at the camera anyway. In one of the shots, one of the older boys had put two fingers behind the head of one of the younger ones, making horns, goofing around. They were happy kids, full of life. Three of the boys and the little girl had round faces, fair hair, light eyes, pale skin. They probably had freckles, too, but the pictures were too faded to tell. The other two boys had military-looking short hair, dark, and dark eyes.

I thought one of those redheads might be O'-Fallon, picking up the driver's license again to see if I could tell which one. But in that picture, the picture of the forty-four-year-old man, the cop, the hair was faded, the round face had begun to soften, the eyes looked dead sad, or just plain dead. His eyes were nothing like the merry eyes of any of those kids, kids without the weight of responsibility driving them into the ground, kids who didn't know what cops see, things, even now, the rest of us can't imagine. No wonder O'-Fallon grew up to look so grim.

O'Fallon's apartment keys were in a little envelope. I could feel them without opening it. There was an address book, too, small and worn, like the wallet. I figured a lot of names would be crossed out, people who had moved or married or divorced or died. Why should his address book be different from anyone else's?

I read the will next, expecting to find it dull reading, the same legalese as any other will I'd ever read, reiterating the laws, instructions that any debts be paid, indicating a burial place, a few pages of dry and boring language with no surprises anywhere. But that was far from the case. I checked the time, then picked up the phone and dialed the precinct.

"Now I really don't get why my name is on this will," I told Brody when he picked up his phone. "O'Fallon has family. He left his estate to his sister. Why didn't he name her the executor of his will?"

For a moment he didn't say anything. Then: "He must have had his reasons."

"He must have," I said, picking up the address book, holding it in my other hand. "Did you notice that this will is brand-new? It's dated two days before he died."

"Yes, ma'am."

Why wouldn't he notice? Noticing things was what he did for a living. I took a deep breath, a suggestion in an article I'd read on anger management. It didn't work. I was feeling duped, stuck with one of life's most unpleasant jobs when it should have fallen to a blood relative. Which, obviously, he had. I felt as if I was shouting now in my own head, if that's even possible.

"Did you ever meet his sister?" I asked. "Did he talk about her? Did she . . . ?" Too loud, too fast, too everything.

"Tim had just lost his mother. Perhaps that's why he redid his will. For an unmarried man, it wouldn't be unusual to leave his estate to his mother. And then, when she'd passed on, to change the will and leave the estate to his sister. And, no, I never met her and I don't recall Tim ever mentioning her. Did you want the Department to do the notification? Is that why you called?"

I took another deep breath, absorbing the news. A stressful job, a code of silence, a recent death in the family, an accidental suicide. Giving Brody the benefit of the doubt. For now.

"No, no, I'll take care of it," I said, thinking about what he'd said earlier when he'd notified me. But I hadn't lost a loved one. I'd lost an acquaintance I barely remembered. That wouldn't be the case for the call I had to make. "As I understand it," I said, "it's part of my job."

"Is there anything . . . ?"

"No, Detective. I'll see you tomorrow then, on Horatio Street."

"Ms. Alexander?"

"Yes?"

"You have the keys. I just want to remind you that the apartment—"

"It's sealed. I understand." Impatient. Still feeling I'd been had.

Was that what pushed him over the line, I wondered, the loss of his mother on top of the stress of the job? But why leave everything to his sister? What about those other red-haired kids from a couple of decades ago, and the two with dark hair? Didn't he want them to know he loved them, too? Wasn't that part of what leaving a will was all about in the first place, especially when the estate would probably be modest?

I opened the address book next and looked up Mary Margaret O'Fallon's phone number. It was an 845 exchange. The address was in Piermont, one of those charming little towns along the Hudson River, in Rockland County, only minutes away from where my own sister lived. He'd left her his money, but he'd never mentioned her. Maybe he and Brody weren't all that close. Though, from the look on Brody's face, that didn't seem to be the case.

I picked up one of the pictures of the little girl, all by herself in this one, smiling shyly at the camera with her head cocked to one side, clearly a kid who had just been told to smile, not one caught in the act of doing so. Most of the pictures of me as a kid looked very much the same way, my father telling me to smile, the smile in the picture overly large and patently false. But parents preferred that to a frown. What did it say about them if you weren't happy all the time? Still, you could almost see how badly I wanted to get away from the camera. Mary Margaret, too.

Mary Margaret O'Fallon, it said. Did that mean she'd never married? Perhaps that was why she'd been left all the money. There were two other O'Fallons on the page, a Kathleen O'Fallon, at the same address, and Dennis. He'd been listed in Woodcliff Lake, New Jersey, that address and phone number, and the name Iris, lightly crossed out, so that you could still read what was there. Underneath, there was an address and phone number in Paramus, a small *w* after it. Dennis's work number.

I looked through the rest of the book, paging through from A to Z. There weren't many names. He didn't seem to have had many friends. I noticed, though, that there were several names with addresses in a row, all on Horatio Street where he lived. Helene and David Castle, and penciled in next to their names, Emma. Then Rob Rosen, and penciled in next to his name, Kevin. And Jin Mei Lin, and next to her name, Yin Yin. Were they all pets, all the ones whose names had been penciled in?

There was the name of a lawyer, the same one who had done the will. There were two doctors listed, one dentist. There were phone numbers for three different liquor stores and one for a Chinese takeout. And there were a handful of other names, men's names, throughout the book: Freddie Ainsley, Dale Benson, Parker Bowling, Chuck Evans, Tommy Finletter, Lanny Smith and Spike Zaslow. They all seemed to have one thing in common. There were no addresses or phone numbers listed, though one of them, Parker Bowling, had a cell phone number alongside his name. There were even some first names without last names in the book, Guy and Sonny and Craig. So what did that mean—that O'Fallon had been gay? Did any of the names, I wondered, belong to the young men in the pictures, and if they didn't, why not, and where were those kids today?

I did one more thing before going to bed. I went up to my office and pulled out the file on the pet-assisted-therapy group where I'd met Timothy O'Fallon. There were very few comments next to each name, just a word or two that might help me help them the following week. I'd put my keys in John's pocket, for example, when it was clear he needed a little push, a push he got literally from Dashiell when I asked him to find what I'd hidden. And after that session I'd written "3," to indicate that it was the third of our six meetings when John spoke, and "Mother," to let me know who it was that John had lost, as if I would forget. I'd also written, "More?" I had the feeling that John had only given us part of the story, that he was holding something back. But there was nothing further, not in the group and not in my notes.

The notes were cryptic, but even now, all this time later, they were enough to remind me of what was important.

Larry's sister had worked for Cantor Fitzgerald and he'd had a fight with her on September 7. They hadn't made up. Brian's brother had been a firefighter. His dad, too. He'd said he should have been one, that he should have died, the way they did, when the Towers collapsed. And Timothy O'Fallon hadn't told us why he'd come, why he seemed so tired, why his eyes looked so sad. Next to his name there was only one comment, "NR," for no response.

CHAPTER 3

As soon as I woke up, I called Mary Margaret O'Fallon to give her the sad news. I got an answering machine and left a message, just my name and number and a request that she call me back. I didn't say what the call was about. I thought, with this kind of news, the least she deserved was a live voice at the other end of the phone.

I tried Dennis O'Fallon next. I got a message for him too, this one letting me know that I'd reached a Lexus dealership that didn't open until eleven. I looked at the crossed-out number for Dennis and Iris O'Fallon and decided to wait and call Dennis at eleven.

I had nearly the whole day before I was due to meet Michael Brody on Horatio Street and only one appointment before then, a pet-therapy visit with Dashiell at two at the Westside Nursing Home on West Thirteenth Street. I opened the small envelope and dumped the keys into my hand, feeling how hard and cold they were. There were only three keys—outer door, door to the apartment, mailbox key. I'd been warned not to go into the apartment without Brody. But I hadn't been asked not to walk by, and my dog needed a walk anyway.

I tried Mary Margaret one more time before leaving the house, just in case she'd been in the shower when the phone rang or down in the basement putting up the wash. I didn't leave a message this time, hoping she wouldn't see the number show up again on Caller ID. I didn't want to alarm her, I thought to myself, then realized how ridiculous that was.

Walking north on Greenwich Street, toward Horatio, I thought of something else that struck me as ridiculous, or at least outdated, the way the cops kept everything so close to the vest. I thought about O'Fallon at the group, not saying a word about what was bothering him, about what drove him to come week after week and sit among us. Sit he did, but silently, cops only talking to other cops about what they saw, not sharing their feelings with anyone. Did just being there help O'Fallon? I wondered.

And when was their habit of silence going to change? Clearly, the system was failing, or there wouldn't be so many cops having tragic accidents, as Brody had put it. It was failing the public as well. Despite the determined effort to protect us, no one was feeling safe anymore. Not anyone. I stopped and turned around to look downtown, as I often did now, to see what was no longer there.

We had breathed in the fine particles of debris, tasted it on our tongues, washed it from our eyes, combed it from our hair. We'd walked on the ashes of the dead—even here in Greenwich Village, a mile and a half north of Ground Zero. And we'd seen the Towers crumble and fall hundreds and hundreds of times—at the moment it happened, then on television, perhaps forever in our sleep.

So why were the police still protecting us from the truth, everything out there now, on television, on the Internet, on the nightly news? The news cameras zoom in on the bloody stains on the sidewalk after a murder, honing in on exactly what used to be avoided. *The New York Times* prints lists of body parts, as yet unidentified, found at the World Trade Center disaster site and now in the hands of the medical examiner: a left foot, a ring finger, a head, for God's sake.

True, the cops still saw things the public didn't. And they saw them on a day-to-day basis, a steady diet of the worst mankind has to offer. But didn't their protection of us, their code of silence make the job even more stressful for them than it already was?

Mary Margaret had just lost her mother. Now I had to tell her she'd also lost her brother. Would she believe the death was accidental? Was there any possibility it was?

All of a sudden I was glad neither of Tim's siblings had been available to answer the phone. It would make more sense to speak to Mary Margaret or Dennis O'Fallon after I'd seen O'Fallon's residence, after I had a better idea if it was just my cynicism that made me disbelieve the story Brody had offered up, cynicism and the knowledge that police suicide is one of the more hideous side effects of the job. In protecting us, the public, from what they see, not exactly appropriate dinner-party conversation when you think about it, they become all the more vulnerable to depression, despair and suicide.

Was that why O'Fallon had come to the post-traumatic-stress group? Not because he'd lost someone in the attack. Not even because of the way the attack changed all our lives. But because of the stress he'd accumulated as part of his job, the steady diet of witnessing horror and keeping it a secret?

Tim had lived on the south side of Horatio Street in one of two identical brick houses. I checked the numbers. Coming from Greenwich Street, Tim's building was the closer of the two. I went up the three concrete steps to the outer door, tried the knob and found it locked, pretty much the way it is in New York City unless there's a doorman to filter visitors. The bells were outside, to the left of the door. The mailboxes were inside, in the tiny vestibule. The mailman could get in using the front-door key that was kept in a special lockbox, the lockboxes themselves all supplied by the post office, all using the same key. I took out Tim's keys and opened the first door, checking the names on the mailboxes. Brody, after all, had not told me not to do that. I opened Tim's mailbox and took out his mail. I hadn't been told not to do that either.

Tim lived on the first floor. I looked through the inner glass door and saw doors on either side of the hall, the one to my right with a rectangular seal on it. The hallway was wider in the center, to accommodate the staircase to the basement below and to the upper floors. Beyond that, at the far end of the narrow hallway, there was another door, this one made of small glass panes and without tape on it. I could see, beyond the glass, a table with a large green umbrella over it and some plants. I hesitated for a moment, then tried the inner door and found that the same key opened it as well.

Dashiell and I walked into the quiet, dimly lit hallway. We stopped for a moment in front of the sealed door, Dashiell moving his head and tasting the air. Then we walked past the staircase and found a second sealed door. At one point, there must have been four separate apartments on this floor, two on each side, otherwise there'd only be one entrance. This time Dashiell put his nose at the bottom of the door where there's space between the door and the sill, space where delivery-men shove menus into your apartment, supers slide in rent bills or neighbors leave notes. I could hear the whoosh of his breath as he blew out air to cleanse his nose and sucked in the odors from the apartment, his tail straight down, moving rapidly.

I tried the knob to the garden door and found it locked, tried the same key once again and pushed the glass door open, standing on the threshold of a double-width communal garden. There was the sound of running water and birds singing. I could smell something sweet, and something nasty, a chemical odor I wouldn't expect to find in a garden. Dashiell sneezed twice, then held his nose high and pulled in the scene. I stepped out.

She was off to my right, sitting on a little stool in front of her easel, a straw hat covering part of her thin, lined face. At first she didn't look up. I watched her dip the tip of her brush onto the palette she held in her left hand and leave a flick of color on the painting. She leaned back to appraise the change and nodded her head. Her lips were moving, as if she were talking to herself, but I couldn't make out the words. Then she turned to where Dashiell and I were standing and she frowned.

"This private garden," she said, getting up, the palette and brush still in her hand. "How you get in here? Netty leave door unlocked again? Door unlocked too many time. This no good. Not safe."

"I have the keys," I told her, staying where I was, opening my hand so that she could see them. She looked frightened. "I have Timothy O'Fallon's keys. I'm the executor of his will."

"Talk louder," she said. "You're mumbling."

"I'm the executor of Detective O'Fallon's estate," I repeated.

"Are you family?" Head back, squinting at me from under her hat.

I shook my head. "No, I'm . . ." Not knowing how to finish the sentence.

"You're not family." Pointing at me with the paintbrush.

"No."

"I didn't think so. You don't look like him. So what? You were his friend?" Pleased with her detective work. But before I could confirm or deny, she bowed her head, once again hiding her face. "I'm sorry. I don't mean to be rude."

I took a chair and pulled it away from the white table with the green umbrella and sat, thinking that that might put her more at ease.

"Were you a friend of his?" I asked.

"His neighbor." She pointed to the windows behind her with her brush. "He was a very nice man. A good man." She nodded. "A sad man," she said.

"What do you mean?" I asked.

"I was painting here on Sunday morning. I heard him crying. His mother had just died. Her funeral was the day before. On Saturday. He was very, very sad. I went back inside to give him privacy. I didn't want him to see that I heard him crying. He wouldn't have liked that."

I got up, dropping the leash and leaving Dashiell at the table and offered my hand. "Rachel Alexander," I said. "I'll be spending some time working here, settling Tim's estate."

"Jin Mei Lin," she said.

She carefully put the brush down on the tray that held her paints and put her hand in mine. It was small and dry, and standing there, I towered over her.

"You're a good person to do this job," she said. "It's too much grief for most people."

Then her small dark eyes left me and settled on Dashiell.

"He doesn't bite," I said, feeling silly as I did, but it was the question nearly everyone asked. Despite the clownlike black patch over his right eye and the Charlie Chaplin mustache, both standouts against his white coat, he was, after all, a pit bull. Carrying a lot of baggage was an unfortunate part of his birthright.

"I see that," Jin Mei said.

It was then that I stepped closer and looked at what she was painting. On the vertical board of the easel, she had taped a photo of a German shepherd, her forehead pleated with concern, her eyes dark and intelligent, her ears, instead of pointing toward the clouds, leaning toward each other, as if in conversation. Below, on the canvas, was the beginning of Jin Mei's portrait of the dog.

"Your dog's eyes are wise," she said, "not mean. She turned to look behind her, at the ruddy Abyssinian on the windowsill, her yellow eyes on Dashiell. "Yin Yin's a good judge of character. If she's staying there, this dog is not a problem."

"Have you lived here long?" I asked.

She nodded. "Detective O'Fallon, too. But not Parker." She wrinkled her nose. "Parker's one of the worst of all the men he took in. When he was out here"—she turned again and pointed to her window—"I went inside, made a cup of tea and waited for him to leave."

"Parker?" I asked.

I remembered a Parker in Tim's address book. Parker Bowling.

Jin Mei nodded. "He's not here now. The police took him out."

"He was arrested?"

She shook her head. "They took him out here, to the garden. They told him he had to go some-where else." She moved her hands as if shooing me away from her. "The detective told him he couldn't stay here because his name isn't on the lease."

"He was living here, this Parker? With Tim?"

"Tim always had someone living here, the men he helped. I already told you, he was a good man."

"Yes," I said, "you did," wondering why Detective Brody hadn't mentioned this Parker, wondering what it meant that O'Fallon had men live here that he was helping, trying really hard not to jump to conclusions. But this was Greenwich Village. And there were hardly any women's names in O'Fallon's address book.

"How long had Parker lived here?" I asked.

"Several months," she said. "No one liked him. He didn't talk to any of us." She swirled her hand around, indicating the whole garden. "Too important to talk to us." She pushed the tip of her nose up with one finger.

"He didn't talk to the neighbors?" I asked.

"Right. He'd come into the garden, sit in a chair, smoke a stinky cigarette, stare straight ahead. He never said, 'Good morning, Jin Mei. How are you today? How is Yin Yin?' Very unfriendly."

"Were you a little afraid of him, Jin Mei? Was that why you went inside when he came out here, because he was something worse than unfriendly?"

Jin Mei shrugged and picked up her brush. "I just didn't like him from day one."

"Was there something else, something he did, something other than his unfriendliness?" I asked.

But that part of our conversation no longer interested her. She dipped just the tip of the brush in white and made a tiny dot in each of the dog's eyes, bringing them to life. Then she put down her brush and took off her hat, smoothing her hair back from her face with both hands. Her hair was a dark, graphite gray, pulled back and coiled into a knot at the nape of her neck. Without the hat, I got a better look at her paper-thin skin the color of masking tape, the pleating near her small eyes, as dark as currants, the crisscrossing lines above her mouth. She looked to be in her seventies, but she might have been older.

Jin Mei pointed at Dashiell. "Would you like me to paint him, maybe for a special occasion? I'm very expensive," she said, "but I'm worth it."

CHAPTER 4

Sitting in the bar at Pastis, Dash next to the table with a bowlful of water, a bowl that matched the decor of the restaurant, I picked at my bacon sandwich as I began to open O'Fallon's mail. I wasn't sure of the procedure. I tried to remember what my sister and I did with my mother's bills, but that was different. We had been named signatories on Beatrice's checking account not long after she got sick.

I pulled an envelope from the bottom of the stack, turned it over and made a note to call O'Fallon's attorney, hoping that she would take care of paying the bills and dealing with most of the paperwork. I suspected I'd have more than enough to do sorting out O'Fallon's possessions and dealing with family and neighbors—grumbling neighbors, to judge by Jin Mei.

I wondered about Parker—who he was, where he was, and how O'Fallon had been helping him. I made a note to talk to the other neighbors. I'd ask Brody about Parker, too, and about the other men O'Fallon had helped.

Brody. As if he were about to tell me what he knew.

I flipped through O'Fallon's Con Ed bill, a packet of coupons for discounts, the envelope addressed to "Occupant," his rent bill, due in a little over a week, an L.L. Bean catalog and the letter I'd been making notes on. I turned it over. No return address. A perfect little handwriting, small and neat and ever so careful. There was only one uncharacteristic flourish. The tail on the *y* on Timothy turned back and underlined his name.

Opening his mailbox, it had never occurred to me that I shouldn't be taking his mail. I'd picked up the packet without looking at it, even the coupons and the catalog, and tossed them into the bag where I had the things I needed for Dashiell's pet-therapy visit. Now holding the square blue envelope, I wondered if I should be the one to open it. I put it down on the table and noticed I'd made a greasy thumbprint on the lower left corner. Too late to go back to Horatio Street and return it to the mailbox. Besides, Brody hadn't told me not to take the mail. He'd only told me not to use the keys to enter the apartment.

Curiosity.

I picked up the envelope, used my knife to slit it open and pulled out the folded sheet of blue stationery. I sniffed it first; no perfume. Then I opened the single fold and read the name. Maggie.

"I know what happened at Breyer's Landing," it said. "I was there. We have to talk."

I picked up the envelope and checked the postmark, Saturday, thinking how strange the mail was. You could mail something in Piermont and it would arrive in New York City in a day or two. You could mail something in Greenwich Village to someone three blocks away and it could take a week or longer to arrive.

I read the note again. Mary Margaret had mailed the note on Saturday, the day of their mother's funeral. The day before Tim died. The note seemed ominous, threatening. Or was that just my suspicious mind-set? But Tim had never seen it. So it couldn't have anything to do with anything.

Except my curiosity.

"I was there," she'd written. What could that mean?

At one, Dashiell and I went for a walk. It was hot but not beastly, and though there was no shade at this hour, there was a bit of a breeze. Whenever we could, we walked under sidewalk bridges to get out of the sun for a minute. Rain or shine, a dog's got to do what a dog's got to do, and before a pet-therapy visit, a long walk is a good idea.

Edna was sitting in her wheelchair near the front door, waiting. "He's here," she said, turning back to the others in the room, five really sad-looking people. "Our little friend is here."

"Our little friend" was the equivalent of calling women "hon" and guys "pal" when you couldn't remember their names. It was, I thought, a rather graceful save for an old lady suffering from senile dementia. Knowing what was coming, I made a graceful save of my own. I positioned myself behind Edna's chair before Dashiell got the chance to put his paws up on the seat, one on each side

of her frail, skinny legs, and lean forward to give
her a kiss.

"He loves me," Edna squealed.

"He does," I said from behind her. "Dashiell
loves his friend Edna."

She nodded. "Comes to see me every day," she
said.

"Once a week," I said, thinking I shouldn't
have corrected her, that, at this time, there was no
point in doing so.

"Tuesdays," Edna said, surprising both of us. "I
remembered he was coming today. I saved him
some of my lunch." Edna reached into her pocket
and took out a stalk of broccoli. That's when I noticed the grease stain on her pocket, like the one
I'd made on the envelope of Maggie O'Fallon's
letter, wondering if Edna had made grease stains
on things when she was younger, too, the way I
did. Did I like hanging out with animals because
it didn't matter to them—neat or careless, fat or
thin, rich or poor, it was all the same? Then I wondered if I'd end up alone, like Edna, someone vis-
iting me on Tuesdays with a friendly dog, making
ten minutes in my endless week bearable.

I opened my bag and pulled out Dashiell's
boar-bristle brush. A short-coated dog, he didn't
tangle if he wasn't brushed. And there was no difference in his appearance before and after. But he
loved the feel of the brush scratching along his
back, and the brushing was part of the ritual with
Edna, who'd had a stroke. She'd fished for the
broccoli with her right hand. My job was to make
sure she did the brushing with her left. Of course
Dashiell wasn't her only therapy, but he was her

favorite one. It's always easier to inspire someone
to pet or brush a dog than to do boring, repeti-
tious exercises while someone counted.

Marlene could still draw, and for her I'd
brought a pad and colored pencils. Her favorite
ritual was touching Dashiell as she drew him,
feeling the lines of his muscular body and the
way they related to each other and then translat-
ing them to paper. I felt the touching helped her
as much as her pride in the finished drawings,
which we'd always tack up on the bulletin board
in the dayroom.

Roger wanted a walk. As usual. I checked with
the nurse and was told it was okay. He held
Dash's lead and we walked over to Fourteenth
Street, where he stopped to say hello to the people eating at a coffee shop with outdoor seating:
two men holding hands across the table, a tiny
Yorkie on the blond one's lap; a couple talking
German who were nonplussed by Roger's greet-
ing; a man with copious tattoos reading the
paper, his eggs sitting untouched on the plate before him, one small semicircle missing from a tri-
angle of his buttered toast. On the steps of St.
Bernard's Church there was a homeless man talking on a cell phone. He and Roger greeted each
other and I thought how odd that was, that
someone talking on a cell phone would interrupt
his conversation to say hello to a stranger. But
when I looked back at him, once again absorbed
in his phone call, I noticed that it wasn't a cell
phone at all that he was holding to his ear. It was
an empty plastic bottle.

Going up the block holding Dashiell's leash,

Roger smiled at everyone. Some people got
sweeter when they got old, some angry at the
dirty trick life played on us, that we start life in
diapers, unable to care for ourselves, and sometimes end up the same way. What kind of a reward was this, I wondered, for a life well-lived,
for hard work, devotion to family, a contribution
to society? But for all I knew, half the people I vis-
ited at the home hadn't lived their lives that way.
Half of them may have been self-centered sons of
bitches from day one and stayed that way from
one set of diapers to the other. Meeting them the
way I did, I'd never know. Nor did it matter.
Doing pet therapy, what you saw was what you
dealt with. Even when snippets of the past were
revealed and acknowledged, Dashiell and I
worked in the moment, doing whatever was
needed at the time we were there.

I wanted more than that when it came to O'-
Fallon. I wanted to know him. There would be no
future, but I wanted to understand the past, wishing he had spoken up just once—would it have
killed him?—in the group where I met him. I
wished I had something more to go on other than
rumor, gossip, slanted opinions and the detritus
of his life; what, and whom, he'd left behind.

But how much could I get to know, coming in
as I had not late in the game but after it was
over—the people all gone, the lights out and the
stadium deserted? Without the presence of the
living, breathing man, how did I now expect to
get to know Timothy O'Fallon, to understand
why he did what he did and what may have been
going through his mind in the hours before his

death? Had it been just grief, or was there more to it?

As I left the Westside Nursing Home, feeling, as I always did, that I'd gotten far more than I'd given, I wondered if Brody had planned on telling me anything else. He seemed to parcel out the information only when he absolutely had to. I wondered if there was some way I could get him to open up, if not about a fellow officer, then about the man who had lived with him, what his relationship to O'Fallon had been and where, if Brody knew, this Parker person was now. But I'd failed to get O'Fallon to speak when I'd had the chance. Why, then, did I imagine I'd be any more successful with Michael Brody?

CHAPTER 5

Detective Michael Brody cut the first of two seals on the door closest to the entrance, then turned to face me.

"There was a man living here with Tim off and on for the past few months. He's been given your name and number, in connection with getting his possessions out of the apartment."

"Living here?" I asked. "With Tim?"

"Tim had taken him in, to give him a chance at cleaning up, getting his life going again."

"Cleaning up? You mean drugs and alcohol?"

Brody nodded, his face telling me he didn't exactly approve of Tim's decision in this case; no way would he, Brody, take a junkie into his home, be on the job twenty-four seven, no break ever.

"Seems an odd thing to do."

"Yes, ma'am," he said, his knife in his hand, one seal still going from the door to the frame, the air in the hallway still and warm. "But that was Tim's way."

"You mean he'd done that before?"

"Yes, ma'am. He had."

"Did it work?" I asked.

Brody slit the second seal. "There's not a terrific track record as far as that goes."

"You mean in rehabilitating drug addicts or in O'Fallon's attempt to rehabilitate addicts, one at a time?"

He took off his sunglasses and looked at me as if we were just meeting for the first time, as if he'd never laid eyes on me before. Perhaps, in fact, he hadn't.

Perhaps I hadn't looked at him either, concentrating on the information rather than the man, both then and now. But I didn't know that this was the time for a look-see, standing this close, tensed for what I would see when he opened the door, Brody looking right at me.

"I'm just telling you to be careful," he said. I could smell his last cigarette, the coffee he'd had at his desk or on the way here. And something else, something that triggered a memory I couldn't quite retrieve. A door opened on the floor above us but it didn't close and there were no footsteps either. Brody leaned closer. "Don't let him rush you," whispering now. "He's going to try. When you're ready to let him get his things, it might be a good idea to have your husband here with you, not be here alone."

"He's dangerous, this—what did you say his name was?"

"He's used a variety of street names. When he called it in, he told the responding officers his name was Parker Bowling. But he's also been known as Dick Parker, Richard Lee Bowling and Parker Lee."

"Is he a suspect?"

"There's been no crime."

The door upstairs closed. We heard the cylinder turn over, the security chain go on.

"I'm just letting you know that he's not a trustworthy individual, Mrs. Alexander. That's all I'm saying."

"It's Ms.," I told him, regretting it immediately. He'd been fishing and I'd taken the bait.

"Alexander's not your married name?" Glancing at the hand holding the leash.

"You said 'he called it in,' Detective. You mean the accident? Does that mean he was here when it happened?"

"Actually, no. He claims he went out early to meet a friend. When he came home a few hours later, he found Tim and called 911."

"He must have been pretty upset."

Brody nodded. "Yes, ma'am. Who wouldn't be?"

"Was he . . . ?"

Brody didn't seem to be listening. He reached into his pocket and took out a card, pulling out a pen and writing something on the back of it.

He was bigger than me, somewhat taller, lots more muscular, his jacket a little tight in the shoulders. I could see where his holster was, pushing at the fabric from underneath. Jacket and tie, I thought, even in the heat of summer. His neck was wide, but not like a football player's. His hair was a mousy shade of brown, cut short, standing up straight like newly mowed grass. When he looked up, I saw that his eyes were brown, but not that deep, dark brown that looks almost black. His were a more washed-out shade, like the freckles some dogs have on their chests and paws, but with flecks of green in it. Old eyes, older than the man. And there was gray at his temples, too, though he looked to be in his mid-forties, and gray in his whisk-broom mustache, trimmed neatly above the line of his mouth.

"I can be here with you when you decide to let Mr. Bowling come to collect his things." Very businesslike now. "If you'd rather not be here alone."

"I wouldn't be," I said.

He raised his eyebrows.

"I'll have Dashiell."

I looked down. Dashiell looked up and wagged his tail. Then he looked at the door to O'Fallon's apartment. I felt the same way. The hallway was starting to feel too small for two people and a large dog. There was no air circulating and the round fluorescent ceiling light made everything appear slightly green. Even Dashiell looked sickly in O'Fallon's hallway. Besides, if I was going to do this, I wanted to get started. I bent and began to unhook Dashiell's leash.

"Is this okay?" I asked.

"As long as he doesn't disturb anything."

"He won't," I told him, wondering what there was that Dashiell might disturb.

"How much time do I have today?"

"Whatever you need," he said, unlocking the door, both locks with the same key, and pushing it open. That was a New York trick—two locks to deter a would-be thief, only one key to carry. Brody stepped out of the way to let me go in first, but of course it was Dashiell who rushed ahead, walking onto the faded Oriental rug and stopping cold a moment later, his mouth open, swallowing the air.

I tasted the air, too. Something like Lysol. Whatever it was, it was overwhelming, used, I was sure, to mask another odor. Still, that was underneath the chemical smell, something metallic and gamy, a smell that brought the food I'd eaten a couple of hours earlier back up to my throat. I thought I could smell smoke, too, the stale odor you get in a place where someone has a long-term habit, or after a politically incorrect party, everything monitored nowadays, even your bad habits. I could see a few ashtrays from where I stood, emptied but not washed. But the odor was faint and I wasn't sure that was the source of the smell. It might have come from Brody, who was standing right behind me.

I stepped into O'Fallon's living room, a book-lined room with an old, worn, oversized, cloth couch with loose back- and side pillows, a plaid blanket lying over the back of it; an oak desk piled with folders and papers; framed photos on every inch of the walls. There were plants everywhere, too, some thriving, others having seen better days, like the couch. I noticed a plastic dinosaur in the dirt of one of the larger ones, an old corn plant that stood in a corner near the windows. There were books piled on the floor, stacks near the desk, and more near the old couch. There was a winter coat over the arm of the couch. What was that about in all this heat? Smack in the middle of the room, there was a gym bag, its contents bulging, the zipper half open. The Oriental rug

had a few worn spots, and in front of the couch a
flat patterned kilim lay on top of it, another small
rug in front of the daybed, which was against the
front wall, under the windows. There were a
small TV, a radio, an ancient teddy bear with
black buttons for eyes, all on one of the wider
bookshelves. A cool north light came in through
the shutters that covered the front windows, the
bottoms closed and latched, the tops partly open,
the light spilling through the slats making lines
on the carpet and up the wall of closets that divided this part of the apartment from the back.

Someone had done an amazing job, I thought.
Where was the blood spatter, the amoebalike
stain on the rug? Where was the shattered wall? I
looked at Brody. He was leaning against the wall
near the doorway, staring straight ahead. I decided not to ask him anything just yet. Perhaps
that was why the blanket was over the couch, I
thought. Or perhaps that was the reason for that
second rug in front of the couch, taken from the
entranceway and put there to cover the place
where O'Fallon's life had leaked from his body.

But that couldn't be. Dashiell had gone
nowhere near that rug, nor had he paid any attention to the couch. In fact, he was nowhere in
sight. Perhaps he was in the kitchen, at the south
end of the apartment, looking for water. And then
I heard him sneezing, clearing his nose for an
odor that interested him, the sound coming from
the west end of the kitchen, the part I couldn't
see. Perhaps the accident had occurred there, O'-
Fallon sitting at the kitchen table with his cleaning kit and his gun, distracted by grief, careless in

the most unforgiving way. Or maybe not. Maybe
he'd left a roast in the oven, I thought, chiding
myself silently for being irreverent.

Brody stayed where he was, near the doorway,
while I walked around, getting a feel for the
place. I sat at the desk for a while, looking
through the folders, all the paperwork I'd have
to deal with as soon as the apartment was unsealed. I picked out a recent bank statement, his
checkbook, a pile of bills that needed to be paid,
and found an envelope to put them in. Then I
noticed a briefcase leaning against the desk. I
put the envelope in that and put the briefcase
near the front door.

I looked at O'Fallon's books—lots of technical
manuals on crime-scene investigation, fingerprints, a book on interrogation, one on forensic
pathology. There was a shelf of true-crime books
as well—Ann Rule, Jack Olsen, James Ellroy,
Philip Gourevitch, and three about the O.J. Simp-
son case. There were books on learning Spanish, a
bartender's guide, some old photo albums. I
pulled one of the albums from the shelf and
slipped it into the briefcase, looking at the pictures on his walls as I walked around, all those
same kids whose photos were in his wallet. A
family man. A serious cop.

Then I went to the kitchen to empty the refrigerator of all the perishables. No need to wait and
make the cleanup any more difficult than it was
going to be. Dashiell was in the kitchen, standing
and staring at me, his brow lined. I felt the same
way. What the hell were we doing here in this
stranger's house?

Brody had moved to the kitchen with me, perhaps as a silent way to remind me he was waiting, to hurry me along. There was no sign of
violence in the kitchen either. I wondered if O'-
Fallon had used a small-caliber gun, if the bullet
that did the damage had never exited his body
and gone into a cabinet or the wall. You could
easily clean the floor in here. Maybe that was it.
Maybe that's why Dashiell had come into the
kitchen as soon as the door of the apartment was
opened.

   I took a bowl from the cabinet and filled it from
a Brita pitcher standing on the sink, putting it
down for Dashiell, but he never touched it. I
opened the cabinet under the sink and pulled out
a couple of D'Agostino bags for the garbage.
Then I took everything that would spoil, if it
hadn't already, out of the refrigerator and put it
all in the bags, tying the handles on top twice to
make sure things stayed put. Last, I took the watering can off the sill so that I could take care of
the plants. There were beer bottles on the sill,
too, and empties all over the counter and on the
table—beer cans, liquor bottles, wine bottles. The
sink had dishes in it and not just one night's dinner dishes. Pots and pans and plates and glasses
were piled almost to the tap. I imagined that
washing those would fall to me now. Unless I
merely pitched them out, too. I remembered that
when Lili and I were doing my mother's apartment, the longer we worked, the more readily we
threw things away, anxious to be done with it, to
breathe the air outside, eat pizza, make love, anxious not to be thinking about death.

I headed for the bathroom to fill the can in the bathtub. That's when Brody moved. Fast.

"Rachel, wait!" His hand on my arm. I turned to face him. "Don't go in there." Grim, he was. I turned again, to look at the closed bathroom door, then back to look into Michael Brody's brooding eyes.

"He was cleaning his gun in the bathroom?"

Brody took the watering can from my hand. "We can get water in the garden," he said. "There's a hose."

I was going to tell him we could use the Brita pitcher to water the plants. What difference did it make now? Instead, I said, "Why don't we just take the plants out."

I put the can back where it had been. Brody picked up an angel-wing begonia from the kitchen sill, its cheerful pink flowers at odds with the reason we were here. He put it on the round table near the second door and went back for another plant. Without speaking, we gathered the rest of the small plants. Then Brody opened the door, unlocked the garden door, propping each open with a plant. I began taking the small plants out while Brody went back to the living room for the big ones.

As I stood holding a coleus and a wandering Jew that for some reason were sitting on the counter instead of hanging from the two hooks in the ceiling over the sink, looking for a good place to put them down, I thought I might suggest the neighbors adopt them sometime before the cool weather settled in. That's when the garden door to the west opened and Jin Mei came out, Yin Yin in her arms.

"Oh, Rachel. You're back so soon."

And before I had the chance to tell her to shut up, wishing I could say it in Cantonese or Mandarin or whatever the hell she spoke so that I could get the message across surreptitiously, I could smell him behind me. Right behind me. There was Dashiell, too, going right up to Jin Mei, lifting his front paws off the ground so that he could stick his big nose in the little Abyssinian's butt.

"We're bringing Tim's plants out," I said. Not knowing what else to say. Not wanting to turn around and look at old stone face. "I thought perhaps the people who share the garden might take a few each at the end of the summer."

Jin Mei nodded. Her straw hat bobbed. Her mouth trembled and for a moment I thought she was going to cry. "Tim promised that when the time came for me to meet my ancestors, he would find a good home for Yin Yin. Now I have to find someone else to do that. It's good Tim's plants have you to make sure *they* get a good home."

When all the plants were placed out in the garden, with Jin Mei's considerable input, I walked back inside, Dashiell following, Brody bringing up the rear. I still hadn't looked him in the eye. I'd only glanced at the ground as he passed me with the corn plant, noticing that the shine on his shoes had gotten messed up by the wet soil in the communal garden. I wondered if he'd noticed. But he probably shined them every night, no matter what.

When he closed the kitchen door, I could no longer hear the birds singing. And there was that smell again, reminding me of where I was, and why. The only sound in the house was the cylinder of the lock clicking into place. And the sound of Dashiell, his nose welded to the bathroom sill.

I followed Brody to the couch. We sat on opposite ends, as far apart as possible without breaking off the arms. I didn't lean back on the blanket. Neither did he. As if death might be catching from the things the deceased had left behind. I thought I'd bring rubber gloves with me when I came back. I was sure I wouldn't be sorry to have them.

"The apartment should be unsealed by late afternoon tomorrow," he said. "Or Thursday at the latest. I'll call you tomorrow and give you the exact time. It'll be okay to"—he turned and looked toward the kitchen—"to use the bathroom then."

"I only came by this morning to see where it was," I said, my forehead as pleated as Dashiell's gets. "I could see the garden from the front door, so I walked through. By. And went out. That's how I met Jin Mei. I didn't go into the apartment, of course."

Brody nodded. "No problem."

So why was I acting as if I'd been sent to the principal's office? I wondered. He wasn't even wearing a uniform, so it couldn't be that.

"Isn't what Detective O'Fallon did a bit unusual," I said, "cleaning his gun in the bathroom rather than at his desk or at the table?"

"No, ma'am. Not particularly."

"But . . ."

"One could sit on the edge of the tub, have the kit on the vanity, avoid the chance of getting oil on the carpet."

One could? What the hell was that supposed to mean?

"So you're saying he was fastidious?"

"Ma'am?"

"Rachel'll do," I told him. "I was asking if he was ..." And then I stopped, shook my head, changed my mind. I wanted to know which way he fell after he was shot, whether he fell backward and hit his head—and did it matter at that point?—or if he crumpled forward, landing on the bath mat or the tile, the gun skittering across the floor, stopping when it hit the door. But what difference did any of that make now? He cleaned his gun at the desk, he cleaned his gun in the bathroom. The man was dead. I needed to inform his sister of his untimely demise, get her here to pick up whichever of his possessions she wanted to keep, settle his estate and get on with my life. I didn't need to be here torturing Brody with my questions. Except for one more.

"What's with the gym bag?" I asked. "Was he going somewhere? I mean, was he planning to, before?"

"That's Parker's. Or so he says. When the uniforms arrived, he was busy packing that with his things."

"Before they told him he had to leave?"

"Yes. And when one of the officers examined the contents of the bag, they found some things they suspected didn't belong to Mr. Parker."

"Such as?"

"A silver ashtray, some gold coins, two wristwatches, a small silver box with the initials 'T.W.O.,' and some clothes that may or may not have belonged to Parker."

"And the winter coat?"

"I imagine he'd planned on taking that as well."

"He and Tim were the same size?"

"Wouldn't matter to Parker."

"You mean he had sticky fingers? It was there, he'd take it."

"*Has* sticky fingers," he said. "Don't turn your back when he's here packing up. And don't be afraid to question anything he claims is his. Anything you're unsure of. Anything that has value."

What difference would it make if he took Tim's clothes? I thought. Tim didn't need them any longer. But for Brody, it was the principle of the thing. So I didn't bother to voice my opinion.

I stood and whistled for Dashiell. Brody stood as well. I picked up the briefcase and Dashiell's leash. Brody took the garbage bags. I walked out ahead of him but he didn't come right out. I waited on Horatio Street. I wasn't sure why. It seemed the polite thing to do.

When he came out, a few minutes later, I opened a garbage can for him and he dropped in the bags. He'd bagged the empties, tying the tops of the bags as I had. It sounded like an explosion when they hit the can.

"If there's anything else I can help you with, don't hesitate to call me. I put my cell phone number on the back of the card I gave you. Don't worry about the time. It's always on."

I took out one of my cards and gave it to Brody. "Same here," I said. "My cell phone number's on there, too, in case you think of anything else I should know."

I turned to leave, but curiosity got the best of me once again.

"Was he your partner, Detective?"

He blinked once.

"No, Ms. Alexander. He wasn't."

He pointed east, his eyebrows raised. I shook my head and pointed west. I'm sorry for your loss, I thought as I watched him head up the block. I was, too. For all the loss he saw.

Even though it was out of the way, I headed toward the river. I'd wanted to get away from Brody and his unspoken grief. And from O'Fallon's apartment. At the moment, I was wishing I weren't quite so curious or quite so stubborn.

Walking south along the Hudson, the breeze felt good on my face. Dashiell seemed to have forgotten the scents that had wafted toward him from under O'Fallon's closed bathroom door. He was now occupied with new smells, the air redolent of the fish and birds that populated the shoreline. My thoughts were still back in that apartment and I was barely aware of my surroundings. I didn't think Brody was being particularly forthcoming with me, which came as no surprise. I hadn't exactly been George Washington myself. Had Jin Mei not been out in the garden, I wouldn't have mentioned having been there earlier. Nor had I bothered to mention Mary Margaret's peculiar little note. I thought I'd speak to her first and find out what it meant, then tell Brody. Or not.

I was thinking and acting as if I were on the job, a habit that had become a way of life for me, something I had in common with Timothy O'Fallon, never mind that it was something he never knew about. He hadn't told me he was a detective and I hadn't told him I was a private investigator. In fact, when someone else in the group had asked me what I did besides pet therapy, I'd lied, the same lie I'd told Brody, the same one that was on the business card I'd just given him. "Research," it said. Perhaps that was more of a half-truth than a lie. No one had asked what it meant and I hadn't volunteered anything further.

Carrying O'Fallon's briefcase and lost in thought, I followed behind my dog, not paying any attention to where we were going. We ended up all the way down at Houston Street before I noticed, turned around and headed home.

CHAPTER 6

The answering machine was blinking. I hit *play*.

The first message began with someone coughing. "Be quiet. I'm on the phone here. Rachel, this is Parker, um, Parker Bowling. I need to get my things from Tim's apartment. I guess you're not home. I'll call you later." I could hear some noise in the background, as if he were calling from a restaurant or a bar.

"Ms. Alexander, this is Maggie O'Fallon returning your call." There was a long pause, just short of disconnecting the answering machine. "You sounded . . . it sounds as if this is something important, but you didn't say what it was about." Then she hung up.

"Rachel, it's me again. I'll try you later." This time he must have been outside. I could hear the sound of traffic, a dog barking, a snippet of a passing conversation. "Not tomorrow," someone said. I heard Parker strike a match. And then he hung up.

"This message is for Rachel Alexander. This is

Dennis O'Fallon calling from Paramus Lexus. You didn't say what you were calling about, whether it was business or personal." He sighed. An impatient man. Then he repeated his name again and left the work number and an extension, saying both twice.

There was a call from someone who wanted to handle my investments, someone who had a method for clearing up my credit card debt who was surprised I hadn't responded to his last three calls, and from someone who said I had been selected to have a free weekend in Florida. I hadn't won any dance lessons or the lottery. But Parker Bowling had called twice more. And he was starting to sound annoyed.

I dialed Maggie O'Fallon and got her machine again. This time I told her I was home and that I'd be staying home. Just in case she called while I was walking Dashiell, I left my cell phone number as well. I couldn't return Dennis's call. He hadn't left his home number.

Parker Bowling hadn't left a home number either. No matter. I wasn't in any rush to talk to him.

I decided to work downstairs, where it was cooler. The brick cottage I rented was small, but had three floors. There were two small bedrooms upstairs, one of which I used for an office, and the bathroom was there, near the top of the stairs. The living room and tiny kitchen were on the ground floor, and there was a large room downstairs that I rarely used. I had a dining room table there but never seemed to invite enough people to dinner to use it. Sometimes I thought I had better skills with dogs than with

people. Sometimes I wasn't sure which kind of
company I preferred.

I thought about cooking something, but I
wasn't in the mood, so I ordered a pizza and took
the briefcase to the round table just outside my
kitchen. I took out O'Fallon's checkbook first,
starting at the latest check in the register and
going backward. He'd not only recorded his
checks and deposits, but his ATM withdrawals as
well. Unlike the way I kept my checkbook, with
more than one item on a line—a check and a de-
posit or a check and an ATM withdrawal—he
gave each item a line of its own.

The checks were fairly ordinary—his rent, his
electric bill, his phone bill. There were regular
checks to a Marie Sanchez, fifty dollars every two
weeks. I guessed that she was his cleaning lady.
She'd gotten a check the Thursday before. I'd
have to make sure to call her sometime before she
showed up again.

There were checks to several liquor stores, a recent check to a florist, one to a doctor, or dentist,
a small amount meaning it was a co-pay. There
was a check for twenty-five dollars to Rob Rosen.
Tim had written "garden" after Rob's name. The
deposits were evenly spaced, one a month, always the same amount of money. It was the ATM
withdrawals that interested me. There had been
seven in the last month, totaling $820. On the line
adjacent to five of the eight withdrawals, there
was a notation: "For Parker." Three hundred and
seventy-five dollars in cash had gone to Parker in
June.

Tim had an IRA at the bank where he had his

checking account. There was $41,654 dollars in the account, not an awful lot to show for twenty-one years of service, but there must have been a retirement account connected to the job as well. I wondered if he'd thought of retiring. So many police suicides seem to occur around that time and he'd put in his twenty years-plus.

The bell at the gate rang. I grabbed some money and Dash and I headed through the garden to fetch our pizza. The delivery kid handed me a card from the pizzeria. Ten of them, he told me, and I'd get a free pie, regular, nothing extra on it. I was sure I'd qualified for several already.

When we got back inside, I put three slices on a plate to cool for Dashiell and pushed O'Fallon's papers aside to keep them clean. Dash watched me eat, a bit disappointed. Maybe even resentful. He usually ate a souped-up diet of raw meat and grated raw vegetables, except when I ate pizza. But he never seemed to remember that each time he had to wait for his slices to cool.

After I had finished two slices, I walked out into the garden, putting Dashiell's plate down on the ground. No sense having to clean up the living room floor when he'd be just as happy eating out-of-doors.

There was a slight breeze. I could smell the lavender growing near the path, the basil from the herb garden. I sat on the steps and thought about what I had to do, hoping again that I could get the attorney to do most of the paperwork. I'd call her first thing in the morning. I wondered if Maggie would want to come into the city and help me sort things. According to the will, only the money and certain named valuables were going to her. The rest of O'Fallon's possessions had been left to the executor, me, to dispose of as I saw fit. I thought this was done when there was no family to pick and choose what they wanted to keep. Perhaps O'Fallon knew better. Perhaps he knew, or thought, that Maggie wouldn't want most of his things. Still, it seemed strange for me to be doing this when he had at least two living blood relatives.

I went inside to look at the photo album, those same kids again, the pictures faded, some even a pale brown, the images on their way to disappearing altogether. I was only on the third page when the phone rang.

"Is this Rachel Alexander?" she asked.

"Yes. Is it Maggie?"

"Yes, it is. I only have a moment. I'm on my break. But your voice sounded urgent and I was wondering what it is you called about. I hope I haven't made a mistake. I hope this isn't one of those calls to ask me to switch to A T and T."

"No, it isn't. I wish it were."

"Oh," she said. "Then what?"

I took a breath. "It's about your brother," I said.

"Dennis?"

"No, it's about Tim. There's been an accident, Maggie. I'm so sorry to be the one to tell you this. Tim is dead."

I heard her inhale sharply.

"He was cleaning his service revolver," I said. "On Sunday morning. I'm sorry this has taken so long, but I didn't hear about it right away."

"He's dead? He shot himself? Mother of God. This is all my fault."

"No, no," I said. "It was an accident."

Mary Margaret was silent.

I wished I could comfort her, but there was nothing comforting to say. I could have told her that her brother went quickly, that he didn't suffer long, or said that at least there was no wife left behind, no young children orphaned, things people say in situations like this. But to what avail? She'd lost her mother last week and her brother this week. There wasn't anything I could say that would erode even the smallest bit of her grief. I'm sorry for your loss, I thought. That's what people said, because what else was there to say?

"Maggie," I said. Then: "I'm so sorry."

I could hear what sounded like a bell ringing, again and again.

"Who are you?" she asked. "Are you with the Department?"

"No, I'm—"

"Then why are you the one calling me?"

"That's the weird thing," I said. I'd walked outside with the phone and was sitting on the steps outside the cottage. There was a three-quarter moon and the sky was cloudless, a kind of inky blue with more stars than you usually see in the city. "I barely knew your brother, but he named me as executor of his estate. It came as—"

"He named you? What does that mean?"

"That his will designated me as—"

"But you just said you barely knew Tim? I don't understand."

"He must have had his reasons," I told her, repeating what Brody had said to me. I told her how I'd met Tim and what he'd said that last day.

I probably should have told her about the tears, but now didn't seem the time. "That's all I know," I told her. "I'm as puzzled as you are. I guess he never mentioned—"

"No, never. I have to go," she said. "I'm at the hospital."

"Oh, I'm sorry," I said again.

"It's not that. It's my job. I'm a nurse."

"Can we talk again, Maggie? I'd like—"

But the line went dead, leaving me with the feeling that I'd botched an important task. I put my head down to my knees, feeling awful. And then, I can't even say why, I went inside, picked up Brody's card and called his cell phone.

"It's Rachel," I said. "I just spoke to Maggie O'-Fallon."

I felt a tear rolling down my cheek, glad this was a phone call and not a face-to-face meeting.

"That'll do it every time," he said. "It went badly?"

"It was terrible."

"It always is. No matter how they react, it's always terrible."

"She says it's her fault."

"That's a common reaction, Rachel. We all like to think we're more powerful than we are. If only *we* had done this or hadn't done that, things would have turned out differently. It's human nature."

"Then . . ."

"You did the best you could. You know what they say about the messenger?"

"Yes, I do. But she was mad at herself."

"Not at you?"

"She was mad at me, too. Very mad."

"Give her a bit of time. Try her again in a day or two."

"Okay," I said. "I will. Detective?"

"Yes?"

"How do you . . . ?"

"Long story. I'll buy you a drink one night and tell you all about it."

"I'm sorry if I bothered you."

"You didn't bother me at all. I'll call you tomorrow, when I hear about the release."

As soon as I put the phone down, it rang again. But I didn't pick it up. Instead, I took the stairs two at a time to the office and listened to the machine pick up, Dashiell barking, my outgoing message and then Parker Bowling, sounding impaired and frustrated.

"She's still not there," he said. "What now?"

Another voice, farther away from the phone, said, "Who am I, fucking Martha Stewart, I got the answer to everything?"

"Bitch," Parker said.

I wasn't sure which one of us he meant. Then I heard the disconnect.

I went back downstairs and poured a glass of wine, sitting at the table where I'd left O'Fallon's album. There were adults in some of the pictures and those same kids again, and again, and again, in different combinations. Family, I thought. So Tim had a brother, too. Dennis. But he hadn't been mentioned in the will. What was that all about?

I paged through the rest of the album, thinking I'd see those kids growing up, thinking I'd be able to figure out which one grew up to be Tim. But they all stayed frozen in time. In the beginning of the album, the kids were ten or eleven through fifteen or sixteen. At the end, the same. Same kids, same ages, same goofy smiles, funny haircuts, high energy, high jinks and, every once in a while, a grown-up in the picture or a more formal shot, the kids dressed up and looking as if they hated it. Nothing written in the album. It didn't say "Tim's fifteenth birthday" or "Aunt Colleen's wedding." No dates, either, no "Summer Vacation, 1979," nothing like that. And no one was holding up a newspaper, the way hostages do so that you know they are alive on a certain date. I could only guess from the fading and my assumption that Tim was one of those boys, that Maggie was the little girl, that the contents of the album were around twenty-five years old, give or take a year or two in either direction.

After looking at the end and seeing that no one had aged, I paged through rather quickly, but near the end of the album, I found a lumpy page. It wasn't a real photo album, the photographs held on by those little black corners my father had used in ours. This was a loose-leaf book with plastic sleeves and a sheet of black paper in the middle of the photos. The lumpy page had two black sheets so that whatever was between them didn't show through from either side. I slipped in two fingers and pulled it out, a newspaper article. It had oxidized to a yellowish-brown color and the paper was very dry. I unfolded it very carefully, noting that it had been folded and unfolded many times. The creases were torn right through in several places. The name of the newspaper wasn't there, but the date was. The article had been published twenty-nine years ago. I began to read.

FATAL ACCIDENT AT BREYER'S LANDING

A local Piermont boy, Joseph Patrick O'Fallon, 12, died yesterday in a dive into the swimming hole at Breyer's Landing. His brothers, Timothy and Dennis, were with him, as well as two cousins, Liam and Francis Connor. The boys, aged 12 to 15, said that although they warned Joseph not to jump from the highest point, he did. When he didn't come back to the surface, the two oldest boys, Timothy and Liam, went in after him but were unable to find him. Francis Connor, 12, ran home to tell his mother, who called the paramedics. The body was recovered later that day.

"The neighborhood boys had been told repeatedly not to use the swimming hole at Breyer's Landing because it is unsafe and there is no supervision," Detective Anthony Rizzo of the Orangeburg Police Department said, "but it was sort of a rite of passage for the local kids, jumping off that rocky ledge into the ice-cold water. I did it myself when I was growing up."

Joseph's father, Detective Colm O'Fallon of the New York City Police Department, said he'd warned the boys too, but to no avail. "If there's a challenge," he said, "boys are going to try to meet it. My wife and I hope that this tragedy might make other boys think twice."

I took Maggie O'Fallon's note out of her brother's briefcase.

"I know what happened at Breyer's Landing. I was there."

If she'd been there, why wouldn't he have known that? Why was she telling him that now, all these years later? And why hadn't the article mentioned her name along with those of her brothers and cousins?

I read the article again to make sure. Then I checked inside each plastic sleeve to see if there was anything else, but there wasn't. I started at the beginning and paged through the album more slowly this time. The boys, three O'Fallons and two Connors, and one little girl, eternally young, nothing recorded after all those charming, goofy, normal kid smiles were wiped off their faces by a tragic accident.

O'Fallon's father had been a New York City detective, too. Grief traveling the marrow of the bones, generation after generation.

I pulled out O'Fallon's driver's license and looked at his face again and then I began to think about Michael Brody, about what cops saw, about how they never told.

I went upstairs to the office and picked up the file from the post-traumatic-stress group where I'd met O'Fallon. I checked my watch. It was nearly ten. I picked up the phone and dialed the first number.

CHAPTER 7

When I woke up, I called O'Fallon's attorney, Melanie Houseman. She said she'd get started on the paperwork, the letter of testamentary that would give me the power to function legally on O'Fallon's behalf, and the death certificate. She asked me to collect and messenger her the bank statements, the lease and any other legal documents I might find.

"I'm sorry to hear this," she said. "He seemed like an awfully nice man."

"I didn't really know him," I told her.

"Is that so?"

"I thought it was odd, his choosing me this way, without even asking. I wonder, did he say anything to you about it, when he gave you my name? Did he happen to say why he'd chosen me to do this for him?"

"He told me his mother had died. She had been the designated executor of the previous will. So naturally he had to make a change. I told him it didn't have to be done in such a hurry and he said that was true, he understood that, but if I didn't mind, he'd appreciate making the changes and signing the new will all in one visit. I figured he was busy and he wanted to get it done, get it off his mind. A lot of the officers are like that, they want something and they want it done immediately. Like lawyers. Now that everything's computerized, I was able to do that for him."

"You said a lot of the officers?"

"My father was a lawyer. His brother was a cop. This started way back when. Before we were Houseman and Houseman, we were Houseman, Riley, Friedkin. For anything personal, not Department business, of course, a lot of the men would come to us. They still do, even more than years ago."

"I guess you give them what they want."

"Mostly, it's speed. That, and good advice. What Tim asked for, same day service, it's not all that unusual."

"Were there many changes in the new will?"

"Well, the executor, from his mother, Kathleen, to you. And the beneficiary was changed from Kathleen to his sister Mary Margaret. That's all. Nothing fancy."

"And he didn't say anything about why he wasn't making Mary Margaret his executor?"

"No. Well, yes, he did. He said that you would know . . . let me think . . . he said that you would know what he wanted."

"Damn. What does that mean?"

"I guess whatever's spelled out in the will."

"Wouldn't his sister have known what he wanted in that case?"

"I suppose. He must have had his reasons."

"So I've been told. That's what one of the detectives said."

"You know, Rachel, had he told me he hardly knew you, I would have strongly advised against this. But he didn't tell me. I didn't have a clue. In fact, that wording was his, the part that says, 'my dear friend.' I guess it's a cop thing. They're not very talkative, not to civilians, anyway. Not even to their own lawyers."

Guys, I thought, not just cops. Someone gets the message through to them before they're toilet-trained: stiff upper lip, don't complain, don't explain, the whole John Wayne thing.

"You're not required to accept this burden, Rachel. It's an awful lot of work. Of course, if you do take it on, you'll be paid for your time and effort. You do know that, don't you? I only ask because an awful lot of people don't, and because Detective O'Fallon never discussed this with you."

"No, I had no idea."

"The executor receives a percent of the value of the estate."

"The only other estate I dealt with was my mother's, and my sister and I were the beneficiaries, so that wasn't an issue. I don't feel right about this, that part of Mary Margaret's money will go to me."

"Oh, don't worry about that. You'll earn it. And it's what Detective O'Fallon wanted. He was clear about that, Rachel, all my clients are. I always explain what's customary. And why."

I was thinking about what she'd just said, about the amount of time this would take. I was thinking about the bills that showed up in my mailbox with great regularity, whether or not I was working. I'd worked for dead people before. That wasn't the problem. But this was the first time a client was dead *before* hiring me.

"I'll arrange a bank account with you as the signatory as soon as you get me the account information. We can write the checks here, but we'll need to send them to you for signing. Meanwhile, I'll get to work on the rest of what you need. Please keep in touch."

"Thanks, Melanie. I'll try not to bother you unnecessarily."

"I get paid, too, Rachel. Getting bothered, as you put it, is part of what I get paid for. Call whenever you need to."

Though I believed Melanie, that there'd be a lot of work, more than I could guess, I still wasn't comfortable with the news that I'd be paid. O'-Fallon had had something in mind. Unless I was able to discover what that was, I wouldn't feel I'd earned the money.

Still, there was the reality of those bills to pay. In fact, there was something else I had to do that morning to keep myself afloat. O'Fallon's rent, I guessed, was governed by Rent Stabilization Laws. Otherwise he would be living in Queens, not Greenwich Village. My fabulous deal had to do with the fact that the Siegals, the couple who owned both the town house across the garden from me and the back cottage that I rented from them, were hardly ever here. They had several other houses and they loved to travel. The deal was that I got the cottage dirt-cheap for making sure their house and their possessions stayed safe

in their absence. I usually checked the house at
least once a week to make sure no one had broken
in and that everything was working the way it
should. They'd notify me when they were coming
back, and at that time I'd hire a cleaning service
and see that everything was ready for them when
they arrived. I always took Dashiell with me to
check the house. If anything was amiss, he'd
know it much sooner than I would. I'd often give
him his search command without telling him
what I wanted him to find. In those cases, he'd
alert for anything that didn't belong where it was,
a perfect way to let me know if the house had
been invaded. And working on command rather
than just being nosy, he'd be sure to search every
inch of the house, not just the places that interested him personally.

One winter, a year and a half earlier, he'd spent
a lot of time checking out a pair of shoes he'd
found in the pantry. I might have missed them
myself. Norma Siegal often slipped off her shoes
when she came into the house. Like me, she preferred to walk around barefoot. I'd even seen her
on the back deck that way and had a conversation
with her in the garden, neither of us wearing
shoes.

After pawing at the shoes and turning them
over, Dashiell took off. I could hear him on the
stairs, hear him opening doors, then sneezing to
clear his nose. Martha was on the top floor in a
small spare bedroom, a homeless woman who
must have noticed that while lights came on at
night, the same lights always came on and went
off at the same time. She'd only been there a day,

and other than the fact that I'd had to replace the lock to the cellar door, she hadn't done any harm. She'd only been keeping warm and trying to survive, like everyone else. I hadn't called the cops. Instead, I'd got her into a halfway house in Chelsea and hoped their training program and support might help her get back on her feet. It was sort of a work/study program for the homeless I'd read about in the paper, and Martha and I both felt lucky that when I called, they were able to take her.

I walked Dashiell first, and when we got back we entered the house through the front door, which was on Tenth Street, just east of the gate I used to get to the cottage. When we finished checking the house, we'd leave by the back door that exited into the garden. That way I'd be sure neither door had been jimmied since my last inspection. For my low rent, I also collected the mail, pitching out all the junk mail and forwarding the bills to their attorney, who would pay them in the Siegals' absence. The Siegals were thrilled to have a private investigator living in the cottage. It made them feel really secure. I was thrilled to have rent I could afford in the neighborhood where I felt at home. That made me feel really secure, a good deal all around.

There'd been no call from Brody all morning. Maggie hadn't called again either. I was hoping she would. I hadn't called Dennis. I was sure Maggie would do that. Then I wondered if she would. Family relationships could be so weird. I thought I'd better ask her when I spoke to her next.

I'd gotten three of the people from the group

last night—Mel, Larry and Brian. Mel kept asking about Dashiell. He barely remembered Tim. Larry referred to Tim as "the Mount Rushmore guy." He said Tim hadn't said a word to him, not in the group, not out. And Brian said he was still having a tough time. He'd gone on Prozac, he said, and he wished he could get off it but when he tried, he was worse than before he started using it. He barely remembered Tim.

I called Scott again and this time he answered. He seemed very upset when I told him that Tim was dead.

"We both got there early once," he said. "We were in the courtyard, just the two of us, waiting for the group to begin, neither of us saying boo. Then I figured, what the hell, and I told him I thought the group was helping me. I did, too. I'd started going out to dinner with friends again. And I was sleeping better. Not great, but better. I asked Tim if he'd been feeling any better. I said I thought Richard was doing a good job, gently directing us toward certain issues, making us see that everything we thought and felt was normal, given the abnormal circumstances we were now stuck with. But Tim didn't share. He listened," Scott said. "He really listened. But he just didn't add anything of his own. I thought he was a really nice man. I mean, I thought he *must be* a really nice man, attentive, caring. But he wasn't awfully forthcoming. It's hard for some people. That's what Richard kept saying, remember? I guess it was too hard for Tim to talk. Did you ever find out who he lost?"

"No," I said, "he didn't talk to me either."

"But you said you were the executor of his will."

"Right. It came as a complete surprise to me."

"You're kidding. I didn't even know you could do that, make someone the executor without asking."

"Don't get any ideas," I told him.

He laughed. "I promise I'll ask you first," he said. Then he asked if I'd called Richard. I said I hadn't, but I would. He asked about Dashiell. And he wished me luck.

I still couldn't reach John and decided to leave a second message. I hadn't called Richard last night. I had both home and office numbers, but I decided to call him at his office and not bother him at home. It wasn't exactly an emergency. He was very effusive when I said my name, then became silent when I told him why I was calling and what little I knew.

"I was just hoping to get a handle on him, to understand this thing. It bothers the hell out of me that I don't know why, that I don't know what he had in mind, making a decision like this. I don't know if you'd feel free to say, but I was wondering if you ever spoke with him privately, if there's anything at all you could tell me about the man that might make these circumstances . . ."

Richard cleared his throat, and for a moment I thought he was going to say, "He must have had his reasons," but he didn't. He said, "I hate this. I hate these complete failures. You try your damnedest to reach someone and they won't let you in, so you can't give them the help you know they need."

"They said it was an accident," I said into the phone.

"There are no accidents, Rachel. Perhaps he didn't mean to do it consciously, but if he was a cop, he knew how to handle a gun, wouldn't you think?"

"His mother had just died. I guess he was pretty depressed."

"I knew there'd be something. There always is. Poor man. I wish he'd called me."

"Had he ever, since the group?"

There was a silence, Richard weighing patient confidentiality when the person in question wasn't his patient. "No. He never called," he said. "I didn't know him either, Rachel."

I thanked him and hung up.

When I put the phone down, it rang. It was Brody this time, saying I could have access to O'-Fallon's apartment. Since I couldn't be sure who might have keys besides the police and me, I called the closest locksmith and asked him to meet me at Tim's apartment. I grabbed a pair of rubber gloves from under the sink, O'Fallon's briefcase, and the leash, and Dashiell and I headed out. The phone started ringing as I was closing the door. I walked back in and stood at the foot of the stairs, listening to Parker's voice as my answering machine was recording it. He was still talking when I closed the door and locked it behind me.

CHAPTER 8

The locksmith's name was Nick. It said so on the front of his shirt. On the back it said "Nick's Locks," in case you caught him going instead of coming. As I unlocked the first door, I explained the deal with the locks, that the upper and lower ones used the same key. As it turned out, all four cylinders used the same key.

Nick began shaking his head. "No good, lady," he said. "Anything you think of, the thieves thought of it two weeks ago. You know those bicycle locks, supposed to be foolproof?"

I nodded.

"Freezing jewelry in the ice tray? Coin collection in a sock? Hollowed out book? Clint Eastwood blew that one in *Escape From Alcatraz*. No, wait, maybe that was what's-his-face in *Shawshank Remdemption*. No matter. It was one of them, right?"

"Tim Robbins," I said.

"Whatever. Emerald ring hidden in a fake light switch? That was a good one, for five minutes. I even had one client built a hidden room. Cost him a pile. Did it work?"

I had the script. I shook my head.

"I rest my case. Nothing beats good hardware. Plus, one of those couldn't hurt none." He was pointing at Dashiell.

Nick had that five-o'clock-shadow look that Don Johnson popularized back when *Miami Vice* was must-see-TV, having a renaissance now with the under thirty set and gay men of any age. Only Nick's, I was sure, was the real McCoy, even at ten-thirty in the morning.

"Another thing," he said. "These things?" He held the cylinder from O'Fallon's front door in the palm of his hand, more like a big paw the way I saw it. "Worthless crap."

In fact, it looked to be the same kind of worthless crap that had kept the cellar door locked before a homeless woman had decided that sleeping in a town house would be preferable to sleeping in the street.

O'Fallon's attorney had told me that whatever I spent would be reimbursed by the estate, that all I had to do was to send her the receipts. Much as I didn't want to be frivolous with Maggie O'Fallon's money, given the long line of untrustworthy men who had lived in her brother's apartment, replacing the locks seemed like a good idea.

"What do you recommend?" I asked.

The bill came to $380 before I noticed the jimmied window. Luckily Nick was still there, writing out the bill at O'Fallon's kitchen table. The bathroom door was still closed. I noticed that, too, but I wasn't in a rush to go in there. I was curious, but more than willing to put it on hold.

The plants and the watering can on the sill had

blocked the damage to the kitchen window. Now that the plants were gone and I had just moved the can so that I could open the window and let some air in, I saw the crack in the wood. I had to stand on one of the kitchen chairs to check the lock. There wasn't any. Instead there was a little rectangle with a different color paint, old faded paint, and two holes where the screws had attached it to the top of the bottom window. I called Nick over to have a look-see. He climbed up on the chair with me, then asked if we could go outside. I told him we could. From the garden, the damage was completely clear, pry marks at the bottom of the window, dents in the wood, probably done with a garden tool, impromptu.

Nick added another thirty-five dollars to the bill and then began to check all the other windows inside and out to be sure the apartment was safe. When he headed toward the bathroom door, I told him to skip that one. He'd checked the window from the garden and it looked pristine. He'd even tried to open it, but the lock held. Plus, I was still postponing that event. I thought I'd function better if I saved it for last, just before I was ready to leave. Or until my bladder insisted otherwise, whichever came first.

The front windows were untouched and had bars on them anyway, another New York phenomenon. You paid a fortune to live here and then, if you lived on the ground floor, your apartment resembled the primate digs at a politically incorrect zoo.

"You want I should throw a new lock on that door to the garden? Piece of shit, the one that's on it. Wouldn't keep out a three-year-old. I'll give you a break on that one, seeing as you're doing a lot of work here, keep the whole shebang under five hundred. Not bad for the peace of mind it'll give you."

I didn't think a three-year-old would be able to reach the doorknob, but didn't say so. I thanked Nick, but told him no, thanks.

"How do you think that kitchen window lock got pulled out?" Nick asked. "Someone wanted in here and had no trouble getting past that one, getting into the garden."

"I understand that," I said, "but there's a limit to what I want to do," thinking my job was to protect O'Fallon's property, not the trees and flowers outside. "I don't even live here," I told him.

Nick screwed up his face. Wouldn't be the first time a locksmith was called to change the lock on an apartment the caller didn't occupy. A scam the thieves thought up two weeks before the locksmiths figured it out, I could have said, but decided to keep my big mouth shut. He was busy trying to figure out if this job was legit or not. I'd handed him the keys that had unlocked both doors. Still, Nick's face was in a knot.

He pulled out his cell phone. "I'm this close to losing a good fee and having to undo all this work, lady. Can you prove you have a right . . ."

I opened O'Fallon's briefcase and took out the will, showing him my name as executor. Then I pulled out my wallet and showed him my driver's license, complete with a picture that made me look as if I lived in a trailer and never ventured out during daylight.

Nick nodded. "Sorry about your loss," he said.

I thanked him. No point in keeping him here an extra half an hour telling him what the story was. Besides, I didn't know what the story was. I was still wishing someone would explain things to me. But dead men don't talk. And while I was sure the ME would disagree with that, the information I wanted wasn't available via organ weights or the path a bullet took ruining someone's young life. I needed words. Why me and not Mary Margaret? That's what I wanted to know.

He must have had his reasons. Maybe the medical examiner would say that, too.

When Nick left, I thought I'd try Brody, ask him about the jimmied window. From the looks of it, it wasn't all that old. Nick thought it had happened a day or two earlier.

He'd looked up at the sky, thinking. "No rain last week, am I right?"

"You're right," I told him. I was getting pretty good at this.

"Could have been longer then, but not more than a week. You see the color of the wood here?" He'd pointed to one of the places where the wood had been fractured, the exposed wood pale and raw-looking. "See the color? If we'd had any weather, it wouldn't be so light." He'd nodded, agreeing with himself.

I picked up O'Fallon's phone, then put it down. The place was tight again, safe. The question could wait until later. I was sure there'd be more of them. For now, I wanted to get to work.

I leaned over the sinkful of dirty dishes to open the window, wondering if whoever had jimmied

the window had managed to get in this way,
scrunching himself into a ball and then stepping
over the sink. You'd have to be a contortionist. I
wondered if it was O'Fallon, if he'd forgotten his
keys, had a neighbor ring him in, then broke his
own window latch to get inside.

I pushed the knob that closed the drain,
squirted in some Dove and ran the hot water. No
use trying to deal with the dishes until they'd
soaked for a while. Doing the dishes was another
task I was happy to postpone, especially since
there was no dishwasher.

When I turned off the water, I heard a voice in
the garden. I couldn't see anyone outside the window. I decided to go out and see who was there.

He was on his cell phone, talking loud. He
seemed to be upset. He was about my height,
maybe an inch or two shorter, in his fifties, his gray
hair slicked back with so much goo it appeared to
be wet but I was sure it wasn't, that it was just the
wet look he'd been after. He was dressed all in
black, perhaps to minimize the potbelly that rested
tenuously on his black belt. Alligator, probably
faux. Even the rims of his retro eyeglasses were
black. He used one thick finger to push them back
up to the bridge of his smallish nose. His skin was
pale but his cheeks were flushed. Perhaps the
yelling had accomplished that.

"Okay," he shouted into the phone. "I hear you.
It's an emergency." I was about to tell him about
the new technology, that he didn't have to shout
to be heard, but I didn't get the chance. "Five. Got
it," he said, slamming the phone closed and sigh-
ing heavily.

"You'd think being a waiter would be a low-stress, easy job, wouldn't you?" he asked me. "Rob's going to have a cat. We have reservations at Lupa, for God's sake. What are you doing for dinner?" I opened my mouth, then closed it again. This, like his other questions, was no doubt rhetorical. I wondered if he was related to my locksmith or if it was just the luck of the draw. He took a step in my direction. "Rachel?"

"Yes. How did you . . . ?"

He put out his hand, not sideways, as if to shake, but palm down and limp, as if he expected me to kiss it. I didn't notice a tiara, so I disappointed him.

"Kevin. Kevin Bell? Jin Mei said she'd met you." He dropped his voice to a stage whisper. "She said you're here because of . . ." He indicated the door I'd just come out of with a nod of his head.

"Yes. I'm taking care of Detective O'Fallon's affairs," I said.

"I don't think he had any," Kevin said. "Not that I wouldn't have been interested, a man with handcuffs and a nightstick. It's got a certain *je ne sais quois*, don't you think?"

"I suppose so, if that's your thing."

"Let's not go there," he said. "We've only just met."

He had a nice smile. Smiling, he didn't look a day over forty-five.

"So you're saying he was gay?"

"O'Fallon? No way. But a boy can dream, can't he?"

"What about Parker?"

"Sweetheart, where are you from, Queens? First of all, this is the Village, not Chelsea. And even there, not *everyone* is gay."

"I didn't ask if everyone was gay. I've only asked you about two people," thinking I was starting to sound like Brody, that I better lighten up. Kevin wasn't obliged to tell me anything.

"Two so far."

"Correct."

"Curious little thing, aren't you?"

"Just trying to understand. I didn't know Tim well. In fact, I hardly knew him at all. I'm trying to . . ."

"That's *très* weird. How'd you get stuck with this?"

"Exactly my point. I don't actually know." I shrugged.

"So, Parker? I'd say whatever you want him to be, that's what Parker is."

"A chameleon."

"Honey, if you want this conversation to continue . . ." He rolled his eyes. "Did anyone before *moi* ever tell you you're no fun?"

I nodded. "Everyone," I said. "That aside, I haven't met Parker yet. Hard to trash someone you never met."

"Oh, sweetie, you're not giving yourself nearly enough credit. It's not as hard as you think. Especially when we're talking about Parker. I'll start. First of all, he's a total bitch. Cold as ice, as if *we* were the interlopers. You know what I mean?" Kevin had stepped closer now, as if there were people around and he didn't want them to overhear him. "And with Tim? Don't ask. He was like butter wouldn't melt in his mouth in front of him and just did whatever he pleased behind his back."

"Like, for instance."

"For instance bringing all his street cronies into Tim's apartment after he was told not to. Repeatedly."

"He did that?" I thought of all those dishes in the sink. Tim hadn't even been there the day before. He'd been at his mother's funeral.

"Oh, please. We'd hear them all the way over to our place." He pointed. "On the other side of Jin Mei. Now *she's* a hoot, you know what I mean. But that's neither here nor there, is it? Parker's the one we're disgusting—oh, I mean discussing— and I can tell you, that boy showed up with his trashy friends, we'd have to close the windows and put on the AC."

"Loud parties?"

"Whenever possible. But would he invite *us?*"

"Never."

I was a quick study. Kevin beamed.

"Rob said it would be a cold day in hell before *he'*d take in someone like Parker."

"And what did Tim do, about those parties?"

"*Tim?* He was furious. He threw Parker out more than once. But Parker would come back, promise never to do it again, and Tim would take him back. He can be very convincing, that Parker fellow. That's how he survives. You might say that being convincing is his profession."

"Did that happen a lot, the back-and-forth thing?"

"Three times that I know of. Last time was the night before Tim's accident. I think that time he meant it, too. We were out here, having salmon *au beurre noir*. I was a chef, before 9/11. Now I'm a waiter. But that's another sad story. Everyone has one. If I had the time, I'd ask you yours. But I don't." Standing too close, his voice way too loud. "Instead of being served tonight, I have to smile and say, 'And how would you like that prepared, madam?' As if I give a shit. How annoying is that?"

"So Tim got mad at Parker often?"

"Especially this last time. You couldn't miss the shouting. Tim told Parker to pack up and go. He said he was sick of broken promises, of lies, of all the stealing. He said he didn't think Parker was even trying. And that was the point of all this, he said, that Parker put in some effort on his own behalf. Something like that. It's not that we were trying to listen. You couldn't help overhearing. And I said to Rob, 'Like *hello*. I could have told him that months ago. This one's a loser, period.' The funny thing is, Tim had no idea how bad it was, how many men were actually at his place, poor lamb. Half of them had come out this way"—pointing to the door I'd just used—"and gone that way"—pointing to the door on the west end of the long narrow garden, the one he and Rob and Jin Mei used. "Rob and I were so upset, we couldn't finish eating. I said, 'We should talk to him.' And Rob said, 'No, we shouldn't. We should butt out.' He's very . . . He's got more dignity than I do. I would have told. But then the next day it was all too late. Tim had that terrible accident. It was an accident, wasn't it?"

"Yes," I said. "Cleaning his gun."

He put two fingers to his lips.

"Did you hear the shot? I was wondering if anyone . . ."

He shook his head. "We were all closed in, the AC on, because of all the noise the evening before. We sleep in the front, so . . ." He shrugged his shoulders. "A waiter," he said. "Look at me, at my age. Do you believe this? Well, I guess I'll see you again. Knock if there's anything you need. My career is calling. I hope you have a life outside of your job, Rachel. I hear that's a good idea."

I lifted one hand in lieu of a comment, but he'd already turned and started walking toward that last door. I headed back inside, Dashiell following behind me.

CHAPTER 9

I was sitting at O'Fallon's desk when his phone rang. I checked to see that the answering machine was on and let it ring through, absorbed in what I was doing and not thinking about the consequences of my act. And then there he was, as close to me as if he were whispering in my ear.

"O'Fallon," the recording said. "State your business, leave your name and number, and I'll get back to you. If this can't wait, call my cell phone." Figuring, they didn't have the number, it couldn't be all that important.

There was a moment of silence and then the caller hung up. I played the outgoing announcement twice more before opening the bottom drawer of the desk and checking the labels on each file. Like most people's paperwork, O'Fallon's was dead boring—a file for his checking account, his rent statements, one on his car, the insurance policy, tune-up records, title. There was a file with instructions for equipment, booklets on how to use a tape recorder, program a VCR, operate the radio I'd seen in the kitchen, change the bags on his vacuum cleaner, use the electric can opener. In another file, he had duplicates of his tax returns for the last three years. I pulled those out and the bank statements and put them in the briefcase to get them to the attorney. I took the last rent statement as well, thinking his rent alone was reason to live forever—the huge main room, a kitchen with a window, and the use of the garden, all for under a thousand dollars a month, a New York miracle. I pulled the folder on the car out and left it on top of the desk. I wondered if he parked it on the street, because if he did, it had probably been towed already. I made a note to ask Brody about the car. If it had been towed, maybe he'd be able to get it back for me without payment of the fine, over a hundred bucks for sure. I didn't know what Mary Margaret was getting—I had no idea, for example, if O'Fallon's death benefits could pass to a sister. But I wasn't anxious to use up any more of her money than I had to.

I picked up an old checkbook and leafed through the register. The car wouldn't have been towed. O'Fallon kept it in an outdoor lot two blocks from here on West and Jane.

Behind the car folder, there was a folder with photographs. I pulled that out and opened it on top of the desk. Same kids, same happy faces, same ages. Then, behind the pictures, a small white envelope with initials on it—RKA. My initials. I opened it and pulled out what was in it, another newspaper article. Dashiell appeared while I was reading and dropped his cement-block head onto my lap. I was about to read it a second time when the phone started ringing again. This time, though, it wasn't O'Fallon's phone. It was my cell.

"Alexander."

"Rachel? Is it you?"

"Maggie? Yes. I'm so glad you called."

"Well, I was thinking. I ought to come into the city, help you with Tim's apartment. You shouldn't have to do all that hard work by yourself. The truth is, I still don't understand why you have to do it at all."

"That makes two of us, but I sure would love the help, if you don't mind." I picked up the keys that were on the side of the desk and flipped them into the palm of my hand. "When can you come?"

"Well, I was thinking Saturday. I can come early, spend the day."

"Are you working every day before that?"

"I am," she said.

"Night shift?"

"Evening. Four to midnight."

I opened my hand and looked at the keys. "What about before that? I mean, suppose I came to talk to you tomorrow. I have so many questions." I looked at the envelope, at my initials, RKA, on it. "Would that be okay? And then you can come in on Saturday and we can go over your brother's things, see what you'd like to have."

There was silence on the line.

"Maggie?"

"Tomorrow would be fine. Come for lunch."

"You don't have to bother with lunch. I just . . ."

"It's no bother at all."

"Okay. And, Maggie? Just so it won't come as a shock when I arrive, I'm going to be driving your brother's car."

"You have the address?"

"Yes. I have Tim's address book. I'll see you about twelve. Is that okay?"

"At twelve, then."

"Oh, I nearly forgot to ask. Did you speak to Dennis? I assumed you would and I didn't call him back. And now I'm—"

"Yes. I told Dennis."

"Will he want to come in as well?"

Maggie didn't answer but the line was still open.

"It doesn't matter. We can talk about that later."

"He's a very busy man, Rachel. He runs a business that's open seven days a week. I'll pick some things for him myself, some remembrances. I'm sure he'd appreciate that."

How odd, I thought afterward, that Dennis hadn't called about his brother, that he had no questions, no concerns. I looked down at the article again, well, the obituary. Maybe not so odd after all. Maybe Dennis O'Fallon had closed up shop years ago.

COLM O'FALLON, NEW YORK CITY DETECTIVE, DEAD AT 44

Detective Colm O'Fallon, 44, died of an accidentally self-inflicted gunshot wound two nights ago in his home in Piermont. Local police reported that Detective O'Fallon was found dead at 7:05 P.M. when his wife Kathleen came home from her rosary group. His cleaning kit was on the kitchen table in front of where he had been sitting. He had apparently been cleaning his service revolver when it discharged, a source at the local precinct reported.

The O'Fallon family had been particularly hard hit during the last year. Detective O'Fallon's youngest son, Joseph, was killed in a diving accident nine months earlier. Seven months after that, his nephew, Liam Connor, 16, who had witnessed the accident, committed suicide.

Detective O'Fallon is survived by his wife, two sons, Timothy and Dennis, and a daughter, Mary Margaret. The family plans a private service and has requested that, in lieu of flowers, donations be sent to Our Mother of Redemption Church in Sparkill.

I got up and walked over to the bathroom, standing outside the closed door for a moment before reaching for the knob. Dashiell pushed his way in front of me. No way was he not getting in there first. I turned the knob, pushed the door open, reached in and turned on the light. Dashiell lifted his head and pulled in the scents.

In yet another surprise, the bathroom where Timothy O'Fallon had accidentally discharged his service revolver while cleaning it, fatally wounding himself, was immaculate. Was it because this was a fellow officer that the police had hired a cleaning service? Because that was not the usual procedure. Still, whatever the reason, I was grateful.

The toilet was across from the door, on the west

wall of the bathroom. The sink and small vanity were to the left of the toilet. And across the south wall was the tub, the shower curtain, a translucent blue, pulled closed, everything just so. The white tile floor was spotless, including the grout. Had there been a bath mat, there was none now. Nor were there any towels.

I bent and touched the floor. No telltale grit, traces of soap, grease, no anything but cool, clean tile. I wondered if they'd bleached the grout to get it so white. I stood, took a breath and pulled the curtain aside, exposing the bathtub and the tiled wall. There was a small, high window overlooking the garden to the left, and on the right side, where there should have been several shattered tiles, there was another surprise. Not only had the service done an astonishing job of cleaning the wall, someone had apparently replaced the damaged tiles as well. But as meticulous and skilled as they had been, I could easily see where the grout was new. Had I not seen the repair, I might have thought Detective O'Fallon had been cleaning a small-caliber gun and that therefore the bullet that did the fatal damage had never exited his body. I might have been convinced that, despite the odds, and despite his experience with firearms, Detective O'Fallon had had an unfortunate accident. Perhaps that had been the point of the careful cleanup. But, in fact, that's not what I thought, because the tiles that had been replaced were nowhere near where they would have been had the detective been sitting on the edge of the bathtub, as reported, cleaning his gun. In fact, the damaged area was exactly where it would have been had a man of six feet one inch tall, the height recorded on O'Fallon's driver's license, held the barrel of a revolver to his right temple and squeezed the trigger.

Jin Mei had said she'd heard him crying. Had he been in the bathroom then, cradling his gun in his hands? Had he been crying in the shower to muffle the sound, afraid, even at the last minute, of seeming weak? Standing at the edge of the tub, looking at the tile wall, the sound of Dashiell's sniffing echoing in the small space, I felt the scenario changing before my eyes. He'd bought grief on the job for twenty-one years, then, for who knew how long, he took it into his private life, taking users off the street and trying to get them to turn their lives around. And he'd failed this time. He'd failed with Parker. How many other times had he failed? What made him keep trying?

His mother had been buried the day before, but grief was already running deep in the O'Fallon family—brother, cousin, father. All when he was not yet a man.

Had the burden gotten to be more than he could bear?

I thought of O'Fallon in the group where we met, stoic and silent. He had come, but he couldn't put his burden down. Now this. Had he killed himself in the shower to minimize the cleanup, to make it easier for whoever would find him, a stand-up guy right down the line?

I pulled the shower curtain closed and took a step back, nearly tripping over Dashiell. Suicide. That surely explained why Brody seemed anxious for me to relinquish my obligation; let the

cops take care of this, let it be recorded as an accident. But unless Detective O'Fallon was cleaning
a water gun, no way would he have been standing in the shower when his gun accidentally discharged. And suicide would explain the
brand-new will and the envelope with my initials
on it. But it didn't explain what it was he wanted
me to do. As far as that went, I still didn't know
any more now than I did at first.

Suddenly I needed to be busy, to be soothed by
work. I decided to do what I could before Maggie
came—clean the kitchen, empty the closets, check
the cabinets under the bookshelves. I was sure
Maggie wouldn't want Tim's clothes, and the
kitchen things looked ordinary and inexpensive. I
could make things easier if I could figure out
what belonged to Parker and pack those things
for him, maybe avoid his coming here altogether.

There were two big closets that opened into the
living room, dividing it from the back of the
apartment. I thought I could start there, do something mindless while I let the new information
gel. I opened the one on the right first. It was a
deep closet, one rack in back of the other, everything in the back in garment bags. I figured that
would be the winter clothes, the things in front
for summer. Except for the coat that had been on
the arm of the couch. That was now hanging
among the lightweight clothing. I wondered if
whoever had hung it up had paid any attention to
which closet was Tim's and which was Parker's. I
wondered if I would know whose things were
whose, until I looked under the clothes, at the
shoes. I took the clothes off their hangers and

carefully laid them on the couch. When the front was empty, except for the hangers swaying there like dancers at the end of a long marathon, I unzipped the garment bags and took out the woolen sport jackets, a navy-blue suit, sweaters in bags from the dry cleaner, folded over hangers waiting for their season to arrive again.

I pulled the shoes out, cop shoes, all of them, except for one pair of loafers. In the very back, there was some luggage. I thought I could pack up the clothes and put the suitcases back in the closet, see if Maggie wanted any of it for any reason. If not, they'd be ready to go to Housing Works. I wondered whether, if I waited until the end, they'd send a truck, take everything at once—the furniture, the pots and pans, even the books. It was the sort of recycling I thought Tim might have approved of: his things sold, the money used to help people with AIDS, people with nowhere else to turn. Not exactly what he'd been doing with men like Parker, but not entirely unrelated either.

I saved a cashmere sweater and a particularly beautiful scarf and set those aside for Maggie. I left the shelf—I'd need a ladder or a chair to reach the things up there—and started the second closet. As soon as I opened this one, I knew I was no longer in Kansas. There weren't as many clothes, but the ones there were seemed new. I thought about all those notations in Tim's checkbook. "For Parker." Expensive sweaters and slacks, sandals, boots, the inside of the closet door plastered with pictures cut from magazines: horses running at full tilt, a skull and crossbones, pictures of rocks. But then I spotted the shelf. And now I didn't want to wait. I took one of the kitchen chairs, carried it over to the closet and climbed up. There were no clothes on this shelf. There was, instead, a sort of shrine, maybe one hundred tiny objects spread out in what seemed like, but I was sure wasn't, random order: the skulls of tiny creatures and the claws of others, bits of marble, like steles, standing between them; a tiny American flag; feathers, rocks and tiny figures, some human, some not, grouped together or standing singly, as if in prayer. There was hair there, too. I didn't know the nature of the creature it had come from. There were coins, some foreign, one gold. There were beads and thread and string that had unevenly placed knots in it, a woman's antique pearl ring. I ran my finger on the shelf between the objects. No dust. Someone took good care of his shrine.

I closed the closet door, trying to figure out if there was a way I could get Parker's things to him without having him come here. Things were starting to add up in a way that made me want to avoid him.

Of course, I could simply empty the second closet and pack it up. Even if everything in it wasn't his, I was sure he wouldn't refuse anything. Did I have an obligation to let him come and pick and choose what he wanted to take, even if some of what he picked and chose wasn't his in the first place? I thought of calling Brody, not to ask him to be here, but to ask him what he thought. Getting Brody to talk? That might be as easy as threading a rabbit through the eye of a needle. So I didn't call. I went back to work.

It was hazy, hot and humid out, but not in O'-Fallon's apartment. With the air conditioner humming, I couldn't hear any street noises, nor was it too warm. The shutters were the way I found them, closed on the bottom and partly open on top, letting the late-afternoon light filter gently into the room.

I tried the cabinets under the bookshelves next and found them locked. No matter, I thought, you could open those locks with a nail file. Instead, I went back to the desk to look for a key, not finding it. I sat in O'Fallon's chair, trying to slip inside the man who used to sit there. Wasn't it James Thurber who said, "I hate women because they always know where things are"? Hands flat on the desk, eyes closed, like a fortune-teller minus the crystal ball and the weird outfit, I dowsed for keys. Nothing. I looked over at the bookshelf nearest the closet door, scanning the shelves for something that might hold keys, though, Lord knows, a cop should know better. It was on the highest shelf I could reach, a little tan honey pot with a lid. I took it down, feeling the heft of it, and put it on the desk. Then I took off the lid and found it was filled to the top with sets of keys. The key to the cabinets, one key fits all, were on a ring with the rest of O'Fallon's keys, one of which was no longer viable now that the locks had been changed. I had two sets of the new keys. I thought I'd give one to Brody, if he had any use for it. If Maggie wanted a set, I'd have mine copied for her. I could ask her at lunch.

There were papers in some of the cabinets, notebooks with notes from old cases. I checked

the dates. There were ten years' worth of notebooks, stopping a year earlier. I would have loved
to read every word, but couldn't do that now. I
thought I'd keep those, if Maggie didn't want
them. The next cabinet had records and CDs. O'-
Fallon had a couple of movies, too, ones he'd
taped from the TV, *Red River* and *Dog Day Afternoon*, *The Godfather* and *Star Wars*, a small, odd
collection. There wasn't any porn, nor any porn
magazines. Not so far.

The next cabinet held the liquor. Again I
thought about how easy these locks would be to
pick. Unless Parker had found the honey pot with
the keys as readily as I had. There was some of
everything, but none of the bottles had much in
them and some were drained and wrung out, not
a drop left to drink, but put back anyway. Which
one of them had been that thirsty? Or was this
something they did together? I thought about all
the empties that had been in the kitchen when
Brody first brought me in here, the bottles he himself had bagged and thrown away. Mostly beer,
but some booze as well. That mess was most
likely left over from Parker's last party. But that
didn't tell me whether or not Tim and Parker had
enabled each other, talking about AA between
drinks.

I thought about where the bullet had destroyed
the tiles, the place too high on the wall for the
shooter to have been seated, the place that had
been repaired. Perhaps all the empties were O'-
Fallon's doing; maybe drinking with or without
company was something he did in an attempt to
numb his feelings, to wash away his sadness,

finding that, over time, the drinking only made things worse or that it took more and more of it to do the job.

I needed some fresh air, even if the fresh air was bound to be as thick as soup. I took Dashiell around a couple of blocks, stopping to pick up an iced tea at Florent, heading back to O'Fallon's thinking I'd get more of the cleanup done before I called it quits. But when we got back and opened the doors, when I found myself in that depressing hallway, I kept going straight. No harm sitting in the garden while I sipped my cold drink. No harm postponing the kind of job no one liked to do.

As I passed the first door on the other side of the hall, I heard a baby crying. I headed for the garden, finding the door unlocked even with no one there. I sat at the round table and watched Dashiell explore the garden, seeing with his nose in a way I couldn't even imagine. I wondered often if he saw the scents in color or if he pictured waves of gray, wishing that, for just a moment, I could live in his skin and know the world as a dog.

The door we'd just come out of opened and there was the squalling baby in the arms of her nanny, a Caucasian child, a nut-brown caretaker, cooing to the unhappy little girl as she walked outside.

"She's teething," she said, rocking the baby in her arms, a short, squat woman with a round, flat face and black hair that caught the light. The baby, who was blond and fair-skinned and looked as if the world were about to end, had her fist in her mouth.

"I'm taking care of Detective O'Fallon's affairs," I volunteered, apropos of nothing, I suspected. This woman did not seem the least bit concerned about who I was or why I was there.

"I know," she said. Then, "Shh, Emma, it'll be okay."

"Jin Mei mentioned me?"

She nodded, looking suspiciously at Dashiell, her shoulder toward him, shielding Emma as if Dash were about to leap at her and end her teething problems forever.

"Do you have a moment to talk?" I asked.

"About?"

"Detective O'Fallon."

"I didn't really know him. Anyway, I already spoke to the police. I told them, I don't know anything." Looking frightened.

No green card, I thought.

"It's sort of personal," I told her, "just for me."

"I still don't know anything, no matter who it's for." A bit too loud. Who was she playing to? I wondered.

"I have to change her," she said, again too loud. "You can follow me if you want to."

I did, up to the kitchen door of the apartment across the hall from O'Fallon's.

"You have to leave *him* in there," she whispered, indicating Dashiell, then the door to O'Fallon's kitchen. I had more important things on my mind than showing her that Dashiell meant no harm, that it wasn't his fault his breed had a history of dogfighting or that it was the breed of the moment, still, for guarding illegal drug stashes.

I opened the kitchen door and sent Dashiell inside, telling him to wait so that he'd know I'd be back very soon.

"Netty Land," she said when we got inside baby Emma's apartment, the door safely closed.

"Rachel Alexander," I told her.

"I know," she said.

The layout of the apartment appeared to be a mirror image of O'Fallon's, also two units combined, a large studio apartment with two doors. I wondered if both buildings had been renovated that way, top to bottom. I followed Netty into the front room that served as living room, bedroom and nursery. I thought Netty would take Emma to the changing table but she sat on the tan leather couch instead, putting the baby down on the rug.

"I don't usually work on Sunday," Netty told me. "But I needed the money. I was here that whole weekend. They went away, to Amish country. They don't spend a whole lot of time with the baby, not if they can help it. It's good for me, anyway. My son is still in Peru, with my mother. I want to bring him here, but I don't have enough money yet. It's expensive," she added, in case I was too dull to get the point.

"Perhaps I can help you a little," I said. "Perhaps we can help each other."

"That would be good. I was here since Friday night. They left right after work."

"Can you hear anything, from across the hall?"

Netty shrugged. "Shouting. I'm sure he heard them plenty, too. She says it's this place, Miss Helene, that they fight all the time because it's too small. She says that's why she can't give me a raise, because they're saving up for a house. She says, Miss Helene, that's why she and Mr. David need a weekend to themselves, because two adults and one baby in this place, it's driving them crazy. 'You don't want us to get a divorce, do you, Netty?' That's what I get instead of a raise."

"I see," I said, giving her problems not much more sympathy than her employers did, wanting to get back on track. "So did you hear any shouting that weekend, from Detective O'Fallon's apartment?"

Netty nodded. "First there was the party. His friends, Mr. Parker's. A bunch of bums, freeloading off Mr. O'Fallon when he wasn't even home. I heard that. I was in the garden most of the afternoon. The baby likes it out there. She watches the birds. I saw the men running out the back when he came home, Mr. O'Fallon. They went through the garden and out the far door, by Jin Mei's apartment. Can you imagine? Grown men acting like that. And then I heard the shouting. He told Parker his free ride was over." Netty leaned toward me, whispering again, the baby asleep on the rug, sucking her thumb. "And then it was quiet, all of them gone. Except him."

"What about Sunday morning? Did you hear the shot?"

Netty shook her head. "The police told me the time. I forgot. Eight something, I think. She was screaming. The teeth, the teeth. And no mama here. I told them, if I heard anything, I figured it was a car, not a gunshot. Who expects to hear a gunshot?"

"You told the police this?"

"I did," she said. "I answered all their questions."

"Anything else you can tell me?"

Netty nodded. "I saw him come back and break the kitchen window, the snake."

"You mean Parker?"

"Yes. I saw him crawl in through the window."

"When was this?"

"Late Sunday morning. Or maybe noon. I was going to give her the bottle outside, hoping she'd fall asleep. I was going out when he was going in through the window."

"So you saw him entering Detective O'Fallon's apartment?"

Netty nodded.

"But not actually breaking the lock?"

She shook her head. "But he did," she said. "The palette knife was right there on the ground where he dropped it."

"Jin Mei's knife?"

"Yes."

"Jin Mei was out painting when Parker broke the lock?"

"No, she forgot the knife the day before. She left it on the table. No matter. No one else uses the garden. Even the others"—she pointed to the ceiling—"they hardly ever come out. Maybe if there's a party for the two buildings, once a year. Otherwise, it's just the first floor."

"What about Detective O'Fallon?"

She shook her head. "Not that I saw. He was at work all the time, not sitting in the garden."

"Did you see or hear anything else? Anything unusual?"

"I told them the same. I didn't see anything

else. I mind my own business. I take care of Emma."

"And you weren't out in the garden earlier, like around eight?"

"I was in here. I didn't get her out until around noon, maybe twelve-thirty."

"And with the air conditioner and the TV . . ."

"I didn't hear the accident."

I went back to O'Fallon's apartment and got two twenties and my business card from my wallet, taking them back across the hall.

"If you think of anything else, would you let me know?"

"I thought you didn't know him," she said, screwing up her face. "I thought he's not your family. Why are you asking these questions?"

"He asked me to take care of things for him. I don't know what it is he wanted," I told her. Her dark eyes looked blank. I don't think Netty Land understood what I was talking about. I wasn't sure I understood it myself. I heard the baby starting to cry. Netty put the money in her pants pocket and closed the door.

I went back into O'Fallon's, going straight for the bathroom again, hoping the contents of his medicine cabinet might speak to me, hoping for an answer from anywhere. I picked up some of the ordinary things I found there, holding them in my hands, putting them back where they'd been: aspirin, Tylenol, Irish Spring soap, razor blades and razor; a bristle brush without a handle, the kind men used to use in pairs; Band-Aids, deodorant; and a prescription bottle, Alocril, the same as I'd gotten from my eye doctor on October

11, 2001, to help me with my irritated eyes, the detritus of the Twin Towers still blowing up to Greenwich Village when the wind came north. Next to that, the same as in my medicine cabinet— artificial tears. Despite the real ones, you had to wash your eyes out several times a day, the irony of that not lost on anyone.

CHAPTER 10

He was waiting at the gate that led to my garden, moving nervously from one foot to the other, a cigarette dangling from his mouth. I saw him in profile first, his black hair pulled back into a long braid that went nearly to his waist, twisted with some kind of cord or string, a feather hanging near the end. He had perfect skin, a straight nose, a strong chin. When he turned, I saw his eyes, a rich, deep brown, more the color of bittersweet chocolate than Turkish coffee, and more lucid than they should have been, given what I'd been led to believe. I knew who he was before he said a word.

"Mr. Bowling, I presume." I didn't offer my hand. Actually, both hands were full, but I wouldn't have offered one anyway.

"Rachel?" He slid the cigarette from his mouth and held it for a moment between his long, thin fingers before tossing it into the street, as if he were reading my stand on his habit before deciding whether or not to waste a perfectly good smoke. I had the feeling he could seduce the gold bars out of Fort Knox without lifting a finger.

I looked at the ember, still alive after the sparks went out, and walked over to crush it with my shoe. I knew I was just being a bitch. No dog was headed our way, Dashiell was nowhere near it and it would have gone out in less than a minute on its own.

"What is it you want?" I asked, not taking out my keys.

"I thought you might want to talk to me," he said, bending closer so that he could lower his voice to a near whisper and I'd still hear him over the traffic from Hudson Street and the whir of the air conditioners.

"Did you?"

He'd said his piece. He waited. The truth was, I did want to talk to him, but I didn't want to say so.

"And you're hoping to get your things," I said.

"I am. The police said that you . . ." He stopped and smiled, showing me his perfect white teeth and the half-dimples his smile made in his cheeks, visible even beneath the artful one-day growth of stubble. I thought about Nick's unshaven face and how different that looked, the real thing versus the fashion statement. "Look at me," Parker said. And I did. Slowly, from head to toe. "I've been wearing the same things for days."

But of course that wasn't true. His chambray work shirt, another affectation unless you count hustling as a blue-collar profession, was immaculate. His jeans were just this side of pressed. Even his shoes, scuffed boots, seemed chosen to complete the picture rather than what he'd been stuck with. His hair was picking up the light from the lamppost. He could have done an Herbal Essence ad with hair that thick and shiny. Whatever it was he needed so badly from Tim's apartment, it wasn't a change of clothes.

"You shouldn't have come here. You should have called," I said.

Parker smiled and nodded. "I did. You were never home."

"You should have left your number."

He looked away and sighed. Then he took a step closer. I felt Dashiell, close to my left leg, inch forward and angle himself so that his head was between Parker and me. Had Parker wanted to come any closer, he would have had to push Dashiell out of his way.

"Look, I didn't know what else to do. I thought if I came here, I might be able to make you understand. I mean, I was living there, it was my home, and when the cops came and said I had to get out, they didn't let me take anything. Not one thing. I was hoping . . ."

I shook my head. "I'm sorry. I'm very busy settling Detective O'Fallon's affairs and you didn't leave me a number, so I couldn't call you back," remembering the cell phone number in O'Fallon's book as I said it. "I just got into the apartment myself and I need to gather things for O'Fallon's attorney. You'll have to wait another day or two."

"That's Tim's, isn't it?" Pointing to the briefcase.

I looked down at the briefcase and back at Parker.

"Yes. Why do you ask?"

"I didn't know you'd be taking anything out."

"You mean before you got your things?"

He nodded, clearly upset, moving from one foot to the other. I wondered how long he'd been standing there and if I'd adopted Brody's attitude before ever talking to Parker myself. He didn't look scary now, just pitiful. Tim had taken him in, hadn't he? Was he now my responsibility, too?

"I can pack up your clothes, if that's what you need. Yours is the closet to the left, isn't it? The one with the shrine?"

"Look, I . . ."

I glanced across the street. "I can drop them off at the Sixth," I said. "You can pick them up there, from Detective Brody."

He began to shake his head again. Not the clothes. Not the shrine. Then what?

I looked across the street again, thinking about those newspaper articles, thinking about talking to Brody about them, old stone face, as if that were going to do me any good.

But Parker might talk, especially if he thought there was something in it for him.

"How about a trade?" I said.

"What do you mean?"

"You said you thought I'd want to talk to you. The truth is, I do. I need information. You tell me anything you can about O'Fallon, I'll make sure you get into the apartment sooner. Deal?"

"Sure, okay," he said, those intense eyes watching me. "When?"

"Right now."

"We're going to Tim's now? Great."

But the more he wanted in, the more I wanted to keep him out, at least until I'd had the chance to check everything out on my own. "Let's take one step at a time," I said. "I haven't eaten all day. You don't want to bargain with a hungry woman."

"We're going in?" he asked, indicating the gate with a nod of his head. The man was shameless.

"Not hardly. We're going to grab a burger."

Parker shrugged. He'd waited this long, he could wait another forty-five minutes, an hour if I ate slowly.

I was going to ask if he was hungry, too, but then I didn't. He looked as if he'd been starving all his life. I just didn't know for what.

I wasn't getting the picture Brody had tried to give me, nor the one Jin Mei had painted of Parker Bowling aka Dick Parker, Richard Lee Bowling and Parker Lee. I needed to sketch one of my own. Most of all, I needed to see what O'-Fallon had seen in this man. I needed to understand why he had taken him in. Even if I had to cut what Parker told me in half, and then in half again, I'd still learn something about O'Fallon's life and that's what I wanted to do now, more than anything.

I headed back to Hudson Street, Dashiell on one side, Parker on the other. We walked over to the White Horse, where we could sit outside. There'd be lots of people there and no one minded a dog being there as long as he was on the outside of the fence. I thought the rule ridiculous. I thought the way the French did it made more sense. But we were in New York, not Paris, and the rules about dogs in places that served food were getting tighter all the time. Some places cared. Others didn't. But the White Horse was close and cheap and there was an empty table near the rail. It would do.

We ordered burgers and Cokes. I had the feeling that Parker would have liked something a bit stronger than a Coke. I thought he was trying to impress me with his sterling behavior and that was okay with me.

"So how did you meet Timothy O'Fallon?" I asked, not one for beating around the bush.

"He arrested me. Petty larceny. I was flat broke and I ate in a restaurant and tried to leave without paying. The waiter tripped me, then the owner punched me and called the cops."

I began to laugh. "No shit? Sounds like the beginning of a beautiful friendship."

"I thought so, too," he said, flashing me a grin that seemed to light up the whole block. "Especially after I told him that I was temporarily unemployed and had recently lost my residence and he said I could bunk with him until I got back on my feet. He said he'd help me out. I couldn't believe I was hearing that from a cop. It was too good to be true. And you know what they say, if it sounds too good to be true, it probably is."

"You mean living with O'Fallon wasn't all you expected it to be?"

Parker reached out, as if to cover my hand with his, but stopped and put his hand down in the middle of the table instead. "It's not that he didn't help me. He did. And I'm grateful to him for it."

So grateful that while he was lying dead in the
bathroom, you were stealing his stuff, I thought.

"But it was hard to live with him."

"How so?"

"His depression. It was relentless."

The waitress came with our burgers and fries.
She had a ring in one eyebrow, another in one
nostril, a chain tattooed around her upper arm.
Her hair was half yellow and half green. By the
time she set down the plates, the fries were half
on the plate and half on the table. I thought it
might be a good idea to slide to the far side of the
bench when she brought the drinks.

Parker took a bite of the burger as if he hadn't
eaten in weeks.

"He was depressed all the time?" I asked.

"Anyone drinks the way he did would be.
Practically nonstop when he got home from work
until he went to bed."

"Did you drink with him? Was that something
you did together?"

"I'd have one drink, you know, to be sociable,
but not like Tim."

"Funny, I thought his letting you live there had
to do with *your* addictions."

He took another bite of his burger.

I waited.

"I've had my problems. I'm not denying that.
And I did slip a couple of times. But that was on
the table, if you know what I mean. My using was
up for discussion. His wasn't."

"Was it the job? Was that what was getting him
down?"

Parker shrugged and picked up a handful of

fries, dipping them in the pool of ketchup he'd made on his plate. "He wasn't going to talk to me about police work."

"Right."

"I just know it was bad. He was one unhappy dude. It didn't surprise me, what he did. Well, it did. But not really."

"Tell me why you went through the window."

For the first time, Parker was caught off-guard, but he recovered almost immediately. Practice makes perfect.

"Lost my keys."

"How, Parker?"

"You're starting to sound like him now and I gotta tell you, it's not attractive."

"Right. Didn't you lose your keys because O'-Fallon finally got fed up with your behavior?" I asked. "Didn't he take them back and ask you to leave?"

"Look, I didn't do anything wrong. If I did, I'd be in jail now, not sitting here and eating this burger." His steady gaze bit into me, making sure I got the point. "He was hot under the collar, you know. I had a couple of close friends over and he didn't like that. I thought, big deal, he wasn't home, what he didn't know wouldn't hurt him."

I didn't interrupt to tell him what a lying sack of shit he was. I was sure he'd been told before.

"I figured, have a few friends in, then get the hell out before he came home. I guess we lost track of time, you know what I mean?"

I nodded. I knew exactly what he meant. I'd seen the decimated liquor cabinet and the empties everywhere, the cans and bottles Brody had bagged and carried out.

"He was pissed, irrational. It was just a few guys having a beer, shooting the shit. Cops." He shook his head, took a few fries, passed them through the ketchup, opened his mouth wide and dropped them in.

There was something sexual about the way he did that, his eyes on me and not on the food, everything in slow motion. I thought it was a survival response, trying to seduce anything that moved to get whatever it was he needed at the time—a smoke, some money, a place to live, his possessions. But it wasn't working on me and I didn't think it had worked on Tim. I didn't know Tim's motive for taking Parker into his home, but whatever it was, I didn't believe he'd been fooled into it.

"He was really pissed, huh?"

"You better believe it. He just blew up and shoved us out the door. No one could get a word in edgewise."

"Same as the cops the next day, not even letting you get your stuff?"

He nodded.

"Only Tim took the keys before he kicked you out."

"No, he didn't. He was too angry to think about something like that. I really lost them. I mean, maybe I left them in the apartment. I don't remember what the hell I did with them after I unlocked the door. You never have trouble finding yours?"

"So what fucking choice did you have, right?

You needed your stuff, you had to break the window to get in?"

"I called him, you know. I figured he had the night to calm down, get over himself. I figured at least he'd let me get my stuff. Worst-case scenario, I figured he'd pitch it out the door."

"But there was no answer."

He nodded, his expression never changing. He was playing the sincerity gambit, portraying himself as the aggrieved person, doing so without a trace of irony. And as far as I could tell, sitting across from him, there was no sign he didn't believe every single word he was saying.

"I figured, even better, you know what I mean? He didn't want me there, fine, to hell with him. He must have gone back to his sister's house, caught an early shift, whatever; I could get in there, grab my stuff and get out, not even have to see him."

"But it didn't work out that way. First, you get there and you stick your hand in your pocket, and there aren't any keys."

He sat back, smiling. "I rang a few bells. Someone always rings you in."

"And the door to the garden was unlocked."

"Usually is."

"Then you pried the window with Jin Mei's palette knife."

"Lock was a piece of shit," he said, "just for show."

"And then what?"

"I went in to get my stuff. What do you think?"

"I think you had a terrific shock when you went for your toothbrush. That's what I think."

Parker drummed his long fingers on the table.

"I've seen dead people before," he said. He picked up his glass and took a long drink. "He need anything?" He was looking at Dashiell. He picked up a fry, danced it up and down in the ketchup and dangled it over Dash's head. A glob of ketchup landed on Dashiell's white fur. Parker shrugged and dropped the fry back on his plate. "So when can I get my stuff, Rachel?"

I took my napkin, dipped it in the water glass, told Dashiell to put his paws up on the fence and wiped his head.

"Where were you Saturday night? Where did you stay?"

He shrugged. "With a friend."

"Does the friend have a name?"

He shook his head. No name. Not one he was about to tell me. Or not one he'd thought up yet.

"What about now? Where are you living these days?"

"My aunt's apartment. Why, you got a better idea?"

"Lucky you," I said, "you always end up with a place to stay, one way or another."

"Yeah, it worked out okay. But I need my stuff."

"Give me the number there. I'll call you, okay?" He wrote the number on a napkin and passed it across the table to me. I opened O'Fallon's briefcase and dropped it in.

"I won't take but five minutes," he said.

"Okay. Friday afternoon, between one and two."

"Not tomorrow?"

"You don't want to be there tomorrow," I told him, not wanting to tell him the truth, that I wouldn't be there tomorrow.

"Why not?"

I waited for him to draw his own conclusion.

"The cops? Shit."

I picked up my burger, broke off a piece for Dashiell, took a bite of what was left.

"I thought they were done with it. I thought that they'd released it. I thought that's why . . ."

Even the cops were allowed to lie to people in order to get the information they were after. What's good enough for New York's finest was surely good enough for me. "Like I'm going to tell them," I said, as sincerely as I could, "sorry, boys, it's not convenient. You can't come back, check around again, see if you missed anything."

I could see him thinking, trying to work out a way around this new information. The check came. He took out his pack of cigarettes, tapped the bottom, offered me a smoke. I took out some money, but Parker held up his hand. He reached into his pocket and took out some bills and counted them, scowling. "I'm a little short," he said, putting the money back in his pocket. "I'll grab it next time."

I paid the check and walked around to the outside of the fence to untie Dashiell's leash.

I turned to leave, then turned back.

"Did you go into the bathroom?" I asked. "Or did you just stand in the doorway?"

Parker stared up at me, then looked around at the other people eating there—young women with halter tops and work boots, couples with baby strollers next to their tables, a couple of guys with tattoos having beers. He got up and came out the exit, as I had just done, coming over to where I stood with Dashiell.

"Let's get away from here," he said. "I don't think anyone else wants to hear this."

The air had cooled off a bit. The humidity was down and there was a breeze. Parker indicated the way he wanted to walk with a nod. We headed uptown, neither of us saying anything. In a moment, I saw where he was going. We walked into Abingdon Square Park, where I had once met the most unusual clients I'd ever had. The park was empty except for a homeless man and his shopping cart at the far end. We sat on a bench and Parker finally lit his cigarette.

"Start with opening the bathroom door," I said.

"The shower was running, the room all steamed up, the shower curtain closed. I think, shit, he's here. He's going to go ballistic when he finds out I broke the lock on the window to get in. I'm about to close the door, leave the fucking toothbrush and the razor, and I would have, except for the water coming over the lip of the tub. It's on the floor, about a half inch high, not quite enough to get over the door saddle. And it's red." He took a puff on his cigarette, blowing the smoke off to the side.

"So what'd you do?"

"I grabbed the towels first and threw them down on the floor so that I could walk in. I still got the shit all over my shoes. I pulled the curtain back and saw him. He was sort of crumpled, on his back, underwater. The gun was near his right hand. The wall, you don't want to know. Looked like fireworks, you know, starting in the middle and exploding out. Only it was blood and bone and brains." Parker shook his head and inhaled deeply on the cigarette. "I shut off the shower. I was going to move his foot and the washcloth off the drain, but it was way too gross in there to stick my hand in. Then I remembered that there was a plunger under the kitchen sink, so I went out and got that."

I pictured the wet, bloody footprints going from the bathroom to the sink and back.

"I used the plunger to move the foot and the washcloth so the hot soapy red water could drain. It took me a minute or so, all that water holding it down. Then I called 911."

"And you packed your things while you waited for them."

"Fat lot of good that did me."

I wondered why he hadn't just grabbed his stuff and left. Perhaps he'd noticed Netty in the garden and knew he'd been seen. Perhaps he knew it would go worse for him if he fled. Perhaps he was really stunned by what he saw, going on automatic when he packed, that's what he'd come for, after all, not thinking clearly. And who could blame him if that was the case?

"When the paramedics came, what happened next?"

"The cops got there first, two young ones. The white one, he went into the bathroom and a minute later I heard him puking. Must have been right out of the academy, his first dead body in a bathtub." Parker grinned. "Looked like shit when he came out of there, even whiter than when he went in. So the black one, another jerk-off, he's like, 'You can't leave that shit in there, not if you want a job tomorrow.' At first, he didn't want to go back, see the body again. But he did. He picked up the bath mat, the towels, dumped them in a garbage bag, puke and all. Then he started in with the Fantastic. Sprayed so much, his partner was coughing in the living room. As soon as he's finished in the bathroom, he tries to light up, the poor bastard. His hand's shaking so much, it takes two matches. He's trying to keep it all together, you know what I mean. But he can't. He's just standing there while his partner starts going through Tim's desk."

"Were they wearing gloves?"

"Gloves? Oh, I get it." Parker laughed. "No, no gloves."

"I see. What next?"

"The paramedics. *They* wore gloves. Knew a guy once, he was a paramedic. He was always afraid of catching something. He wore double gloves. I go, 'Why don't you pick another line of work, asshole, one where you're not dealing with all those dangerous fluids?' You know what he says? He says, 'You tell me what's not dangerous and I'll do it.' That's what he says." He shook his head. "So I go, 'How about being a clerk at a 7-Eleven?' And he goes, 'Right, like that's not going to get me shot.' And I go . . ."

"The paramedics?"

"Yeah, yeah. They go into the bathroom, they stay—what, two seconds?—and they come back out. They go hang out in the garden, smoking, waiting to be told what to do. I mean, you talk to them, it's like they're doctors. It's like they're better than doctors. But then you see them in the flesh, it's more like slapstick. They don't know their ass from a hole in someone's head. If not for me, O'Fallon would have still been lying underwater."

Parker tossed his cigarette across the park. I thought about the Crime Scene Unit showing up, finding the integrity of the scene destroyed, everything trampled, touched, contaminated. But did it really matter when someone took a gun to his own head?

"The cop who was going through the desk," Parker said, "he began to ask me a lot of questions—who I was, what was I doing there, like that. Then the other one looked through my bag and said I couldn't take it. That's when the detectives showed. Man, it was standing room only in there. One of them took me outside, to the garden. He's like, 'You can't stay in the apartment, it's got to be sealed pending investigation of the accident.' Some accident. The man wanted to be dead. He got tired of waiting, took things into his own hands. I don't have any argument with that. He's better off now, far as I can tell."

It was hard not to react to that. But if I did, Parker didn't notice. He was on a roll and he just kept talking. "I'm telling you the God's honest truth," he said, looking toward Hudson Street. "It's what he wanted."

He stood and reached for my hand. I shook my head. "I don't need any help getting up," I told him.

Parker sat down again.

"And I don't need company."

"No, it's not that. It's something else. It's about the town house."

"What town house?"

"The one on Tenth Street. The one you take care of."

"What about it?" Wondering which neighbor he'd wheedled that out of. Why not? Endearing himself to strangers was his single talent. In that, it seemed, he was the quintessential con artist.

"If you need any help, you know—painting, repairs, like a live-in super—I could be of use to you, just until the Siegals come back, of course. When are they due back, by the way?"

"What the hell are you talking about?"

"You don't have to worry. I'd work for my keep. I could cook for you, clean the house, do the wash. I'd do whatever you needed, Rachel, whatever you asked." He leaned a little closer. "You might feel safer having a man nearby, for protection."

Had his aunt given him a time limit? Or was he always looking ahead, knowing nothing lasts forever? This time I got up. And so did Dashiell. Parker started to get up, too, but I put my hand out to stop him. "Don't move," I said. "Don't even think of moving. Because I already have someone who does whatever I ask him to and I'm thinking of asking for a little favor right now."

His forehead pleated, Parker looked confused. That's when he seemed to notice Dashiell, as if it hadn't registered before that he was standing there, his eyes locked on Parker's, his tail straight out behind him, barely stirring the air.

"Just sit here for a while, Parker. Don't get up. And for God's sake, don't speak."

I was out of the park and doubling back toward home when I heard him, the weasel.

"You won't forget your promise, Rachel, will you? I told you everything, just like you wanted. You won't forget about Friday?"

"I never forget a promise," I said, thinking of the promise I'd somehow made to O'Fallon even though I wasn't aware I was making it at the time.

The leash in one hand, O'Fallon's briefcase in the other, I took a long way home. Weaving up and down some of the dark, narrow streets between Bleecker and West Fourth streets, I peered into the tall, lit-up windows of town houses, wondering what the lives of the people who lived there were like, people with chandeliers and grand central staircases, with libraries and formal dining rooms, people with money and jobs they could actually talk about. Passing their elegant homes, I wondered if the people who lived there ever thought about people who lived half in and half out of the gutter. People like Parker, O'Fallon, people like me.

CHAPTER 11

When I was two blocks from home, my cell phone rang. The conversation was short and one-sided. "I'm on Perry Street," I said. Then, "Yes." And "Yes" again.

Once again there was a man waiting at the gate that led to my cottage, smoking a cigarette, this one standing with his back to me. But this one wasn't jiggling around. He was standing perfectly still and I had the feeling he was used to waiting. I had the feeling he could do it for a long, long time, no problem.

There was a weariness in his shoulders and something about him that made him look shabby and used. I wondered what it was he had to tell me. I wondered what could be so important that it couldn't wait, and why he'd crossed the street to wait for me rather than asking me to stop by the precinct. When he turned around and I saw the mileage on his face, the wear and tear, I knew that whatever it was he'd come to say, it wasn't good.

He didn't smile when he saw me, lift his hand, toss away the cigarette, take a step in my direction. He stood his ground, waiting until I was standing next to him, waiting for me to talk first even though this meeting had been his idea.

"What happened?"

He pinched the bridge of his nose with two fingers, let his hand drop. I thought it would go right back where it had been, to his side, but he put it around my arm instead. "Where can we talk for a minute?"

I thought about the way I'd felt a couple of hours before, not taking out my key, leading Parker away from where I lived, from where I felt safe. Then I took out the keys and opened the gate. Brody held it, closing it behind us, stepping aside to let me lock it, then testing it to make sure, a careful man. We walked down the tunnel made by the town house I took care of and the one next door, brick all around us, our footsteps loud and hollow, coming back at us as we walked. The only light in the garden was the one on a timer, at the back of the Siegal house. The house lights were on, too, a ploy to induce people into thinking that someone was at home, a ploy that hadn't even fooled a homeless woman who'd barely had her wits about her. My lights were off, the cottage dark. No one could see it from the street. Lights on, lights off, it didn't make a dime's worth of difference.

We walked over to the steps. I moved the key toward the lock. Brody took my arm again.

"Let's stay out here," he said. "This is nice."

We sat on the steps. I leaned the briefcase against the rail and unhooked Dashiell's leash. There was a blue ceramic bowl outside, nearly as dark as lapis. He walked over to it, took a noisy drink, checked the perimeter, then lay down in his favorite spot, under the oak.

There were lights on in some of the apartments that backed onto the garden, and air conditioners making a white noise, so that aside from an occasional horn or passing motorcycle, we couldn't hear the traffic on Hudson Street.

"I had no idea this was back here," Brody said.

"That's one of the things I like about it. That, and this, being able to sit outside, think my own thoughts, look at the stars without worrying about getting mugged."

"You just let a strange man in here. You're much too trusting."

I turned to look at him. "A man with a gun." I reached out to touch it through his jacket, changing my mind before I did. "But you're not going to mug me with your service revolver, are you, Detective? You're going to do it with words."

He unbuttoned his jacket, letting it fall open.

"Have you spoken to Parker yet?"

"Yes, why?"

"When did you speak to him?"

"Tonight. Just before you called. I found him waiting for me when I got home. He wants his stuff. He seems real anxious to get it."

"You didn't bring him in here, did you?"

"No, Detective. I thought he might be armed."

"This is serious, Ms. Alexander."

"Right. And I understand that cops never make jokes to ease the tension. I'll try to behave myself. He was here, standing at the gate, like you were.

I had no idea he'd show up here, but I thought I'd take the opportunity to ask him some questions. I have a lot of questions, Detective, and I haven't been getting a lot of answers. We went over to the White Horse, had a burger. He talked about breaking into the apartment on Horatio Street, finding Tim in the bathtub, the shower going. He told me about the two rookie cops who contaminated the crime scene and handled everything in sight without gloves. And he stuck me with the check."

"So he hasn't been back to Tim's place yet?" Deadpan. Had I thought I was going to rattle him, I'd have been severely mistaken.

"No. But he's been calling a lot. That's why he showed up. I never seem to be here to answer his calls. What's up?"

"Did he tell you where he was staying now?"

"Yes, he did. With an aunt."

"And did he give you a number where you could reach him?"

"Yes. He wrote it on a napkin. Why? Do you want it?"

He shook his head. "She's been reported missing," he said, his expression not changing.

"By Parker?"

Brody laughed. Well, perhaps it was more of a snort of derision. "No, ma'am. She's an actress. She had a small part in an Off-Broadway play, right here in the neighborhood."

"At the Louise Lortell?"

"Yes, ma'am."

"Detective?"

"Yes?"

"I think you ought to be calling me Rachel."

He nodded.

"Would you like a beer?"

He shook his head.

"So, she didn't show up for work?"

"She missed the Sunday matinee. They called and couldn't reach her. They left a message. I don't know what they figured, but they put the understudy on, Sunday night as well. The theater is dark on Monday. They tried to call her Tuesday. Same thing. No luck. So today they called it in. It's not like her, they said. She's never missed a performance. A real pro. At it since she was eleven."

"Has anyone talked to Parker?"

"He told one of the detectives he was going to live with an aunt of his, that he'd lived with her before and she'd agreed to take him in again when we took him out of Tim's apartment."

"He told me the same thing."

"Tonight?"

"Yes, this was the only time I talked to him."

"So he hasn't been to Tim's?"

"No. I already told you that. If you're not going to believe me, you can go back to calling me ma'am."

"Yes, ma'am. Just trying to get this straight."

"I told him he could come on Friday, that that's the soonest I could do it. So did anyone talk to him after you heard his aunt had gone missing? What did he say? Did he say where she was?"

"He says she went to Europe. He says she gave him the keys and said he could stay at her place until she gets back."

"Europe? In the middle of the run of a show? I wouldn't think so."

"We asked Parker where we could get in touch with her and he was quite vague, said he had no idea where she might be, not even what country she went to."

"Let me guess. There's no record of her on any flight."

"Correct. And her passport? Expired over two years ago."

"Are you looking for Parker? Is he going to be charged?"

"With what?" He ran a hand through his short hair. "There's no body, no evidence he did anything wrong."

"But you think he did."

"You don't want to know what I think of Parker."

"Did Tim?"

"Ma'am?"

"Did Tim want to know what you thought of Parker?"

"No, ma'am. He never asked."

"So, now what?"

"We're looking into the aunt's whereabouts. I just wanted you to be aware of this. The offer holds. If you want me to be there when you let Parker take his things, I will. Unless you have a boyfriend who could . . ."

I shook my head. "Ex. I don't think he'd fly in from California for this."

"I'm sorry," he said. I thought he meant it, too.

"I wanted to talk to you, too. I saw where the tile was replaced. Tim wasn't cleaning his gun."

Brody didn't move.

"It wasn't an accident."

"There's no need for Mary Margaret to hear that."

"None at all."

"And no need for you to repeat what you just said to me, not to another living soul."

"No need."

"That's good. A man's career shouldn't have to end on a note of shame."

"I understand. But, of course, Parker knows."

He nodded.

"He said Tim had been . . ." I stopped, not thinking he'd want to have this discussion, not thinking there was anything I could tell him about job-related depression, about cop suicide, that he didn't already know.

"I'll take that beer now, if you don't mind."

I got up and unlocked the door, picking up the briefcase and dropping it onto the table outside the kitchen. I opened the refrigerator and took out two beers. For some strange reason, when I turned around, I expected Brody to be standing right behind me. But it was only Dashiell who had followed me inside, his tail thumping against the cabinets now that I'd noticed him, now that I'd gotten the message.

I put down the beers, opened the refrigerator and took out the plastic container with Dashiell's food—raw turkey, brown rice, a medley of grated vegetables. There was only one portion left, so I put the container down, checked his water bowl, gave him a pat on the head and took the beers outside.

"It's a funny thing, the way people do things," Brody said.

"What do you mean?"

"There was this woman a few years ago, lived on Charles Street, not too far from here. She decided she'd had enough, decided to take her cat with her."

"How do you know that?"

"We found her clothes down on the old pier, all folded just so, as if she were going to put them back on after her swim, the shoes lined up, socks balled up and stuffed in the shoes, cat's collar on top of the pile."

"How do you know it didn't belong to a small dog?"

Brody grinned, opened the beer, dropped the pull-tab into his pocket, pulled out a pack of cigarettes.

"Do you mind?" he asked.

I shook my head.

"Well, first off, there was a box of Friskies at her apartment, a litter box in the john, one of those jungle-gym things covered in carpet in the living room. There were a couple of catnip mice under the bed, a couple of small balls, one made of crunched-up foil, in the bottom of the closet, one of them in one of her shoes. And two, we found the cat."

"And the collar fit?"

"Not after eleven days in the water."

He took a long pull on the beer. I popped my can and did the same.

"Did you meet the dwarf yet?" he asked.

"What dwarf?"

"The redheaded one, lives upstairs from Tim."

"Not yet," I told him. "But I have a feeling I might get lucky tomorrow."

"Not if you play cards with the dwarf, you won't. He'll ask you, guaranteed. You say no, he's going to make out like it's personal, like you have something against him."

"Because he's got red hair?"

Brody smiled.

"And if I say yes?"

"You'll lose your shirt."

I could see the Big Dipper in the dark sky. "Don't worry about Friday," I said. "About Parker. I'll be okay."

"Don't underestimate him, Rachel."

"I won't," I said. "Anyway, I have a gun."

"I know." He looked at me, searching for a tell-tale bulge. "Where do you keep it?"

"Bedroom closet, top shelf, way in the back."

"And the bullets?"

"In the kitchen cabinets, behind the ziti, I think."

"Handy."

Now I was the one who was deadpan.

"You any good?"

"I am," I told him.

"But?"

"I don't like them. It makes it too easy when things are rough." I shook my head. "He's not going to give me a hard time. It wouldn't get him anywhere. It can't get him the apartment back. And if he gives me a hard time, he doesn't get to collect his possessions. He's going to be slimy, he's going to be manipulative, but he's not going to be dangerous."

"But . . ."

"No poker with the dwarf. It is poker, isn't it?"

Brody grinned this time.

"Poker it is," he said.

There was a little can with sand in it at the side of the path. He got up and pushed his cigarette into the sand. He turned and handed me the empty beer can. I called Dashiell over and tossed him the can. He walked toward the tunnel, dropping the can into the recycling container at the near end.

"Good trick," Brody said.

"We're full of them."

I walked him through the tunnel, thanking him for taking the time to let me know what was going on, unlocked the gate with the key and pulled it open.

"You forgot to tell me his name."

"Doesn't matter. You'll know him when you see him."

"Short arms. Short legs. Red hair."

"Irwin Del Toro."

"Yeah, right."

"He swears it's real."

"You're much too trusting," I told him.

"No woman's ever said that to me before."

"Now *that* I believe."

I started to close the gate. He put his hand out to stop it.

"If you change your mind about Friday . . ."

"I can call anytime, day or night."

"I didn't understand it before. But I do now."

"Understand what?"

"Why Tim chose you."

"What do you mean?" I asked.

He pulled the gate closed behind him.

"Why, Michael?" I put my hand on top of his. "What did he want me to do?"

He shook his head, slid his hand from under mine and headed across the street, back toward the station house. I stood there watching him leave, Dashiell at my side.

CHAPTER 12

The box office at the Louise Lortell Theater didn't open until noon and when I knocked on the door, no one answered. There was no one named Bowling listed on the poster outside. But there was an Elizabeth Bowles among the cast names. Perhaps they were still hopeful she'd show up for the next performance with a whopper of a story about where she'd been. I wasn't so hopeful myself, not after what Brody had told me. And not after reading the article I found in the Metro section of the *Times* that morning.

ACTRESS VANISHES, POLICE INVESTIGATE

The police are investigating the mysterious disappearance of the actress Elizabeth Bowles, who was appearing in a play at the Louise Lortell Theater. Bowles, 53, who lives in Greenwich Village, did not show up for a performance last week and has not been seen since the evening before, when she left the theater after the show. Her nephew, Parker Bowles, 34, said she took a trip to Europe, but there is no record of her flight and her passport, police say, expired several years ago.

"Elizabeth would never walk out in the middle of the run of a play," the director, Herbert Lewis, said. "She's the consummate professional. If you want someone who will inhabit a character fully and never miss a curtain, you hire Elizabeth. We're all very concerned, very worried."

Police say that Parker Bowles, who is unemployed, has been living at her apartment off and on the last two years. Neighbors say they hadn't seen Elizabeth for several days and that on Sunday, they saw her nephew and two friends throwing out what appeared to be women's clothing and shoes. But police were unable to find these items. Mr. Bowles, also known as Parker Bowling and Dick Parker, denies knowing anything further about the disappearance of his aunt. Though the information he gave to the detectives was inconsistent, at this point, police sources say, there is no crime, so there is no suspect. However, a detective at the Sixth Precinct did say they did not believe Ms. Bowles had gone to Europe.

Though she primarily worked on the stage, Elizabeth Bowles appeared in eleven films, including *Strangers on a Train* and *Zorba the Greek*. She was never married but was said to have had numerous affairs, including one with the actor Anthony Quinn.

I still had time before picking up O'Fallon's car and heading up to Piermont, so I walked over to O'Fallon's building and rang the bell for the apartment over his. The voice that answered was husky and I wondered if I'd woken him, if he'd been playing cards half the night and hadn't gotten to bed until the sun came up, letting my imagination run away with me.

I stated my name and business and he buzzed me in. I climbed the stairs and as I lifted my hand to knock, the door opened and there he was, looking up at me, a scowl on his face.

"I already talked to the police."

"I know."

"So what's the deal here? You a cop? No, doll, anyone can see you're not a cop. Your neck's not thick enough. And your shoes. Tuh. No way. Not a cop. So what the hell do you want?"

Beyond him, I could see the living room, the same size as O'Fallon's but very different in appearance. The wall facing me was covered with posters. Brody hadn't mentioned that Del Toro had had a varied and jaded career in show business, a stint with Barnum & Bailey, nightclub appearances, some TV work. In the middle of the room there was a traditional poker table, covered in green, eight chairs around it. I could smell the cigars from the last game even though the ashtrays had been emptied.

"I didn't see nothing. I didn't hear nothing. I don't know nothing. Case closed. Period. End of story." He began to close the door. I put my hand out to stop it, feeling like a bully.

"No gunshot?"

"Not a one."

"No fight?"

"Fight? What fight?"

"The day before. He had a fight with Parker and some of his friends."

"Friends. You mean those freeloaders who used to come here, carry on, drink Tim's booze, trash his apartment?"

"Those very ones."

"Has he eaten yet today?" Pointing at Dash.

I nodded.

"Good. Then you can come in." He turned around and waddled toward the sofa under the windows, hiking his legs up with his hips as he walked. He took a little backward hop to get seated, his feet a good fifteen inches off the floor once he was up there. Looking around, I could see that even in his own home, everything was scaled too big for him. I figured there must be a stool at the sink, another in the bathroom, a stick with a pad on one end for reaching light switches—God knows what else to make the environment user-friendly.

I grabbed a chair out from around the poker table and turned it so that I'd be facing him. "I was hoping . . ."

"I don't bite," he said. "You could sit here, doll." He patted the couch cushion. Dashiell walked over to see what he wanted. I stayed where I was. He put a hand on Dashiell's head, gave it a pat.

"In my day, I worked with the big cats. It was a comedic thing, you know, big joke seeing a little person controlling them with a whip and chair. Got a lot of laughs. Got me a lot of money at the time. Funny or no, a tiger's still a tiger. Animals don't scare me. It's people you got to watch out for."

"Mr. Del Toro, are you sure you didn't hear anything? I don't understand why no one heard the shot."

"Where do you live, little lady? The suburbs? You think anyone in New York would single out a sound and say"—hands dramatically to his cheeks—" 'Jeepers, did you hear that, a gunshot!' Never going to happen. Could be I did hear it. Could be I thought what I heard was a car backfiring. Could be some other horrific noise was happening at the same time and my air conditioner was on, the TV, the water running, whatever. Could be I was in church, praying to grow taller. There are just so many jobs for leprechauns, pixies, elves and trolls. A person has to earn a living, no matter what the fuck his height is. You understand what I'm saying?"

"I do," I said.

"Could be you can't hear much from one floor to another in this old building."

"Is that so?"

He rolled his eyes. "Have I ever lied to you, doll? I mean, so far."

"Mr. Del . . ."

"Good. Glad that's settled."

I got up. Dashiell got up. Irwin got up. He walked to the door, then turned back to face me.

"You play poker?" he asked.

"No," I lied. "Never have."

"Perfect. Tonight at eight. Every Thursday at eight. You don't have to call in advance. Just show up."

"Mr. Del Toro . . ." I said.

"Call me Irwin. Everyone calls me Irwin, at least to my face."

"Irwin, if you can't hear much up and down, how do you know about Parker's friends coming here and carrying on and drinking Tim's booze?"

"Easy. A couple of them are buddies of mine." He seemed to tilt his head to the wall with the posters. "No way they're going to drink and not invite me to join them."

"You mean men you worked with?"

He scratched his head, as if he were trying to figure out how to answer me.

"Probably wrapped it in a towel. Probably didn't want to disturb anyone, especially on a Sunday morning."

"But . . ."

"He was the most considerate man you'd ever want to know, doll. I felt tall around him."

I looked at one of the posters, from a small circus, Gerber's Traveling Oddities. One of the pictures was of Irwin getting out of one of those tiny cars. Even with the makeup and the fake nose, you couldn't miss him, not with that bright red hair.

"What would you have done if you were?" I asked.

"Tall? High wire." He stretched those short

arms out to the side, lifted one short leg, closed his eyes.

"You'd have been something, Irwin, really something."

"I know. He always said that, too. He said I was a tall man stuck in a short man's body. He said everyone was stuck, one way or another."

"When you talked to Tim, did you go downstairs or did he come up here?"

"Either way."

"And did you drink, you and Tim?"

"You mean booze?" He screwed up his face, cocking his head like an attentive dog. "Me? Yeah. Tim? No. He drank club soda, or maybe coffee. You said you were taking care of his affairs?"

"I am."

"What are you, with the bank or something? You his lawyer? What's the deal?"

"A friend."

"No way, doll. Tim was dry, going on eleven years. You don't know that, you weren't a friend."

"Correct," I said.

He raised his eyebrows.

"I was more of a slight acquaintance."

"I don't get it, doll."

"Neither do I, Irwin. Neither do I."

"What's he do?" He was pointing at Dashiell again. "I had a trick dog, I could get TV work. I can't just go on, make an ass of myself. It's not PC, you know what I'm saying. I'd get the fucking Little People of America on my case. You can't be an undignified dwarf anymore. But I could make an ass of him. Don't worry, doll. You'd get a cut. I'm a fair man."

He turned to Dashiell.

"Roll over," he told him. "Speak." Then he turned to me, palms raised toward the heavens. "Help me out here, doll. You must have taught him something, big dog like this."

"Nothing fancy," I said. "He sits and gives his paw."

"Impressive."

"*Semper paratus*," I told him. "Like you said, he's a big dog. I had to train him."

"They get all the girls, you know." He pointed up, at the ceiling. "The high-wire artists. People think it's the lion tamer." He shook his head. "Not so. Never been so. You single, doll? You seeing anyone?" He raised his eyebrows, looked me up and down, as if I were a piece of merchandise he was about to bid on.

I raised my hand like a stop sign.

"A guy can dream," he said. "You change your mind, doll, you know where to find me. Don't let my small stature fool you. I can show you a good time."

He reached for the doorknob. I raised my hand again. "Open it," I told Dash, indicating the door with a tilt of my head. Dashiell pushed in front of Irwin, grasped the knob, turned his head and backed up.

Irwin squinted at me. "Always something up your sleeve, eh? I like that in a woman. Don't be a stranger, doll. You hear me?"

I stopped at O'Fallon's apartment and dumped out the briefcase on his desk, refilling it with the things I wanted to take to Maggie's house—one of the photo albums, the coin collection, the silver ashtray that Parker had tried to steal. I decided to take the file on the car as well, in case there was any trouble at the lot.

My cell phone rang as I was on the way to pick up the car.

"Alexander."

"Rachel. I'm sorry I couldn't get back to you sooner. I was away."

"Who is this?"

"It's Ted Hank. I was John's partner. I guess you hadn't heard."

"Heard what?" I asked, though I thought perhaps I knew.

"John's dead, Rachel. He died of AIDS five months ago."

"I'm so sorry."

"He talked about you. And about Dash. He said he thought it was so weird, a private investigator doing pet therapy."

I stopped in the street. Dashiell began to sniff at the wrought iron around a tree pit, coleus growing around the tree, a plastic water bottle lying on top of two of the rich red leaves.

"He knew that? I never told anyone in the group . . ."

"I'm sorry," he said. "I didn't mean to give you a double shock. I should have kept my mouth shut."

"No, just tell me how he knew."

"I don't know. I figured you told him. Not so?"

I didn't say anything right away, so he kept on talking.

"No harm meant. No harm done, I hope. It's not some big secret, is it? I mean, in order for you to get work, people have to know, don't they?"

"Might he have told anyone else? Do you think he . . ."

There was silence on the line. Someone blew his horn on Washington Street. A dog across the street, a short-legged Jack Russell, all full of himself, began to bark at Dashiell.

"I couldn't honestly say."

"No harm done," I said a little too quickly. "I appreciate your calling, and I'm so sorry to hear about John."

O'Fallon's car was a beat-up Toyota Celica. I was glad I'd brought along the file with his papers. The monthly fee for the lot was worth more than the damn car and was due the next day. I'd see if Maggie would agree to come in by bus on Saturday and then drive Tim's car home. If not, I could even pick her up. Either way, it would save the estate about three hundred dollars because I could just pay the day rate until then. One less bill to deduct from Maggie's inheritance, one less thing for me to worry about.

And one more. Had John told O'Fallon that I was a private investigator? If I'd been named executor because of that, it wasn't just curiosity I was feeling. I wasn't just acting out of habit. I was on the job. I was getting paid to discover something, to do something. The only trouble was, I didn't know what it was.

I opened the back windows halfway for

Dashiell. As I pulled out of the lot, I heard him sneezing, clearing the way for new scents, ready to pull the world in as fast as it was passing, trying not to miss a thing. It was a lesson that wasn't lost on me.

CHAPTER 13

The house, along the Sparkill Creek, was one of the little saltboxes that faced a winding two-lane road, their long, narrow backyards sloping down toward the water. The O'Fallon house was painted gray with white trim. I parked along the road so that I wouldn't block Mary Margaret's car. She was at the open door as soon as I got out. She waited as we walked toward the house, asked if the dog was housebroken, then invited us in.

She had the kind of strong, trim body you often see on nurses and she was dressed in a trim, no-nonsense way as well, a pretty woman who did nothing to augment the gifts nature had given her. Her red hair was pulled back in a knot at the nape of her neck. She was in a pantsuit in shades of tan, no makeup, no nail polish, no jewelry. A little brown bird trying very hard not to be noticed.

Dashiell and I followed her inside. If I'd expected to be hit by the lingering odors of her mother's long-term illness, vaguely concealed by Lysol, Fantastic and Soft Scrub, I was pleas-

antly surprised. The windows were open, sunlight pouring in, the living room bright and
airy, everything in its place. The house had so
much sparkle I would have bet Maggie made
the beds with hospital corners, even here at
home.

We walked through the living room to the
kitchen. In New York City, it would be called an
eat-in kitchen. But this was a house. Houses almost always had kitchens you could eat in. The
table was set for lunch. She pointed to the place
farther from the sink and refrigerator and asked
me to sit. Then, surprising me, she took an old
saucepan from under the sink, ran the water cold
and filled the pot for Dashiell. She stood watching him drink noisily from the pan before really
looking at me.

"Does he need something to eat? I could give
him some turkey if he's hungry."

"No, he's fine, thank you." Again, a surprise.
And then another. She had a full-time job and,
until recently, another one at home, caring for her
sick mother. I expected a tuna sandwich, perhaps
a tossed salad with bottled dressing, but Maggie
was taking eggs out of the refrigerator, then butter and cheese. That's when I noticed the omelet
pan on the stove, the little pile of fresh herbs on
the counter.

"I don't buy this nonsense about eggs being
bad for you, do you, Rachel?" She was melting
butter, whipping the eggs. "It sometimes seems
there's nothing left to eat, if you read what's in
the papers and take it seriously." She grated just a
touch of cheese into the whipped eggs, poured

the mixture into the pan and began to chop the herbs, her hand moving quickly, the rhythmic sound of the knife on the cutting board filling the kitchen.

"This is so kind of you," I told her. "I didn't want you to trouble yourself like this."

"It's no bother at all," she said. "I haven't had time for company in a while. It's lovely to have someone here for lunch." As if I were a neighbor or old school chum dropping by for a chat. As if I weren't here to talk to her about her dead brother.

During lunch, she talked about the gentrification of Piermont, all the new construction, the rising prices of the houses, even the small ones, like hers, along the creek. The old Victorian houses facing the Hudson River, once considered white elephants, were never on the market more than a week, she told me, and sometimes strangers would ring the bell, even along the creek, but most definitely along the river, and ask if this house or that might be going on the market anytime soon.

"Are you planning to sell?" I asked.

"Where would I go?"

I finished the last of my omelet, wiping the plate with a piece of toast, thanking her again for the delicious lunch. When I got up to put my plate in the sink, she flapped her hand at me.

"Just leave it, Rachel. We can have our iced tea out on the back patio. The dog might enjoy that better than sitting in the living room."

Dashiell and I followed her out. I wasn't sure she'd believed he was house-trained. Some people who've never lived with a dog have trouble believing a dog can be unobtrusive and appropriate, even in a living room. But it was cool outside under the shade of an awning, and in no time Dashiell was down at the water's edge, turning back to catch my eye in the hope I'd throw a stick for him to retrieve.

I put O'Fallon's briefcase across my lap, taking out the folder I'd brought along to convince the guy at the lot that it would be okay for me to take the car. But before I asked Maggie if she'd consider taking the car on Saturday, I thought of an even better plan.

"I was wondering if I could leave Tim's car here? The payment at the lot is due tomorrow. It seems an awful waste of money. I don't know if you can use the car, or if you'd want to sell it?"

Actually, according to the will, the car was now mine. But the last thing I wanted to contend with was Tim's old wreck of a car that might not even pass inspection without expensive repair work. I'd have to take the time and trouble to sell it, paying to park it at the lot until I did.

"Of course, if that helps. You can leave it."

"Perhaps Dennis might be able to help you sell it."

"Oh, I don't think Dennis would be wanting that at his Lexus dealership. The only kind of used car he'd sell would be a pre-owned Lexus."

I shrugged. "I have all the papers here." I tapped the folder. "I'll just need to know what you get for it if you sell it, for the final income tax form."

"You don't even get away with that when you're dead," she said. "You'd think . . ."

"The lawyer will take care of that," I told her. "She seems very efficient and most helpful." She must be dealing with all of this for her mother, too. Just the thought of handling two estates at once was overwhelming. I wonder if that had occurred to Tim, too. I wondered if that was why he hadn't named Maggie his executor, if it were that simple, nothing more than that he didn't want her to have to do this twice.

"How will you get back to the city?" she asked. "I don't think . . ." She was looking at Dashiell now, lying down on the slope of cool earth near the water's edge.

"I can take a car service back," I said, thinking that if I hadn't been so preoccupied, I would have thought of this earlier, left Dashiell at home and taken the bus back to the city, a subway after that. But even if I ended up with a car service, it would be much cheaper than a month's worth of parking at the lot.

"I doubt they'll take you with a wet dog."

Dashiell was wading in the creek. In no time, he'd find a reason to go swimming. I hadn't, after all, told him he couldn't.

"I see your point," I said. "Well, I guess I could keep the car another couple of days. I could pay the day rate at the lot. It won't be so bad."

"How about if I drive you over the bridge? You can grab a cab there. Would that be okay?"

"That would be great, if you don't mind."

"No problem. It's on the way to work anyway."

"Terrific." I put my hand back into the briefcase. "Even though you're coming Saturday, I brought some pictures from Tim's apartment. I thought you'd want them. I didn't see any reason to wait."

Maggie looked, but didn't say anything.

"They're old ones," I said. "The only recent one was of your mother." I didn't have that one with me, the one Tim had left on the desk before taking his gun into the bathroom, before pulling the trigger on what should have been the rest of his life. "I was hoping we could look at some of the ones in the album and that you might tell me which one is Tim."

"Of course."

"I brought a couple of other things from the apartment as well. I'm sure there's more there you'll want."

She nodded.

"I was thinking of sending the clothes and the kitchen things to Housing Works. The kitchen things are pretty inexpensive, not nearly as nice as the ones you have." I decided not to mention the scarf and the sweater. Maybe that was a dumb idea to begin with, picking out things for a person you didn't know. "Is there anything special that you can think of that you want me to put aside, because I'll be working there again tonight, and all day tomorrow?"

"I'm not, I don't . . ."

"It's awkward, doing this. I'm sorry if . . ."

"Don't apologize. It's all got to be done. Let's look at the pictures now, and I'll show you which one's Timothy."

I took out the album I'd brought along and placed it on the redwood table in front of us, moving my glass of iced tea off to the side, flipping the album open to the middle.

"That's Tim"—her finger pointing to one of the grinning redheaded boys. "This one's Dennis."

"The Lexus salesman."

"Yes. And here's our Joey."

"Joseph Patrick."

"Yes. Bless his soul. And this one's me, of course."

"The only girl."

She looked up, her mouth open, as if she were about to speak, perhaps to tell me what that meant. But I already knew. It meant being the one stuck at home, taking care of your mother.

"Have you always lived at home?" I asked.

"I have," she said. "And this is Liam. He was my first cousin. And this one's Francis. I had a terrible crush on him when I was eleven. Oh, I thought the sun rose and set on Francis Connor, I was that smitten."

"Tim had some newspaper articles among his things," I said. "One about Joseph. One about your father."

"Dennis once said we were like the Kennedys, only without the money or the fame."

"I—"

"Do you believe in curses?" she asked.

"I don't know. I've never thought about it."

"Oh, you'd think about it a lot if you were in this family."

I looked back at the pictures of the smiling kids, then back at Mary Margaret.

"No one knows why it happened to them either," she said.

"To the Kennedys?"

"Yes, and it goes on and on. Like ours. It didn't stop with Jack or Robert or that terrible incident with Teddy. There was that rape trial, and the Skakel nightmare. On through the generations. I don't expect our troubles are over either."

"You mean the accidents in your family?"

"My father used to say, 'We're not here for fun. We're here for sorrow.' " She was looking straight ahead, watching Dashiell racing back and forth at the river's edge. " 'That's our lot here on earth,' he said before his accident. 'Our reward comes later.' "

"Sounds as if you were raised to be a very responsible person."

"I was, not like the kids coming up today, so self-involved—just me, me, me. Even the young nurses, fresh out of school. It's a service profession. Some of them, they're in it for the social life. They're in it to find a doctor to marry. You do what's right," she said. "That's what I grew up with, what we all grew up with."

"Were you and Tim close?" I felt as if I was treading on thin ice, expecting Maggie to break down and cry at any moment. But her eyes were dry. She was in control.

"Oh, I worshiped Timothy. We all did." Smiling now.

"He was the oldest, wasn't he?" To keep it going.

"Yes, the firstborn. We all looked up to him. We all wanted to be just like him, to do everything he could do."

She hadn't answered me at all, so I asked again. "So you were close? As grown-ups, too?"

Her back straight, her head high, she sat perfectly still, the sibling who'd stayed at home and nursed her mother, working full-time, keeping the house immaculate, taking care of the old lady as she slipped from one world to the next.

"So you saw each other often?" I asked.

"I loved him," she said without looking at me. "We were family. Family's everything. But he was so busy with work."

"And you were working long hours at the hospital and taking care of your mother."

Do you see Dennis much? I wanted to ask. But I didn't. I thought I'd said too much already. I thought about the letter, the short note that had arrived after Tim had died. I didn't mention that either.

I gave Maggie the keys to the car, leaving the folder on the table. While she changed for work, I went to check the car, to see if there was anything in it I needed to take. There was the usual stuff in the glove compartment: empty and half-empty packs of cigarettes, the repair manual, a flashlight, a greasy rag, a package of Kleenex, an unopened roll of red Lifesavers and a plastic cup. The trunk was empty except for the spare, which looked brand-new, and the tool kit, the jack, flares, a few wrenches. I checked the floor in the back and came away with dirty hands, sand, cigarette butts, empty soda cans. I checked under the passenger seat and found more tissues, Scott this time, the box crushed on one side as if someone had stepped on it. And then I sat in the driver's seat and reached under it as far as I could, pulling out the notebook. It was one of those the kids used to buy every fall for school, like the ones I'd found at Tim's apartment. Only this one was current. I took it inside, put it into the briefcase, then went into the downstairs bathroom to wash my hands.

I thought I'd sit outside with Dashiell until Maggie was ready, but then I remembered something from my first job as an undercover agent, when I worked for the Petrie Brothers before going out on my own. I was placed at a hospital on Staten Island, ostensibly working as a nurse's aide. In fact, I was there because of theft. Whenever I tried to take notes, the head nurse would open the bathroom door, see my white shoes and the pink uniform that was two sizes too big hanging down to my ankles. Then she'd yell at me to get back to work. In order to make notes so that I could write my daily report, I would stand on the toilet, then crouch down, using a little nib of a pencil and a folded three-by-five card to jot down names and things I saw. Then I'd slip the folded card and the pencil into a cigarette pack and go back to work. So I went back out to the car and looked inside the cigarette packs I'd seen in the glove compartment, but there was nothing there. I looked at the matchbooks, too, and this time I did find something. On the inside flap of one of them, written in pencil. It said, "Alexander." And then my phone number. I slipped the matchbook into my pocket and went back to wait with Dashiell.

Maggie, in a white tunic, white pants and white thick-soled shoes, came out with two towels. She gave me one to use on Dashiell. She spread the other one on the backseat of Tim's old car, tucking it in carefully to protect the stained, torn uphol-stery seat. She opened the back windows, too, perhaps to dilute the smell of wet dog, which made me feel rude and foolish.

Crossing the George Washington Bridge, Mag-gie said I should use my judgment about the things in Tim's apartment. She said she was sure I'd know what to hold on to and what to let go, but if there was a doubt about any particular item, she'd help me when she got there. She asked if ten was too early. I told her it wasn't. Then she asked me what the cross streets were, letting me know that if she had been there at all, it hadn't been for a very long time.

As the cab drove down the Westside High-way, I looked out over the water, the afternoon light making ripples of bright silver where it moved, leaving it a deep blue-gray in places where there was the illusion of stillness. Though I had only been gone for a few hours and hadn't been all that far away, something in me flut-tered, someplace there was joy at being back in the city.

That's when I remembered that Parker was due to show up at Tim's apartment in the morn-ing, Parker whose aunt had gone missing during the run of a play. The napkin he'd written his aunt's number on was on Tim's desk. I'd simply make up another story and postpone his visit. I needed more time to look things over by myself before he got the chance to spirit away anything I might find telling. And I needed time to figure out a way to keep Maggie O'Fallon from seeing what I had seen in the bathroom. The last thing on earth she needed was to upgrade her brother's death to suicide. I told the driver I'd changed my mind, to take me to Horatio Street instead of home.

CHAPTER 14

As soon as I got inside O'Fallon's apartment, I dropped the briefcase on top of the desk and picked up the napkin, holding it under the light so that I could read the numbers Parker had written there. I dialed, still working on my story as I listened to the phone ringing at the other end. A machine picked up saying that Carolyn and Mark were sorry they couldn't come to the phone but that my call was important to them, so would I please leave a message after the beep. I didn't.

The apartment was stuffy, so I opened the kitchen window and one of the front ones, letting a breeze blow through. Parker had given me a wrong number. Had he done it on purpose, so that I couldn't call him to cancel? He'd waited long enough to get his things. Whatever it was he wanted to retrieve, he wanted it badly. Not his clothes, though. I was as sure as I could be that if Parker needed something to wear, he was willing and capable of shoplifting it. And probably had. Was it the shrine? I opened the closet

with his things, going through the clothes this
time, my hand in every pocket, collecting whatever I found and dropping it into a plastic food-
storage bag. Then I pulled over a kitchen chair
and studied the shrine, picking up a tiny skull, a
smooth rock, a small feather, and not picking up
what appeared to be nail clippings, hair, desic-
cated feces, hoping I was wrong about the last
item but not willing to do anything to find out.

There were boxes on the floor of the closet,
comic books in one. Those could be worth money.
I wondered if they were Tim's, but I didn't see
Tim as someone who'd collect *Batman* and *Spider-
Man*. Still, you never know.

There were running shoes in one box, a pair of
new boots in another. And in the corner, as if it
had been tossed there, perhaps when Parker had
heard someone at the door, a beaded purse, small
and elegant. I picked it up and put it on Tim's
desk, wondering if perhaps the purse had belonged to Tim's mother, thinking I'd ask Maggie
when I saw her. I put the plastic bag on the desk,
too, figuring I'd dump it and go through the
things I found, though none of it looked particularly telling at first glance.

There was a soft rap at the kitchen door. When
I opened it, there was Jin Mei with a cup of tea.

"I noticed the window was open. I thought
you might like a cup of tea."

I took the cup, celedon green with a brush-
stroke drawing of bamboo on it, and asked her in.
She shook her head.

"I'm working, too," she said, "catching the afternoon light for my painting. Saturday, the same time

as now, four o'clock, all the neighbors want to meet in the garden, to remember Tim. We'd like you to come."

"Of course."

She nodded. "I knew you would."

"Is anyone inviting Tim's family?"

"That will be your job."

"His sister will be here anyway on Saturday. I'll call his brother and ask him to come, too."

"Good."

"What about Parker?" I asked. "Will he be here?"

"Irwin said he'd call him. Irwin said it would be bad karma not to invite Parker."

"Bad karma for whom?"

"That's what I wondered." Jin Mei smiled and nodded.

"Is Irwin calling Parker? Does he have his number?" Thinking I could run upstairs, get it from him, cancel tomorrow's visit, tell him Saturday, after the memorial, would be a more sensible time. Or Sunday, after Maggie had taken the things she wanted, after I had packed up the rest for Housing Works.

Jin Mei shrugged. "If he doesn't call him, it's fine by me."

"Thank you for the tea, Jin Mei."

"Don't work too late. You need to sit still and be quiet tonight. You have too much on your mind. I can see that."

"True."

"You need to empty your mind, sit in the garden, look up at the stars, feel your"—she circled one hand—"to the universe."

"Connection?"

"Yes. You need to do this."

"I promise," I told her. "I will."

When I'd closed and locked the door, I remembered that there was a cell phone number for Parker in Tim's address book that was with the papers I'd dumped out of the briefcase. I went to the desk, sat in Tim's chair, put the teacup down on the napkin from the White Horse with the wrong phone number on it and opened the address book. I picked up the phone and dialed, hoping Parker had it turned off and that I could leave a message and not have to talk to him. But when the phone rang, I heard it in Tim's living room, the sound somewhat muffled but clearly coming from someplace in the room. I put the handset of Tim's phone down on the desk and looked around, but I couldn't see a cell phone anywhere and I wasn't sure exactly where the sound was coming from.

"Find it," I told Dash, expecting to see him rush around the way I would have, looking everywhere for the phone. Instead, he ambled over to the couch and pushed his nose under one of the side cushions, flipping it up onto the arm of the couch. When he turned around to face me, the phone was in his mouth. Not only that, there were other things stuffed in the corner of the couch, as if Dashiell had uncovered a magpie's nest.

I hung up Tim's phone to stop the ringing, taking the cell phone from Dashiell, telling him he was a good and handsome dog, indispensable and efficient as well. I glanced at the stash in the corner, but wanted to know Parker wasn't coming before doing anything else. His cell phone here, right in my hand, I wondered how I'd get in touch with him now. Without thinking, I opened the phone, thinking I'd call Irwin, ask if he had a number for Parker. I reached for Tim's address book, but it occurred to me that Parker might have Irwin's number on his cell, which was already in my hand. But before I got the chance to see if he did, I saw something else. Parker had two messages.

I knew I had no right to listen to Parker's messages, but that had never stopped me in the past and it surely wasn't going to stop me now. What I found might not be admissible in court, but I wasn't trying to make an airtight case. I was only trying to find out what the hell was going on. And when I saw that the first message was from Elizabeth Bowles, there was no way on earth I would have closed the phone and put it back where I found it, where Parker would expect to find it the next day if I couldn't reach him before to tell him not to come.

"Parker, it's Elizabeth again and the answer is still no. Under no circumstances will I have you living in my home again. If my brother were alive, he'd be telling you the same thing. And don't come asking for money either. Been there. Done that. It's over."

The message had been left after Tim had kicked Parker out of the house. He hadn't heard it. No matter. This was obviously not the first time Elizabeth had told him that he couldn't move back in with her. He'd made another plea anyway. Just in case. But he was more than likely expecting exactly what he got, another rejection.

Was that why he hadn't retrieved his phone when the cops were here? Was this the reason he was in such a rush to get his things back? Because if anyone heard what I'd just heard, there'd be no doubt that Parker hadn't been given permission to stay at his aunt's apartment.

I played back the second message.

"P, it's me, Andy. See you in hell" was all it said. Caller unknown. At least to the phone and to me.

There was a wallet stuffed in the corner, too, with about eighty dollars in it. Two watches, both expensive. A man's silver ID bracelet with the name "Christopher" on it. Magpie indeed. I wondered if Parker had been sitting on his stash when the cops were looking around. I wondered, too, how much they'd looked around once they'd determined the death to be a suicide.

I made one more call, this time using O'Fallon's phone, and then got back to work. I dumped the plastic bag with the contents of Parker's pockets in it onto the kitchen table, not wanting to get his things mixed up with the things on Tim's desk. I picked through the pile: pens and pencils, tissues and handkerchiefs, a folded-up scarf, a pair of leather gloves with the price tag still on them, a comb, a man's gold bracelet, matches, opened packs of cigarettes and change. I couldn't make much of anything new out of what I'd found but thought the stuff should go to the same person I was going to give the cell phone to, Michael Brody. Parker was his problem, not mine, unless of course he was somehow the cause of Tim's death. But the cops didn't seem to think so. As far as I knew, he wasn't even questioned at the precinct, only at the apartment. While they did suspect him in connection with the disappearance of Elizabeth Bowles, no one seemed to think him culpable in Tim's death. No one except me. I was pretty sure that Parker had helped Tim down the long path to suicide, that he beat him down, that he'd made it more and more difficult for Tim to feel there was any point to his life, any saving grace to cling to, any reason to live. But if that was prosecutable, the jails would be far more crowded than they already are, souls pressed as tightly together as subway riders during rush hour.

I began to put everything back in the bag when I read one of the matchbook covers. Hell. The message hadn't said, "See you in hell." It had said, "See you in Hell," a bar on Gansevoort Street.

I went back to the couch, the one with the nest of goodies, the couch, I was sure, where Parker had slept. Only this time, I tore it apart. I took off all the cushions, finding more treasures hidden in corners. Why not? The couch had been both his bed and his nightstand. Where else could he put his things? And things of Tim's he meant to remove from the apartment, seeing first if they'd be missed before taking them to a local hockshop or selling them in the street.

When I'd finished poking into every corner, I unzipped the worn pillow covers and reached inside. In one, wrapped in a dishtowel, there was cash. I sat down and counted it. Parker had hidden $3,235 there, Parker who, as far as I knew, did not have a job. Another reason why he was so anxious to retrieve his possessions.

I spent another three hours at the apartment, packing things up. I had personal effects, photos, some books and valuables for Maggie. I put those things on Tim's bed after pulling that apart to make sure there wasn't a bird's nest in that one, too. I had a huge pile of things, packed in shopping bags, suitcases, and just loose, for Housing Works. I'd call in a day or two, ask if they'd come and pick up everything at once. Ironically, the charities were nearly as fussy as the heirs. There were always things no one would want, things you'd eventually have to pay someone to come and haul away. I had a third pile, neatly folded and packed in plastic bags: Parker's clothes, everything from his closet except the shrine and the small purse. When I finished, I left everything as it was and went upstairs to Irwin's apartment.

"You're early, doll." His hair was gelled flat and the gel made it appear darker. "The game doesn't start for another hour. I'm glad you're here. You can help me make dip."

"I don't make dip," I told him, "and I didn't come to play."

"Alas," he said. "I thought that might be so when you showed up without the obligatory six-pack, but *c'est la vie*. What can I do for you?"

"I was wondering if you called Parker yet, to invite him to the memorial on Saturday."

"Not yet, doll. It's on my list." He tapped his temple and I thought of Tim holding the gun to that very spot on his own head, then squeezing the trigger. Jin Mei was right. I needed some quiet time.

"Will you give him a message from me? I told him he could come and collect his things tomorrow afternoon, but it turns out, he can't. I have a dentist appointment I'd forgotten about."

"Nothing serious, I hope." He was squinting up at me, his face a study of cynical disbelief. Irwin had good radar. I decided I'd better stop bullshitting and stick to the business at hand.

"I packed up his clothes. He said he needed them. If I can leave them with you, he can . . ."

"Sure, doll, sure. No problem."

I went back downstairs and brought up the shopping bags and one suitcase full of clothes. It took me three trips to get everything upstairs. Irwin never touched a bag. He just pointed at where he wanted me to put everything. Fair enough, I thought. It wasn't his job in the first place.

"There are a few other things I'll give him after the memorial. Will you tell him that, too?"

"You can tell him yourself. He'll be here for the game."

"Sorry," I told him, "no can do. I have an appointment tonight, too, and I don't like to keep a gentleman waiting." I checked my watch as if I had to rush, but the truth was, I wasn't meeting Brody for several hours. I thanked Irwin again and told him I'd see him on Saturday.

He motioned for me to bend closer. I did. "It's going to be a sad one," he whispered. "But you can always cry on my shoulder. Don't forget, doll, I'm here for you, whatever it is you need."

CHAPTER 15

I was halfway home before I
changed my mind. I stopped into one of the ubiq-
uitous Korean delis that never close and, amaz-
ingly, has everything you'd ever think to ask for
crammed into a space the size of a country
kitchen. I bought a six-pack, a large bag of corn
chips and two containers of ready-made dip. I
strongly suspected that Irwin was kidding about
the dip. Still, as I told him, *semper paratus* was my
motto. Or one of them.

If Irwin was surprised to see me back at his
apartment, he didn't show it at all, not a man I
wanted to play poker with under normal circumstances, which mine never seem to be. Anyway, I
was nothing if not a good sport. In fact, in keeping with said motto, I'd made one other stop on
the way to the game. I'd stopped at O'Fallon's
apartment and dropped off his briefcase. I didn't
want any curious eyes seeing that I had O'Fallon's notebook or, worse, Parker's cell phone, and
I thought it might look pretty hinky taking the
briefcase with me if I went to the bathroom. I took

off Dashiell's leash and left that on top of the briefcase. I also picked something up, my poker money. I took three hundred of Parker's stash, stuffed it into my pocket, and Dashiell and I headed up the stairs. If Irwin was as good a player as Brody had indicated, I was going to lose for sure. Losing Parker's money wouldn't be nearly as painful as losing my own.

"Just when you thought you were out . . ." he said.

"You pulled me back in."

And so he did, his hand on the waist of my jeans, walking backward and tugging me along. He stopped short of the poker table, standing on tiptoes to try to get a look inside the bag I was carrying.

"You're not Greek, are you, doll? You never mentioned your last name?"

"Not Greek. A Jew bearing gifts. I believe that's considered kosher."

He smiled.

I handed him the bag.

"Six-pack, chips, dips. You're a find, doll."

The bell rang. He handed the bag back to me. "In the kitchen. Anywhere there's room. Beer in the fridge."

I carried the beer and chips into Irwin's kitchen, seeing the stool at the sink and a folding stepladder leaning against the wall adjacent to the kitchen door. I put the beer in the fridge. There was already a whole shelf of beer in there. I opened the cabinets until I found a large bowl and dumped the chips in there. I was taking that back to the living room when the door opened and there stood Parker with three other men.

"Rachel," he said.

"Hello, Parker. Nice to see you again."

He looked at Irwin, then back at me.

"I invited her," Irwin said. "At least *she* brought something."

I held the bowl of chips aloft. "A six-pack, too. Thirsty work, playing poker."

Now they were all squinting at me, Parker because I was there, Irwin because he thought he'd caught me in a lie—he had, too, at least one—and one of the other three because he had a cigarette dangling from his mouth, the smoke making him squinch up his eyes. I guess the other two were just waiting to be introduced, hoping the mark had a ton of money to lose. And that she did.

"Enough chitchat," Irwin said. "Let's play cards."

There was a light hanging over the poker table, the wire running across the ceiling and down the wall. Irwin shut off the rest of the lights and we took our seats, all except one of Parker's friends, the one with the cigarette, who went to get the first round of beer. I thought about going back to the kitchen for the dips, but didn't bother.

"We're still on for tomorrow, right, Rachel?" Parker asked, fidgeting with the money in his pocket. Or maybe he'd found the set of keys he'd lost because whatever it was he was fooling with was making a jingling kind of noise.

"As a matter of fact, you're not," Irwin told him. "Rachel here was kind enough to pack up your stuff and leave it with me. You can take it tonight when you go."

Parker looked betrayed. "But you said—"

"Dog has to go to the vet," I said. I turned to smile at Irwin. He smiled back approvingly, one con artist appreciating another.

"But you said—"

"You said you needed your clothes," I told him. "They're right there." I pointed to the stash of things against the wall.

"But there's other stuff that's mine."

"I can give you the rest on Saturday, after the memorial."

"What memorial?" Rattled now.

"I was going to tell you all of this, in due time." Irwin picked up the deck and began to shuffle. "Everything in due time. But first introduce your little friends to Rachel."

"Bill, Ricky, Ape, Rachel." Not telling me who was who. Though I had a sneaky feeling the one with hair on the backs of his hands might be Ape.

"Gentlemen."

"Don't count on it," Irwin said. "Now, you told me you've never played poker before. Shall I go over what beats what?"

"Nah. I'll catch on," I told him. "Anyway, I can't stay too long. I have this appointment."

"With a gentleman," Irwin told the others, "a real one, I suspect."

"So why can't we get the rest of my stuff now if you can't do it tomorrow? I'm here. You're here."

"Right. I'm *here*. I'm not *there*."

"Bitch." It was the one who was smoking. He took the cigarette out of his mouth and bent it into the ashtray, leaving it only half out so that the smoke kept coming and coming. It sounded like

the voice from the answering machine, but that
person had said his name was Andy. Maybe they
all used as many names as Parker did.

"You talk to a lady like that," I told him, "you'll
go right straight to hell." I watched for a reaction,
but there was none. He just reached for a beer and
pulled out the tab.

Dashiell walked over to the window, poked
aside the curtain and looked down at the street.
The compressor of the air conditioner kicked on.
Irwin picked up the cards.

"Win or lose, I'm out of here in an hour.
Agreed?"

"You can leave right now," one of Parker's
friends said, either Bill or Ricky or perhaps even
Ape. "Who invited you, anyway?"

"I did." He had a big voice for a little person,
deep and resonant. And he knew how to use it. I
thought of what he'd told me, that he'd worked
with the big cats, not a man to be pushed
around. "Parker, your stuff is here, and if it's still
here when I wake up in the morning, it'll be
there"—pointing to the windows, his finger
curved so that if he were actually at the windows, he'd be pointing to the garbage cans. "As
for the rest of your things, there's a memorial for
Tim on Saturday, at four o'clock, in the garden.
Rachel was kind enough to say you could get the
rest of your things after that. Meanwhile, you
have clothes." He looked at Parker. We all did.
He was wearing a denim shirt, the wrinkles
from being folded on a shelf still visible. His
jeans looked new, too, either that or dry-cleaned,
the way they do it on the Upper East Side. "As

for the rest of you deadbeats . . . Bill"—he was looking at the one with thinning blond hair, a short-sleeved plaid shirt, green pants, not a fashionista like Parker—"Ricky"—the one who was smoking, the one you wouldn't want to be alone with on an elevator or in a dark alley, unless you had your pit bull with you—"Ape"—the hairy one, the tallest of the three, the beefiest one, too—"you drank enough of his whiskey and stole enough of his possessions to show your ugly mugs there, for decency's sake, pretend you're respectful of the dead, pretend you're saying a little prayer for the good detective. But that's up to you, of course. I imagine if I mentioned that Jin Mei will no doubt be preparing some food for the mourners, you might actually show. But I'm hoping you'll come because it's the decent thing to do."

"What would you know from decent?" Ape asked him. "How about you and Ella, was that decent?"

Irwin turned to me to explain.

"This is going to be good," Ape added. He had a high voice for such a big man.

"He's referring to a faux marriage I had at one time with a Miss Ella Vanilla, the fat lady in a circus I was with back then. He thinks I done her wrong, leaving the way I did, Ella still madly in love with me." He turned to Ape. "Nothing lasts forever," he said. "Except maybe death."

"No maybe about it," Ricky said. He got up and went to the kitchen. A moment later I realized he'd actually gone to the bathroom because he'd neglected to close the door.

"Comes from living in a tent," Irwin told me.

"He was with you in the circus?"

"A rigger," he said. "When sober. And not in jail." He tapped the deck of cards on the table twice. "Where's Andy? I thought he said he was coming."

Parker shrugged. "He did. Must be not. Or coming late. You know how he is."

"Time and poker wait for no man." He was sitting on two pillows so that he could reach the table. He shuffled the deck and asked me to cut. I tapped the top card. Irwin announced the game and dealt. The conversation, if you can call it that, was clearly over. We anted, bet, folded, played the game. When an hour was up, I decided to stay another. When it was time to go, I was $175 ahead.

Irwin gave me a pat on the ass when I got up. "It's customary to tip the house before you leave," he said. "You know, for the beer, the chips and the dips."

I dropped two twenties on the table. Easy come, easy go.

"Next Thursday?" he asked.

"Wouldn't miss it for the world. See you gentlemen on Saturday, I trust."

None of the gentlemen at Irwin's poker table got up when I did. Parker, in fact, even failed to say good-bye.

As Dash and I headed down the stairs, someone was coming up. He was just at the age when hard living starts to show, his skin rough, his face deeply lined, his hair faded and dull, eyes as old as a cop's eyes. Or a drifter's. Hands deep in his

pants pockets, he just kept coming, as if I weren't
there. I stood aside and let him pass. When I got
to the first floor, I heard Irwin's door open. I unlocked O'Fallon's door, grabbed the leash and the
briefcase and headed home.

CHAPTER 16

Something called the Certificate of Preliminary Letters of Testamentary was in the mail from Melanie Houseman's office. So was O'Fallon's death certificate. Dashiell began to explore the garden as if it were a brand-new place, every inch of it worthy of his attention. I sat on the steps and opened the mail, but it was too dark to read. I didn't think reading a death certificate was exactly what Jin Mei had in mind, even though I was, as she had suggested, in a garden.

I decided to do a round of tai chi, to see if that would clear my mind. As soon as I took the first stance, Dashiell came to stand near me to bask in my increased energy. By the time I'd finished the form, I felt clearer. I went inside to read the mail.

There were only a couple of items on O'Fallon's death certificate that I was interested in, but I read every word. It seemed, somehow, disrespectful not to. The single sheet had been issued by the Department of Health, and after the identifying information, O'Fallon's full name, age and last-known address, there was a box that

said, "Date and hour of death or found dead."
The date he died was there. The time his body
was discovered was there as well. There would
be no exact time of death. There had been no wit-
ness, no broken watch, no one claiming to have
heard the shot. Eventually the ME would record
an approximate time of death, a period of several
hours during which evidence reveals he might
have died. Because Jin Mei had heard him crying
early in the morning and Parker had called 911
around noon, the time of death would probably
be recorded as between eight and twelve that
morning.

I didn't know if any more specific information
would be coming my way, unless I could pry it
out of Brody. I imagined that because O'Fallon
had been fully submerged in hot soapy water, the
ME might make a narrower assessment of the
time he'd died, that the particular deterioration
caused by or prevented by the water would help
him to pinpoint a tighter time frame.

After "Death was caused by . . ." there was a
caution. It read, "Enter only one cause per line."
But only the first line remained, the other two
having been crossed out so thoroughly that even
holding the form under the light, I was unable to
read what had been deleted. What
was left was, "Immediate cause." And typed
alongside that, in capital letters, PENDING FURTHER
STUDIES. It said the same thing, all in caps, farther
down the page, after "Manner of Death." None
of the other choices—homicide, natural, suicide,
undetermined—had been checked.

Near the bottom of the page were my name and

address, as executor, and the name of the funeral home designated in O'Fallon's will, Redden's on Fourteenth Street. After that, there was a statement certifying that all the foregoing information was a true copy of the record on file at the Department of Health. It also said the Department of Health did not certify the truth of the statements, that they had accepted the facts as stated but had not verified them. And even though, with this statement, they had neatly passed the buck for any sort of responsibility, their seal was affixed in the lower right-hand corner.

I had the feeling that Brody would tell me that "pending further studies" simply meant the tox screens weren't completed yet. I slipped the death certificate back into the envelope, pulling out and reading the preliminary letters of testamentary next. It was this document, issued by the Surrogate Court of the County of New York, which allowed me legal authority over Timothy O'Fallon's estate. The note from Melanie said that the checking account had been opened and that I could stop by my local branch of Chase to sign the signature cards. After I had done so, her office would begin to pay O'Fallon's bills, sending me the checks to approve and sign.

The mail included a postcard from my Aunt Ceil, who was on vacation in Denmark, a phone bill, a letter from my congressman and a check for $80 from AT&T. If I cashed it, they would automatically become my long-distance carrier. I tore it up, dropped it in the garbage and picked up the phone.

I called Maria Sanchez, figuring if I told her the

sad news sooner rather than later, she might be able to fill O'Fallon's time and not suffer the loss of income.

"You need cleaning?" she asked.

I told her no, I didn't.

"I'll give you a good price."

I told her no again.

"You want the key back?"

I told her not to bother, that the lock had been changed.

There was a silence on the line, and then she said, "Because of me?"

"No," I said, "not because of you. I did it before I knew about you."

"Then because of Mr. Parker?"

"Yes," I told her, "that's right." It wasn't the whole story. But it would do.

"He was a pig," she said.

"Pardon?"

"Mr. Parker. Always dishes in the sink, a dirty bathroom. He never let me vacuum the couch he slept on. A real slob."

Jin Mei was right, I needed time off. Even after a round of tai chi, I was still on overload. I fixed Dashiell's dinner, looked longingly at the nylon bag with my swimsuit, cap and goggles, but there was no time for a swim, not if I was going to be here when Brody came. I grabbed an apple and curled up on the couch with O'Fallon's notebook to see if there was anything I could learn about Parker while I waited for the bell from the front gate to ring. But it was later than I thought. Or maybe Brody was early. I hadn't yet bitten into the apple or sampled O'Fallon's notes when he arrived.

Walking barefoot down on the cold stone floor-ing of the tunnel, I could see Brody waiting on the other side of the gate. He stood with his hands at his sides, looking as if he could do that all day. I imagine he could have gotten a job at Bucking-ham Palace, guarding the queen, or perhaps he could work as a mime, pretending to be the Statue of Liberty, his face painted green, his breathing barely discernible.

I unlocked the gate and pulled it toward me. For a moment, he stood there, still not moving.

"I don't have the answer to your question," he said.

"Which question?"

"Why. What it was Tim wanted."

"That makes two of us."

He hesitated and for a moment I thought he was going to leave. I stepped back and waited. After an-other moment, he walked in. I watched him walk down the tunnel and head for the garden before I closed the gate and locked it with the key. I could have had a system where I buzzed people in with-out having to walk out to let them in, but then I'd be depending upon other people to make sure the gate clicked shut, people whose security didn't de-pend on it the way mine did. I had seen how peo-ple handled a similar situation at the dog run, being careful to secure the gate when they went in, being careless when they left. I didn't want to bet my life that the kid who delivered pizza or the UPS guy would give a shit if my gate was locked or not. I didn't want to be surprised one day by a visitor I would not have invited in, especially considering the work I did.

Brody walked to the center of the dark garden, stretched his back and then turned around to see where I was. I headed toward him, feeling suddenly that I was at least as hungry as I was tired, thinking it might not be such a bad idea to have to walk out to the gate one more time, to pay for a pizza or some chicken Milanese.

"Have you eaten?" I asked.

He shook his head.

"You forget meals, too?"

"Sometimes."

"That's a bad habit. At least that's what my mother used to say."

Brody smiled. A real smile.

"You have your phone with you?"

"I do."

"Okay, dial this number." I gave him the number of the pizza place, not even embarrassed that I knew it by heart.

"What do you want on it?" he asked.

He knew the number, too. I began to laugh. It felt really good. I waved a hand to him. "Whatever," I said, "except anchovies," and started to laugh again. "And mushrooms."

He nodded.

"Don't get meatballs on it either," I told him.

"How about sausages?"

I shook my head.

"You want a plain pie?"

"Okay."

"Why didn't you just say so?" He took out his phone and just held it for a moment. "My wife used to say she didn't know how I was still walking around, all the meals I skip, the junk I eat."

"Used to? You mean, except for tonight, your eating habits have improved? Or did she just give up on you?"

He nodded. "Totally. Three years ago."

"I'm sorry," I told him.

"Yeah. Me, too." He dialed the pizza place. "Let's stay out here," he said. "Is that okay?"

"Someone told me I should spend time in a garden today, that I needed to clear my mind."

"Always a good idea."

"Difficult to do."

"Not for him."

Dashiell was rolling on his back in the ivy.

"Guess he needs to empty his mind, too."

He took off his jacket and put it over the top railing. "What's he got on his mind?"

"He hasn't said."

He nodded. We sat for a while without talking. It had been a long day. Sometimes it seemed they all were. I bet Brody would have agreed but I didn't bother to ask his opinion. When the bell rang, we could hear the sound coming from behind the closed cottage door. While I was unlocking the gate, Brody took out money to pay for the pie. I tried to argue with him, but he insisted. The truth is, I never care about stuff like that. I could pay, or he could. I can open a door for myself, or be gracious when someone else does. My view of myself isn't locked into trivial expressions of courtesy or generosity. And I was too hungry to have a prolonged argument.

There were a table and chairs in the garden, but I sat on the top step. Brody followed me, putting the pie behind us, in front of the door.

Dashiell came over, his tail swinging happily from side to side.

"Ignore him," I said. "No matter what he claims, he's eaten already."

Speaking of gracious, I got up, stepped over the pizza box and went inside to get some beer, napkins and paper plates. While I was there, I picked up Parker's phone and the matchbook and slipped them into my pants pocket. I took O'Fallon's notebook and slipped it under one of the couch cushions.

"The reason I asked you to come here tonight . . ."

"I thought it was the other thing, about O'Fallon, about why he named you as executor. I didn't even know you could do that."

"Do what?"

"Name an executor without permission. It seems . . ."

"Do you have a will, Detective?"

"Yes, as a matter of fact, I do."

"Did your attorney ask you whether or not you had informed your executor of your decision and had received said person's approval to be so named?"

"I see your point. So, if not that, why did you call?"

"Dashiell found something at O'Fallon's apartment, something I thought you'd want."

"What do you mean?"

"Parker's cell phone. I called it, to cancel the appointment I had with him. I'd told him he could come to Tim's tomorrow, to get his things. Then I changed my mind. I wanted more time to look at things myself, before he started claiming them. The number he gave me, for his aunt's place, it was a wrong number."

Brody nodded.

"I remembered seeing a cell phone number in Tim's address book, so I called that. I was at Tim's apartment at the time and the phone rang there. The only trouble was, I couldn't see the phone and I wasn't sure where the sound was coming from, so . . ."

"You asked Dashiell to find it."

Dash looked at Brody when he heard the words, then looked at me for clarification. I waved a hand at him, to tell him he wasn't working, he was just waiting for pizza, nothing more.

"Right. And he did. And that's why . . ."

He was looking at Dashiell again. "You said you'd been a dog trainer?"

"That's right."

"So you taught Dashiell how to do pet therapy?"

"No. He didn't need me for that."

Brody raised his eyebrows.

"It's innate. All predators know how to tell the weak from the strong. For the wild ones, once they do . . ." I drew my pointer across my throat. "That's how they survive."

"Sounds like the predators I deal with."

"Except that domesticated predators, like dogs, don't think of humans as prey."

"How do they think of us?"

"As family. So when we're hurting or in trouble, they don't have us for lunch. They nurture us."

Brody looked at Dashiell.

"All I had to do was teach Dash manners so that when he goes to a nursing home or the church where I met Tim, he behaves appropriately."

Brody took a pull on his beer. "What about protection work? Does he . . . ?"

I nodded.

"Is that why you didn't need me at O'Fallon's when I offered to be there?"

I nodded again.

"That's good," Brody said, "very good. What else?"

"It depends on the circumstances, on what's called for."

"Any rescue work?"

"He wasn't down at Ground Zero, if that's what you're asking. And anyway, most of those dogs specialized in cadaver recovery."

"And Dashiell, does he do that, too?"

"I've started him on that. It's not that it's really something new to him. If I give him a scent and send him, he'll do his best to find it, no matter what it is. Except . . ." I stopped, looking first at Dashiell and then at Brody, both of them concentrating hard on me. "Except that if a dog's only done rescue work, if he's only come up with living people, he can get really depressed after a day of finding bodies. Or body parts. So I'm getting him used to it, just in case."

Brody turned away. Maybe he was skipping the news, too.

"Some people think it's the handler's reaction that causes the depression with cadaver work, that to a dog, it's all the same."

Brody was shaking his head.

"I don't believe that either," I said. "Anyway, there's another side to it. Even when the work is brutal, it's what he wants to do. He really loves to work. It's a religious experience for him. It's therapy. It's self-defining. It's not the icing on the cake, it's the cake itself."

Brody was smiling. He reached out and touched my arm.

"I know, I know. I get carried away. It's just that most dogs never get the chance to . . ."

"You don't have to explain. I know exactly how he feels."

"Oh," I said. Another thing his wife had complained about, perhaps.

I ate some pizza. Brody did, too.

"Sometimes I think it's just easier than real life," I said.

"What is?"

"Work." I leaned back against the rail.

Brody took a deep breath and let it back out.

Dashiell began to vocalize, a kind of singsong sound he made to let me know he was running out of patience. I shot him a look and he lay down.

"It's hard getting the training materials," I said. "I know most of the groups training cadaver dogs use chemical scents—you know, the pseudo formulas. But until we understand it all, until we know exactly what the dog's keying on, I'd rather use the real thing."

"Any bodies buried here?"

"Not quite that real. I've used extracted teeth, and some blood products. My dentist has been very helpful."

"Good," he said again. "How far along is he?"

Gesturing toward Dash with his half-eaten slice of pizza, getting the dog's hopes up.

"Maybe halfway to where I'd want him. All the scent work he's done helps. He's got the culture down cold—how to quarter, how to keep his mind on the task at hand. But he still needs more experience with . . ."

"The dead?"

I nodded. Cadaver recovery wasn't something you'd ordinarily talk about, but sometimes, in order to be useful, you ended up doing things you never imagined you'd do. If anyone would understand, I knew Brody would. He took out a cigarette, lit it, kept the match in his hand. He wasn't in any rush to get Parker's cell phone. He had no idea what was on it. But I did. I pulled it out of my pocket.

"This may be one of the reasons why Parker was so anxious to get back in there and to do it when none of you guys were around. Also, I think I saw him, the guy who wanted to see Parker in hell."

"That would be me."

"No . . . listen." I handed him the phone.

He flipped it open, then played the messages, his eyes getting darker as he listened.

"I found this, too." I showed him the matchbook from Hell.

He looked down at the phone, but didn't say what he was thinking.

"The matchbook was in a jacket pocket. I found it when I was packing up Parker's clothes. The cell phone was another story. It was hidden under the couch cushions. That's probably why the uniforms didn't find it. My guess is that Parker was sitting on his stash the whole time. Literally."

Brody remained silent.

"There was cash there, too," I said. "It's still back at O'Fallon's apartment." I picked up my beer, put it down again. "They really messed up. Parker said they were very young, right out of the academy."

Brody had no comment. He just sat there, the smoke from his cigarette curling toward the center of the garden like a graceful wave good-bye.

"I met the dwarf," I told him. "In fact, I played poker with him."

"How much did you lose?"

"I came out ahead," I said.

"No kidding."

I wondered if I should add that I'd used the money I'd found as a stake, that there was more there now than when I'd found it.

"Parker was there," I said instead. "And a bunch of his deadbeat friends."

"Which ones?"

"Bill, Ricky and a hairy-looking guy they called Ape."

"Nice company you keep." He put the cigarette out against the side of the steps, then remembered the can with sand in it.

"That time when I spoke to Parker," I said, "he told me he went out to meet a friend the morning Tim . . . of Tim's accident."

Brody was studying me now with those sad eyes of his.

"Who did he say he was meeting, and did you ever talk to . . ."

"He only gave a first name, said that was all he knew. He said the guy never showed up."

"I thought Parker was out all morning," I said. "I don't get it. If the guy never showed up . . ."

"He said he hung out, met someone else while he was waiting, got into a conversation."

"And does this other person have a name?"

"Bert."

"Bert. Again no last name?"

Brody shook his head. "Giving useful information to the police isn't one of his priorities."

"He say where he met this Bert?" I asked him.

"He did."

"And someone went there to see if anyone remembered seeing him at the time he claimed to be there?"

Brody laughed. "You neglected to read me my rights. This'll never hold up in court. Yes, someone went there. Parker's covered for the time he claims he was out."

"Which commenced prior to the time Jin Mei heard Tim?"

"Yes, ma'am."

I picked up a piece of the pizza and gave it to Dashiell.

"I thought you said he ate."

I shrugged. "Life is too hard without pizza," I said, "even for a dog."

Maybe it was too hard even with pizza. Brody didn't say so, but I had the feeling that's what he was thinking. I told him I'd gotten the death certificate. I asked him what "pending further investigation" meant. He told me they were probably waiting for the tox screens to come back.

"Do they expect anything?"

"No. It's routine." He reached over and took

the matchbook from Hell. "Like collecting evidence at the scene. When it's a suicide and it doesn't appear to be staged, it's not all that important." He compressed his lips, lifted a hand in the air, shook his head.

"Not really your personal opinion?"

"Definitely not. You always want it done by the book, no matter what you think it is. Opinions change. You want to have that evidence, just in case you might need it."

I could see the muscles in his cheeks jumping, see the tension in his shoulders, the disappointment that, whether or not it had been necessary, an important job had been botched.

"Thanks for this." He dropped the phone into his jacket pocket; the matchbook, too.

I thought about O'Fallon's notebook, but the cops had seen the previous ones and had left them at his apartment. I thought that was reason enough for me to look at the notes first, then decide if they were something Brody would want to see.

When the rain started, it was just a fine mist. For a while, we stayed where we were. Then Brody got up, picked up his jacket and headed for the gate, Dash and I following behind him.

"There's a memorial for Tim on Saturday, at four, in the communal garden. His sister and brother will be there. Will you come?"

He squeezed my shoulder, letting his hand stay for a moment. "I will," he said.

While I was locking the gate, I heard the rain beating on the cars parked along Tenth Street. I saw Brody start to run. I did the same.

CHAPTER 17

I hadn't had time to look through O'Fallon's notebook when I'd found it. I didn't know how long Maggie would take to change into her uniform and I didn't want to be asked to leave it with her. I thought it more expedient if she didn't see it in the first place, at least not until I knew what sort of notes her brother had made and thought he needed to hide under the driver's seat of his car.

After Brody left, I made a cup of tea and had Dashiell find the notebook for me. I was feeling guilty that he'd just been hanging out with me but that I hadn't been giving him enough to do. Riding in a car or watching me pack up someone else's belongings, even finding Parker's cell phone, these things did not qualify as work for a strong, intelligent dog. Talking to Brody about the cadaver-recovery work I'd been doing with Dashiell made me promise myself I'd get back to it soon. I'd packed up a lot of O'Fallon's possessions and gotten rid of his car. I thought I'd probably be finished with the apartment in a week or so. It wasn't unusual for a landlord, even here in New York City, to forgo a month's rent when a long-term tenant has died. After all, by putting in a little bit of money—a new refrigerator, a new kitchen floor, a better sink in the bathroom—he could raise the rent sufficiently that in very little time he'd more than make up what he'd lost. Getting rid of a rent-stabilized tenant, one way or another, always benefited a landlord. Even if that was not the case, O'Fallon's rent was cheap for New York and the estate could afford to pay for another month if that was what I needed. Dashiell and I both needed time. I decided to take the next day off, to work with Dashiell and go swimming at the Y.

I took the notebook from Dashiell—he had done one of the things he loved best: he'd found something that was out of place—and sat down on the couch to read. Opening it for just a moment at Maggie's house, I'd seen Parker's name in it. So I expected the notes to be mostly about him. But that wasn't the case.

This notebook, unlike the ones I'd seen at O'Fallon's apartment, was not about the cases he was working on. This one was more like a diary, more personal. I had the feeling that when I read the others, they would be heading down this road, becoming less about work and more about O'Fallon.

The first surprise was that O'Fallon had recorded money he'd given to Parker, and in some instances, what the money was meant for. He had clearly been trying to see that Parker could earn a living, one essential of being self-sufficient. He had no intention of taking care of him any longer than he had to. He'd given him money for a short course in food preparation, something that would allow him to get a job as a cook. I thought about Parker offering to cook for me. So he hadn't been lying. But then a page later, O'Fallon had written "no go re food course." Parker had said he was mugged. "Promised to look for work and pay money back," O'Fallon had written, but he had not been fooled. Nor had he given up either. At the bottom of that page, he'd written, "Try harder." An admonishment, I thought, to himself.

And then in the middle of the notes about Parker, about his growing passive-aggressive attitude, his continued use of alcohol and drugs, the petty theft of O'Fallon's possessions and whatever else he could get his hands on, there was a change of topic. O'Fallon had apparently been doing research on police suicide and had been making notes on what he'd read.

It was one of those notebooks with a marbled cover, a little rectangle where you could write your name and the subject matter, but O'Fallon hadn't written in either space. I wondered if he had carried it with him. Or perhaps he wrote the notes sitting in his car, the windows closed, the air conditioner on, closeted from the rest of the world, but not from his own problems, not that at all.

I wondered if the notebook was his way of reflecting, of making decisions, because the major issues he was grappling with were all in it.

"Stress inherent in the work," he'd written at

the top of one page. Then there was a list: "irreg-
ular hours, long hours, rotating shifts, a feeling of
uselessness, lack of respect from the public, bore-
dom, secretiveness, loyalty to the club and not the
truth"—that last one underlined—"dealing with
violence, misery, death." There was a blank line,
as if he had been thinking, as if, perhaps, he'd
been reluctant to continue, and then: "Fear of appearing weak." And under that, another list,
"Signs of Weakness." O'Fallon had written:
"Seeking professional aid, letting on that not
everything is okay, admitting a lack of control,
admitting failure of any kind, any show of emotions, any discussion of emotions, feeling any
emotions." The last underlined.

When the phone rang in my quiet house, I was
startled. I looked at the clock before I sent
Dashiell for the phone. It was past midnight. I'd
been reading for over an hour.

"Alexander," I said, expecting to hear someone
in trouble, someone needing my help.

"Did I wake you?" he asked.

"No. What's up?"

"You know the garden around Saint Luke's
Church, on Hudson Street?"

"Yes."

"What's Dashiell's command for cadaver
work?"

" 'Find bones.' Why?"

"Perfect. Take him there, to Saint Luke's. Tell
him that, tell him to find bones."

"What are you talking about?"

"I buried something there for him to find."

"You did what?"

"It's not deep. I know there wasn't enough time for that, for the scent to migrate to the surface. I talked to someone."

"What do you mean, you talked to someone?"

"Never mind that. You said it was difficult getting material for training sessions. I made some inquiries and got you something. That's all."

"But why?"

"Let's say it's a present."

I heard him light a cigarette.

"Isn't the garden locked at night?"

"Not tonight. The first gate you come to will be open. When he makes his find, leave it there. I have to"—he paused, cleared his throat—"put it back."

"Oh."

"Don't forget your slicker. It's still raining."

And just like that, the phone went dead.

I sat there for a moment, stunned. But it was what I wanted. Exactly what I wanted. And it was already tomorrow, the day I promised myself I'd work with Dashiell. I ran upstairs to the office and got Dash's tracking harness and a long lead. I put on heavy socks and waterproof boots. I took the jar of Vicks and ran down the stairs, grabbed my slicker, shoved the Vicks in the pocket and suited Dashiell for work. Ten minutes later, I was at the gate to Saint Luke's Church, looking around me like a thief, then opening the latch and slipping inside, carefully closing the gate behind me. There were no lights on anywhere, not in the garden and not from any of the windows. The rain had nearly stopped by now, but steam was rising from the paths, the mist was so thick that had there been any lights on, they would not have illuminated the garden anyway. It was a large place, snaking around the church, the school, the building that housed the thrift shop. I switched the leash from Dashiell's collar to his harness so that when he pulled hard, which he would as soon as he was on the scent, he wouldn't be giving himself a correction. A correction would stop him cold, the last thing I wanted. I bent and whispered, "Are you ready? Find bones," adjusting the leash so that it would slide through my hands as he went and I followed.

Dashiell's head was above the ground. He was air-scenting. He turned it from side to side and then began to move, quartering the area of the courtyard where we had entered, searching a section at a time at a speed I could barely keep up with. Then he pulled me to another part of the yard, and now he was moving in a straight line. He stopped, pushed his nose into the pile of leaves in front of him, then sat and barked once, looking toward me, then back at the ground in front of him. He pawed at the leaves once, then barked again. I caught up quickly, testing the air. Nothing. I thought about using the Vicks anyway, but decided to wait. I didn't want to lose my own sense of smell unless I absolutely had to. I didn't know what Brody had borrowed. He hadn't said. But unless he'd buried a rotting corpse in the church courtyard or borrowed whatever Dashiell had found from the morgue, it wasn't all that likely that the odor Dash had followed would be discernible by me.

I knelt on the wet ground and carefully began

to brush the leaves away with my hands. There was loose soil underneath. I brushed that away, too, until I saw it. Dashiell began to speak, not a bark, but a low mumbling noise he made when he was excited or wanted something. Kneeling next to the shallow grave, both of us looking at the single bone, I put my arm around him.

"You did good," I told him. "You did great."

All I could smell was the musky odor of the damp ground. For Dashiell, there was much more. I could hear his tail stirring the wet leaves behind him. I put some leaves back where they'd been on the odd chance someone would happen by before Brody returned. Then I stood, and so did Dashiell. Suddenly I broke away, running across the lawn. I stopped and turned to face him, patting my chest. When he leaped in the air, I put out my arms and caught him. He turned and began to lick the rain off my face. Then he put his wet cheek against mine and held it there. "You did it," I whispered, squeezing him against me. "I *knew* you could."

Leaving St. Luke's courtyard, I carefully pulled the gate closed behind me, not happy that it would remain open for the rest of the night. But then I saw him across the street, sitting in a parked car. Well, I didn't exactly see him. What I saw was the ember of his cigarette, flaring as he inhaled. I could have walked over to the car, to thank him. But I didn't. I didn't wave either. Had he wanted to talk to me then, he would have gotten out. He hadn't. He was waiting until I left to retrieve the bone and lock the gate. I started to run and didn't stop until I was standing in front of my own gate, trying to catch my breath.

As late as it was, I was too elated to feel sleepy. I had thought that Dashiell's previous search work would help him learn human remains recovery more quickly, and now it seemed I'd been right. I dried Dashiell, ran a bath and peeled off my wet clothes. Sitting in the tub, head back, eyes closed, I heard the phone ring. I heard my own outgoing message, Dashiell barking. Then I heard his voice.

"I know what you did," he said. "Just remember, there are consequences for every act."

There was something familiar about what he'd said, something too familiar. I got up, put on my robe and, still dripping, walked into the office and hit *play* on the answering machine, listening to Parker's message a second time. Then I took the stairs two at a time, picking up O'Fallon's notebook and paging through it quickly. I knew what I was looking for would be on the right-hand side, but I couldn't remember exactly where it was. And then I found it, about two thirds of the way down the page. It was with the material about police suicide. It said, "No shot fired goes unheard. There are consequences for every act."

That was in pen. And on the following line, in pencil, perhaps as an afterthought, he'd written, "Could God love someone like Parker? And, more to the point, what about someone like me?"

CHAPTER 18

I had thought I'd wait until Saturday before asking Maggie anything more, before I mentioned the letter she'd written that Tim hadn't lived to see, before I tried to find out what was going on with this unlucky family. But reading Tim's notebook made me change my mind. When I woke up on Friday morning, half the day was gone. But Maggie might still be home. I pulled out her letter and read it again. Then I picked up the phone and made the call.

"It's Rachel," I said when she picked up.

"Is there something wrong?"

I didn't know if it was her mind-set making her ask, her recent experience, or the tone of my voice. Whatever it was, hearing the fear in her voice, I couldn't go on. It was true that there was no more time for beating about the bush. I had to understand more of what was going on before seeing Parker again. That would be the next day, if not sooner. But I couldn't push Maggie, not over the phone, not after all she'd been through. I was going to have to find out what I needed to know on my own.

"Oh, nothing at all wrong," I told her. "I was just confirming tomorrow, to make sure you're coming."

"I am, yes."

"And I wanted to tell you that Tim's neighbors are having a memorial in the afternoon, out in the garden. They asked me to be sure to invite you and Dennis." The truth was, I'd forgotten to call either of them. "I was going to call him next."

"A memorial, how lovely of them."

"I'll call Dennis," I said, hoping she'd tell me she'd do it. But she didn't.

I looked up the number of his Lexus dealership and dialed, waiting for a secretary to pick up, but it was the same voice that I had heard on my answering machine, the call I'd never returned because Maggie had said she'd do that herself. I was feeling the weight of speaking to another grieving relative. I was thankful he was at work so that I could make it short.

"It's Rachel Alexander, Dennis."

"Oh, yes."

"The reason I'm calling is that Tim's neighbors are having a memorial for him tomorrow at four, in the garden behind his apartment. They asked me to be sure to ask you to come."

"Tomorrow at four?" he asked, sounding distracted, perhaps working on the computer as we spoke.

"Yes, just a small group. I imagine people will share some memories of Tim. And while you're there, if there's anything from his apartment you'd like to have . . ."

There was an awkward silence.

"I hope you can make it," I said.

"Of course, of course," he said. "At four?"

"Yes, four."

"Um, can you give me the address? I don't know that I have his latest."

I wasn't sure exactly how long Tim had been in the apartment, but from his low rent I knew it was at least fifteen years, probably longer. I gave his brother the address and instructions on how to get there. I told him I was looking forward to meeting him. Then I hung up, thinking again about why Timothy William O'Fallon had thought a stranger would be better able to handle his estate than a blood relative, starting to understand his decision.

I felt knots in my shoulders and when I looked down at my own lap, both my hands were resting against my thighs, balled into fists. I was in no shape to deal with Tim's brother and sister, with reading the rest of O'Fallon's notes, with much of anything. I decided that Jin Mei had hit the nail on the head, but instead of meditating in a garden, I'd do it where I did it best, in the pool at the McBurney Y. I fed Dashiell and took him out for a long walk. Then I grabbed my swimming gear and one other thing and headed out.

Floating on my back in all that blue, I couldn't have thought about the O'Fallons had I wanted to. There was something about being in the water that emptied my mind and let it float as free as my body did. I had done twenty-five minutes of lap swimming, concentrating only on my breathing and feeling my body moving in the water. I had stretched my legs at the shallow end. And now, floating, my eyes closed, I felt at peace. I took a hot shower, got dressed, and feeling relaxed for the first time since I'd heard of Timothy O'Fallon's death, I began to walk home.

On the way home, I remembered that I was out of fresh vegetables for Dashiell's meals. I stopped at Integral Yoga and got a couple of bags of food—carrots with the tops on, dandelion greens, green and yellow squash, and some fruit for me. Then I headed to Horatio Street, but not to O'Fallon's apartment. I opened the bag with my swimming gear and took out the plastic bag and a spoon. Then I bent next to one of the few tree pits that weren't planted with summer flowers, dug a little hole and dumped the extracted teeth into it, covering them with dirt and tamping it down. Picking up my groceries, I headed home to go back to work. But just a block away, there was a dead pigeon lying against the curb. You don't see that very often, considering the number of pigeons living in the city. So I decided to make good use of this poor soul. Looking around, hoping no one was headed my way, I knelt, slipped a dog bag over one hand like a glove and plucked a couple of feathers from one bent wing. Then I took a detour, a third of the way down Jane Street, made another hole in another tree pit and buried the feathers there, a possible false find to sharpen Dash's training.

There was a notice in the mail saying O'Fallon's body had been released. When I got inside, I called the funeral home he'd designated in his will and arranged for them to pick it up. He'd requested cremation, but he hadn't specified what was to be done with his ashes. Perhaps he assumed that I could figure that out as well.

Instead of doing more work, I took Dashiell for a long walk along the river. When we got home, I thought I'd better make Dash's food before going back to O'Fallon's notebook, have it ready when mealtime rolled around. I put on the radio, a Bach concerto was playing, and spread the greens out on the counter. Chopping dandelion greens and carrot tops and grating squash and carrots was another form of meditation for me, something that kept me in the moment, that kept my mind free of the buzz that usually filled it. When I was finished, I stirred in some yogurt and put the mixture in the refrigerator, taking out some ground turkey to defrost so that I could add it to the vegetables at mealtime.

Finally, I sat on the couch and picked up the notebook, but I didn't open it. I started instead to go over the things I'd learned, to think about them—about Maggie's letter, about the location of the tile that had been replaced in O'Fallon's bathroom, about Parker's aunt who had gone missing, about how distracted Dennis O'Fallon had been on the phone. When I opened the notebook, I noticed a small red smear on the corner of the page I was about to read, as if O'Fallon's thumb had been bleeding when he'd turned the page to continue making notes. I wondered if he'd cut his hand in a work-related incident or if he was tense and bit his cuticles, the way my ex-husband used to—cool on the outside, knotted up within.

And then I started to think about Maggie again. She'd seen her brother at their mother's funeral service and written him that evening, not long after he'd left her home. What was that all about?

There was a list of items stolen, meticulously recorded on the left-hand page, items taken by Parker. Maybe Tim didn't care about his things, only about trying to give this man he'd taken in a chance. His life didn't seem to be about material possessions. It's hard to believe he would have become a cop if he had cared about money and possessions. But still, you'd hate to have your things just disappear, to look for a cigarette lighter, a pair of cuff links, a watch, and find it isn't where you left it, to realize that it wasn't misplaced, that it was gone forever.

It was late, but the turkey was still frozen and Dashiell needed a walk anyway. I had thought to leave the teeth for him to find in the morning, but decided to give it a try then. It was eight-thirty. The street wouldn't be crowded. People were already home from work and the transvestite hookers who worked the meat market and used Horatio Street as an outdoor hotel were not yet on the job.

I grabbed the leash, my keys and some pick-up bags. Dashiell was already waiting at the door. As soon as I opened it, he ran to the wrought-iron gate, then back to me, then back to the gate. His ears were back and there was a manic look in his eyes, all the enthusiasm in the world balled up and shoved into the very idea of a walk around the neighborhood, one of the many things I loved about dogs. And one other, the joy they got from

working. Of course Dashiell didn't know he'd be
working on this walk. He didn't know that until
we got to Twelfth Street and I told him to find
bones. I tapped the closest tree pit, this one
planted with pink impatiens, and repeated the
command. He checked it out in no time, moving
on to the next and then the next. We snaked down
one side of the street, back up the other, staying
between Greenwich and Washington streets,
working our way to Horatio and the tree pit with
the buried teeth.

When we were coming around the north side
of Jane Street, Dashiell stopped, his head hanging
over the tree pit with the buried feathers. I
thought he'd turn to look at me, that I'd tell him,
"No, leave it, find bones," but that's not what
happened. He bent his head over the earth that
covered the feathers, shook it once and then
headed for the next tree.

I decided to keep my mouth shut and let him
work. I could see the alertness in every muscle in
his body. He didn't need to be interrupted with
praise or petting. I had no doubt that he knew exactly what he was doing. I had no doubt he'd stop
at the tree pit where I'd buried the teeth, sit, turn
to look at me and bark once. Which is what he
did. "Piece of cake," he might as well have been
thinking. "Next."

I didn't have the spoon with me, so I used a
plastic pick-up bag to scoop away the earth. I let
him peer down the small hole. I told him he was
the greatest dog ever born. And then I picked out
the teeth, turned the bag inside out and made a
knot in it, dropping it in my pocket.

I was only a couple of doors away from O'Fallon's building. When I stood, I saw a young couple coming out, the man carrying a baby stroller down the steps and placing it on the sidewalk, the baby screaming at the top of her lungs. It seemed Emma was still having teething problems. He was very tall, a chunky man with an awkward gait. His wife was small with something steely in her posture, a determination in her stride, even when she was accompanying a yowling baby. I was going to introduce myself, but they headed the other way, perhaps in the hope that a walk along the river would put the unhappy baby to sleep.

The house on the corner of Horatio and Greenwich streets was being renovated. We walked under the sidewalk bridge hung with dusty plastic sheets. The first-floor windows were covered with opaque plastic to keep the dust out. Or maybe it was to keep it in. If that was so, it wasn't doing a very good job. I could feel the grit of construction debris under my shoes and taste the dust in my mouth as we walked between the ghostlike building and the long, low Dumpster at the curb.

Back at home, I mixed the ground turkey into the vegetable mix and gave Dash an extra large portion. He'd finished eating before I put away the rest of his food. I didn't feel like cooking for myself, so I picked up the phone, called Pepe Verde and ordered chicken Milanese, and while I waited for my food to arrive, I laid out the things I wanted to take with me in the morning. It was going to be a long day, Maggie there early, then the memorial, perhaps dealing with Parker and the things he'd left behind, some of which, as he had apparently figured out, would not be where he'd left them. I thought I'd put him off again, at least until Maggie had gone home. I didn't think Maggie O'Fallon needed to deal with Parker Bowling on the day of her brother's memorial service.

I planned to go to bed right after eating, get up early and get to O'Fallon's. I needed to make sure the shower curtain was closed. I thought I'd throw some towels over the rod, too, make it less likely the curtain would be opened. I had no idea how curious Maggie would be, how much she'd want to know, or to face. Perhaps in her heart she already knew the truth. Perhaps she knew more than I could guess.

I decided to sit outside for a few minutes before going to bed. As it turned out, I sat in the garden until all the lights in the neighboring buildings had gone out. And then I sat there even longer. There was a cloud cover and I couldn't see any stars. Even the moon was difficult to make out, a shadowy crescent, pale and undelineated. Instead of lying under the oak tree or poking his big head into the ivy, looking for God knows what, Dashiell sat with me on the top step. He leaned against my side, his cheek against mine, as content to be in my company as I was to be in his. It must have been nearly two before I locked the door and followed Dashiell up to bed.

Even then, sleep wouldn't come. Just a few days earlier, I hadn't recognized Timothy O'Fallon's name. Now I was unable to get it—or him—out of my thoughts even when all I longed for was to go to sleep.

CHAPTER 19

    I got to O'Fallon's apartment at eight, two hours before Maggie was due to arrive. I decided to tackle the kitchen first. I wanted to get rid of that mound of dirty dishes before she came. I put on rubber gloves, ran the water as hot as it would get, and then stood there looking at the mess Parker and his buddies had left. Then I shut off the water, drained the sink and began to double-bag the musty ashtrays, the cheap unmatched glasses, the plates and platters and pots and pans that nobody would want, carrying them to the trash cans out front, two bags at a time. I saved two glasses and two cups, in case Maggie and I wanted water or tea, and a large bowl that I filled with water for Dashiell. I began to go through the kitchen cabinets next. I didn't think either Maggie or Dennis would want an open box of Ritz crackers, almonds from the year one, half a six-pack of diet ginger ale, Cheerios, enough Campbell's tomato soup for a small army, an open box of linguini.

The shelves were grimy. If the place were a

condo or a co-op, I would have called Maria
Sanchez to come and clean everything before it
went on the market. But it was a rental, and cleaning up before re-renting would be the responsibility of the landlord. I merely closed the empty
cabinets and scoured the empty sink.

There was more to do in the kitchen but I
wanted to make sure the bathroom was taken
care of before Maggie came. The bathroom, I
thought, trumped everything.

I found some towels and a bath mat at the very
top of Tim's closet. I took those down and filled
the empty rack with hand towels. Then I closed
the shower curtain, hoping it would stay that
way. And thinking it might discourage Maggie
from moving it, I hung two large bath towels over
the shower-curtain bar, as if they'd been put there
to dry. I put the mat in front of the sink, then
opened the medicine cabinet and dumped everything into a garbage bag. The less time Maggie
spent in the bathroom, the better.

I still had forty minutes left. I'd left the couch
pillows upturned. I put them back the way they
should be, smacked the couch in a few places to
give it better shape, tightened the cover on the
daybed, opened the shutters to give the room
more light and then started on the desk. I'd left a
lot of papers there, things I wasn't finished with.
I stacked those neatly and slipped them into the
briefcase, wiping the dust off the desk with a
paper towel. Now all that was left was a cup that
held pens and pencils, a small bronze statue of a
horse, the small purse I'd found in the corner of
Parker's closet and the photo of Kathleen O'Fal-

lon, the one the police had found on Tim's desk at the time they found him dead in the bathtub.

I wasn't sure what to do with the photo. I surely didn't want to tell Maggie the circumstances under which it had been found. But it was a lovely portrait and I thought she might want it. So, as a compromise, I propped it up against the books on one of the shelves adjacent to the desk.

When I looked back at the desk, there was one more thing to put away, that small purse. So I stood it on the shelf, right next to the photo. But when I looked back at it, I realized I'd made a little shrine of my own. So I took the purse and dropped it into the bottom desk drawer, out of sight.

For a moment, I thought about emptying out my mother's apartment. My sister Lili and I would take turns dredging up some of the awful things our mother had said to us when we were growing up, laughing at the memory of them, as if they hadn't cut to the core at the time. And then we'd realize, as if for the first time, how final this departure was and we'd begin to cry. Sometimes it was an object that got to us, like the shoe box we found with pictures of us as kids. "She loved us," Lili had said, as if that were a complete surprise to her.

I sat in Tim's chair, looking at his mother's implacable face. Maggie looked very much like her, someplace to the west of placid. Perhaps "unfeeling" was the right word, though it seemed cruel. But if she had closed herself off, who could blame her? We all did what we had to in order to survive.

I wondered if the facade would hold up when

she got here, when she was in the place where her
brother had lived and died, a place, as far as I
could tell, where she'd never been. I wondered
what sort of surprises Maggie would discover
among her brother's belongings, and if she'd cry
the way Lili and I had, tears we thought would
never stop.

I wondered if she and Tim had said anything
beyond hello at the wake because it was that very
night that Maggie had sat down to write her
brother the note I had found in the mailbox the
first day I was here. "We have to talk," she'd said.
Why hadn't they talked that afternoon? Even
with a house full of people, they could have
found a moment to themselves, surely he could
have stayed later, if that was what it would have
taken.

Tim's closet was nearly empty, the clothes and
shoes packed up for Housing Works. I decided to
put those bags and suitcases into the bottom of
his closet, to get them out of the way. It was ten to
ten. I walked through the apartment feeling
pleased. I thought that aside from the wear in the
living room rug, the dust I was sure was on all the
books, particularly those on the higher shelves,
and the fact that the place could have used a paint
job, it might pass muster with Maggie. I sat on the
couch to wait for her to come when my cell phone
rang.

"Success the other night?"

"You mean the bone? Yes, he found it."

"Any problems?"

"None at all. Thanks for this. It was just what
he needed, what we both needed."

"Good," he said, "that's good. And the false hides, did either of them fool him?"

"You did that, too? No. He pretty much went straight for the bone. An ulna?"

"A radius."

I didn't think I'd get an answer had I asked him where he'd gotten it. So I didn't. I waited, wondering what he had to say that couldn't have waited. I was going to see him in a few hours, unless something came up at work. Was that what he'd called to say?

"I'm at Tim's apartment," I told him. "Are you still planning on coming later, for the memorial?"

"Yes, I am."

"But?"

The bell rang. I went to the intercom and hit the button that unlocked the front door, thinking I should have asked who was there, even though it was ten, the time Maggie had said she'd be here. Though I hardly knew her, I couldn't imagine her not showing up on time.

"We found Parker's aunt."

There was a knock at the door.

"Where was she?" I asked, opening the door for Maggie. I held up one finger, to tell her I'd be off the phone in a minute.

"In the Hudson," Brody said. "I wanted you to know before you read it in the paper."

I waited, but he didn't continue. "What would I find, if I read about it in the paper?"

"Not too much."

"Some details about her career, I imagine."

I heard a phone ringing on the other end, someone yelling.

"But not that she was dead when she went into the water," he said.

"Oh."

"Her neck had been broken first."

Maggie was still standing in the doorway, just looking. I motioned for her to come in, then closed the door behind her.

"Was there ID? Did they know who it was right away?"

"Yes. And yes."

"Odd."

"Not as odd as you think."

"How did, um, she get found?"

"Is someone there?"

"Yes. Exactly."

"Mary Margaret?"

"Yes, that's right."

"There was a mark on one ankle. Someone had tried to weigh her down but the rope didn't stay tied."

"Someone? You mean Parker?"

He didn't answer me right away. I heard him strike a match. "The putz couldn't even do that right," he whispered. "How hard is that, to tie a knot that stays tied?" I pictured him shaking his head, taking a drag on the cigarette, the ashtray on his desk brimming over. Or maybe he'd just dumped it. Maybe there was a cloud of ash rising from his wastebasket as we spoke. "She'd been in the water about a week, time enough in this weather for her to come back up to the surface. A civilian spotted her, called it in on his cell."

"So it seems Parker had a place to stay the very first night."

"So it seems."

"He told me he'd stayed with a friend."

"Told us he'd gone drinking with his buddies, that they'd stayed out all night."

"He ought to get his stories straight."

Maggie was holding the picture of her mother, standing with her back to me. I turned around, too, facing the door, and lowered my voice.

"Where is he now? In jail?"

There was another silence on the line, this one longer.

"Michael?"

"Believe me, we'll find him."

This time I was the one who had nothing to say.

"The closets at her apartment were full of his things, most of them new," he said.

"Freshly shoplifted?"

"Could be. He had a nice little shrine set up on the coffee table. There was almost nothing of his aunt's personal effects in the place. You'd think he had been there for years, that it was his apartment, not hers."

"He threw her stuff out?"

"When the detectives spoke to him earlier, he claimed she went on a trip, took her things with her. He said she left him a note to that effect, saying he could stay there until she got back."

"Let me guess. He neglected to save it."

"That's what he said."

"And he had nothing to do with . . ." I turned around to see if Maggie was listening, but she was gone. That's when I heard the shower curtain being ripped back.

"I've got to go," I said, ending the call and running toward the bathroom.

The door was open. She stood in the middle of the room, staring at the tile wall, her body so still I thought she might no longer be breathing. But then she made a little noise, almost like a cough but not quite. When she turned around, her face was composed.

"Where shall we begin?" she asked. As if nothing out of the ordinary had happened here, as if she didn't understand the meaning of what had been right before her eyes.

"Maggie, I—"

She waved a hand at me, took a deep breath. "Are there any other photographs?" she asked. I stepped out of the way and she walked past me, through the kitchen and back to the living room. I put some water in the kettle and lit the stove. "I gave this to Timothy just last week," she said, holding the photograph of Kathleen, the one that had been found on his desk the afternoon he'd been found dead in the bath. She looked around for a place to put it. I figured she'd take it, take all the family pictures.

"Let's put the things you want to take on the daybed for now."

She walked over to the daybed, Tim's bed, carefully smoothed the cover I'd smoothed less than an hour before, and put the photo down. Then she began to look at the pictures hanging on the walls.

"It's all the family," she said, her hand to her lips. "When we were young."

I followed behind her. Dashiell did, too, staying at her side.

She began to take the photos off the walls and I went to get the paper towels, so that we could dust them off, wishing I'd thought to bring some boxes so that she had a place to pack them. While she dusted and stacked the framed photos of herself and Tim and Dennis and Joey, I made two cups of tea and set them on the table. Then I picked up the briefcase from the floor near the desk, taking out the letter Maggie had written to Tim after seeing him the week before.

"Come in the kitchen. Let's have a cup of tea," I said, walking to the table ahead of her, the blue envelope in my hand.

"What's that?" Standing behind her chair.

"I've been collecting Tim's mail," I said. "The lawyer for the estate, Tim's lawyer, pays the bills and sends me the checks to sign. She'll take care of all that. But this was in the mailbox the first time I came."

I pulled out my chair and sat. Maggie remained standing.

"He never read it then?" She pulled out the chair and sat, putting her hands around the mug. "No, of course he didn't. I didn't mail it until Saturday night. He couldn't have read it, could he?"

"No, he couldn't have read it."

I took the letter out of the envelope and handed it to her. She moved her cup aside, wiped the table with her hand to make sure it was dry, and put the letter down in front of her, smoothing it flat with her hands.

"Will you tell me about Breyer's Landing, Maggie?"

She took a sip of tea, looking into the cup after she'd put it back on the table. "They say hot tea cools you off in summer," she said.

"There's not much here. It was either tea or water."

"This is fine. I always find a cup of tea comforting, don't you?"

Dashiell lapped some water from the bowl I'd put down, then sighed and slid down noisily next to Maggie's chair. Then there was only the sound of the air conditioner, the compressor cycling on.

"It's up on Clausland Mountain, in Upper Nyack. The boys would ride their bikes up old Tweed Boulevard and then hike in to the swimming hole. It was forbidden to go there, of course. For one thing, it's part of the army's property. For another, it was dangerous. It was a deep hole in the mountain where the water would collect from melting snow, rain, any sort of runoff. Of course there was no lifeguard, no supervision of any kind. It was just a hole filled with icy water, surrounded by rocks, inside and out. All the parents made a point to tell their children not to go there, but they all did. All the boys, anyway. That's how they'd prove themselves, by jumping in," she said, her voice cracking. "It was the way they'd show how brave they were, how little they valued life. Or so they thought."

"You couldn't be cool if you didn't do it."

"Exactly. Of course, they didn't invite me. They didn't want girls there. If a girl jumped in, it would spoil it. It would no longer be considered

a brave thing to do if a girl could do it." She
stopped to sip her tea. "There was a rumor that
this girl Nancy Shapiro went once and dived in.
She was a Jewish girl, from over in Orangeburg.
We didn't know her. And I only heard it was so. I
couldn't swear to it."

"But you never did?"

"No. I was never allowed to go."

"But you did."

"Twice. I was there when Joey hit his head and
drowned. And I was there again when they
pulled him out."

"Tell me about it," I whispered. I wanted to
reach for her hand, but they were both around the
warm mug, her eyes down, seeing then, not now,
not me.

"It was a Saturday. They all left on their bikes,
my brothers and my cousins Liam and Francis,
the five of them. It was always the five of them, always together. I asked Tim if I could go and he
said, 'Don't be ridiculous.' And when I asked him
why, he said, 'You're a girl.' As if any fool would
know the reason without asking. Any fool but me.

"After they left, I took my bicycle and followed
them. I'd heard them talking once or twice, about
what roads they took. And I'd been on Tweed
Boulevard. I just wasn't sure exactly how to get to
the swimming hole, to Breyer's Landing. I wasn't
sure where to leave the road and walk in or which
way to go once I did. It was all trees, one spot
looking pretty much like the next. I wasn't even
sure I'd find them at all because I couldn't be
close enough for them to see me. Besides, I didn't
ride as quickly as they did, not going up that

mountain. Part of the way, I had to get off and
push my bike, it was that steep."

"But you saw their bikes."

"I did, yes. And that's how I knew where to
head into the woods. But I didn't leave my bike
there. I took it way beyond where they'd stopped
and hid it behind some bushes, some overgrown
forsythia along the side of the road. Then I wandered for a while. But finally I heard them, their
voices. That wasn't so hard. They were shouting.
As I crept up closer, careful where I stepped, I
could see why. It was at Joey. He was way up on
top of the rocks, near where the waterfall came
down into the pool. You could see even from
below that the rocks were slick, that it was a pre-
carious place to stand. They were all yelling at
him, telling him to come down, telling him not to
jump, not from way up there. He'd picked the
highest spot, the very highest, ten feet or more
above the water. I crouched in the bushes, afraid.
He was stubborn, Joey. He was the smallest one,
so he had to be the scrappiest. He'd take on anyone, Joey would, especially if they called him a
baby. That was the worst."

"He was twelve?"

"And me eleven, barely ten months apart. Irish
twins."

"What happened next?"

"He looked so small up there with his shirt off,
so pale and skinny. I thought he'd jump, to show
them. I thought he'd think he had to, or it would
be the end of him, that they'd never let him live it
down."

"And he did? He jumped?"

Maggie looked up, startled, as if she'd forgotten I was there. "Not right away. Not before I had the chance to look good and hard at Francis."

"What do you mean?"

"That's why I'd followed them. I didn't care anything about their precious swimming hole. I was madly in love with my cousin Francis. I would have gone anywhere just for a glimpse of him, just to be near him. You remember how it was when you were eleven?"

Maggie looked up again, her eyes shining.

"I do," I told her.

"He was a beautiful boy with the most startling eyes. They were so alive. Mischief was the fire in them, I guess"—Maggie smiled to herself—"because he was a daredevil, that Francis Connor, braver than the whole lot of them put together."

"How old was he?"

"Twelve, like Joey, only Francis's birthday was three months earlier, so he wasn't the baby. They were the best of friends, Francis and Joseph. 'Find one, you'll find the other,' my father used to say. It was true, too. They were inseparable."

"Had Francis made the jump?"

"I don't know. I'd only ever followed them that one time. How's that for the luck of the Irish?"

"No one ever said? No one talked about it?"

She shook her head. "No. If that was their road to manhood, they wouldn't tell a mere girl now, would they? It was something between the lot of them. They never talked about anything they did when they went off together. But I had the feeling Joey was the last to try it." She shook her head. "Me, even from the lowest spot, I wouldn't have done it, the water that cold, and black as the devil's heart. If you put your hand in, you wouldn't see your own fingers, and when you pulled it out, to make sure it was still there . . . because in no time at all you couldn't feel it, your hand would be blue."

"When did you do that?"

"Do what?"

"Put your hand in."

She stared straight ahead with flat eyes. "After," she said, "after they took him out."

I nodded. "Maggie," I said, "you said you didn't know if Francis had made the jump."

"That's right."

"Then what made you think he was so brave?" Thinking that love is blind, even when you're eleven. Maybe especially when you're eleven.

"It was because of the fire, what he did then, that's where you could see how fearless he was, the second youngest of the boys, but the one to rush in and do the saving when it was necessary."

"What fire?"

"It was the winter before Joey's accident. They were playing cowboys and Indians with a couple of younger kids from Nyack. And the game got out of hand."

"How so?"

"They'd made themselves the Indians and the two other kids were supposed to be the cowboys. They didn't mind. It meant they'd be the good guys. But then the Indians captured one of them and tied him to a tree."

"And then what?"

"They piled some dead leaves around his feet,

leaves and small dry sticks. They said they were going to burn the white man at the stake. At first Freddy, he was the kid they'd captured, he thought it was all part of the adventure. It was playacting to him, the same as any other game. And I think it was meant to be. I really do."

She stopped and just looked at me, desperate for me to believe along with her.

"But something changed," I said.

"It was just an accident. Truly." She reached across the table for my hand. "One of them had stolen some cigarettes from my father's pack. They did that all the time. Cigarettes, even booze sometimes. And the match, I guess it was, started the leaves on fire. The wind was up and the fire grew too quickly for them to stamp it out. So they began running around and shouting, not knowing what to do, except for Francis. He was the one who untied the ropes and got little Freddy free. Then he took off his own jacket and wrapped it around Freddy's legs and rolled him on the ground."

"Was he burned badly?"

"Not as badly as Freddy. That poor boy, he was only ten, he had a lot of damage to his legs. If not for the patches of snow, it would have been worse. The fire would have moved faster. The woods might have gone up. But after Francis got Freddy free, it seemed to wake up Timothy, Dennis, Joey and Liam. They began to throw handfuls of snow on the fire and then they were able to stamp it out."

"Did they ever tell your parents?"

"They had to tell them something. Francis's

jacket was ruined. Everyone had part of their clothes or shoes burned."

"They must have been furious."

"Not at all. They never knew the truth. No one ever told the truth about anything back then. You just swept it all under the rug and went on."

"What did they say happened?"

"They said there was some kid from Nyack, Freddy Baker, in the woods and he was smoking and accidentally started a fire. They said he ran away and they put the fire out, that that's how they'd gotten burned. The way they told it, they were heroes."

"What about Freddy Baker? How did he get home? What did he tell his parents?"

"There was no Freddy Baker. That's just a name the boys made up, to have a scapegoat."

"But what about the real kid, the kid who was injured, whatever his name was?"

She picked up her cup and put it down again without drinking. "People are pretty resilient, Rachel. I've certainly learned that, being a nurse. You see someone at death's door and a few weeks or months later, they're back living their lives."

"As if nothing happened?"

"Not necessarily. But they go on. What choice is there?"

"So how did Freddy, or whatever his name was, get home? Wasn't he burned too badly to walk?"

"He was," she said. "Francis carried him."

"All the way to Nyack?"

She nodded.

"And on the way, they worked on Freddy's cover story?"

"I guess they did." She smiled. "I'm sure they made him the hero in it, too. That's how they did things."

"And they were believed?"

"My father was angry, of course. He told them they should stay closer to home, that they should stick to themselves, to family. He said they were foolhardy and headstrong, but you could tell, he admired them, too. He wouldn't have wanted boys who were Goody Two-shoes. He loved the fact that they were wild, that they were brave."

"They must have told a damn good story," I said, thinking Maggie was doing the same thing with me.

"They could talk the silver out of your teeth, those five. That's just the way it was. My parents liked things to be pleasant, so you grew up telling them the things you knew would make them happy. When you had a problem, you kept it to yourself. We were all good storytellers. It's in the blood."

"Were you there that day, the day of the fire?"

She shook her head.

"Then if they didn't tell the truth, how did you find out what happened?"

"Joey. He made me swear I'd never tell."

"He told you everything?"

Maggie took a sip of tea and made a face. It must have gotten cold by then.

"He told me a lot. But . . ."

"Not that he was planning on that jump."

"No, not that."

"You couldn't have stopped him, Maggie. No one could."

"No, I surely couldn't have stopped him. I do know that." Close to tears, it seemed. But not crying.

"Was that what you wanted to tell your brother?"

She looked up, startled. "Was what?"

I pointed to the letter. "Is that what you meant? That you wanted to tell him it wasn't his fault that he didn't stop Joey from jumping, that no one could have."

"Yes. That was what I meant to tell him."

I got up and put the fire on under the kettle. I should have thought to bring something to eat. But we could always order something in when we got hungry. I hadn't emptied the kitchen drawers yet. I was sure O'Fallon had take-out menus. Everyone in Manhattan did.

Maggie got up and began to wash both our cups. "Is that lovely garden part of Timothy's place, too?" She was standing on her toes, leaning over the sink and looking out the window.

"It's a communal garden for this building and the one next door. That's where the memorial will be."

She sat down, leaving the clean cups on the counter. I sat down, too, waiting for the water to boil, for Maggie to tell me more, hoping to learn something that would make everything else make sense. I wondered if that was it, the boys growing up wild, doing some terrible things, if that's why Tim took in all those men and tried to turn their lives around. Did he do it to try to make up for the things he'd done as a boy, for burning poor Freddy Baker, whatever his real name was, at the stake? But lots of boys did things like that, and worse, and they didn't grow up and take dangerous drifters in off the street, spend money on them, risk life and limb trying to help strangers get their lives in order.

"Liam's suicide must have been a shock to the family. He was so young," I said, hoping to get Maggie started again.

"Sixteen. He'd wanted to be a priest. That was the plan. But after he died, that was the end of it," she said. "Everything changed."

"What do you mean?"

"The two families. It was the end of their being so close. For a while, we just didn't see them much, not my aunt and uncle, not Francis. Then they moved away. And everything was different after that."

"How so?"

"Well, it was just Timmy and Dennis then. After a bit, they went their separate ways. Dennis met some new boys in school and started hanging out with them. He spent a lot of time away from home. Tim was by himself a lot or away from the house, too. But when they were home, they didn't have much to say about where they'd been."

"That was the time of your father's accident, wasn't it?"

"It was. That happened right before the Connors moved to Pennsylvania. It's not that far away, but they might as well have moved to the moon, the way things turned out."

"You never saw them?"

She shook her head. "Not after my father's funeral. That was the last. My mother and Aunt

Margaret kept in touch, mostly letters, but then long periods would go by when neither one of them wrote. I was named after Margaret. She's my mother's older sister and my mother really loved her. I think she was heartbroken when the letters stopped coming. But then, near the end, they would talk on the phone. When Margaret called her, my mother would brighten up. She'd seem content for hours afterward. I was glad of that, glad they got to talking again at the end."

"Did they come to the wake after she died?"

"Oh, no. They couldn't. Uncle Jim is in a wheelchair and Margaret's frail as well. But I spoke to them. They knew, of course. They sent some lovely flowers."

"What about Francis? Did he come to the wake?"

"Francis? Oh, no. With Liam gone, it was Francis who gave his life to God."

"He became a priest?"

She shook her head. "A monk. Perhaps a silent order, I don't know for sure. After they moved, I never saw him or heard from him again. Well, teenage boys don't write letters to their cousins, do they? And now he has a monastic family. Now he has more important things on his mind. Anyway, people lose touch, what with this and that. You know how it is."

I did, too. I'd barely spoken to my own sister in the last year. In fact, her house was five minutes from Maggie's. I could have arranged to visit her the morning I was up there, but I hadn't.

"But at the end, after my mother had asked me to call Aunt Margaret for her, well, that was good, that they were back in touch. They talked for a long time, that day, and a few other times. But I don't know what they talked about. I don't know if my aunt mentioned Francis. My mother didn't say and I didn't ask. We all had something more pressing to think about, and anyway, that was all so long ago," she said, "when we used to play together and I had that silly crush on him."

The water was boiling. I asked Maggie if she wanted another cup of tea or if we should get back to work. "Both," she said. I said I'd go out and get some boxes while she looked through Tim's books and gathered the rest of the photographs. She said that would be helpful.

"I can't remember what he looked like," she said when I handed her the mug of hot tea.

"Francis?" I asked.

She shook her head. "No, my father. Unless I'm looking at his picture, I can't remember his face." She looked at me and took a deep breath, as if she'd just remembered why we were here and who this was about. "We all grew up too fast. Tim didn't have much of a childhood," she said. "None of us did."

I took Dashiell with me, glad for the chance to get out, to get away from the very stories I had encouraged Maggie to tell me. Outside, the sun was shining. There were people going about their lives—kids on skateboards, traffic passing, dog walkers walking other people's dogs, nannies with babies in strollers, pathologically skinny young women with designer shopping bags looking for a place to pick at lunch. We headed to the little deli across Washington Street, where I picked up three smallish boxes and a couple of muffins to go with the tea, wishing I could take a long walk instead of going back inside to deal with all that grief. Standing on the corner, waiting for the chance to cross the street, I glanced downtown. I was no longer sure exactly where the Twin Towers had stood. I didn't know which of the smaller buildings that I could see now had been visible before the attack and which had been hidden by the World Trade Center. Like Maggie, I would have needed a photograph to remind me. I turned away, back toward the traffic heading our way from the meat market, waiting for the chance to cross.

CHAPTER 20

Where'd you get the bone?" I whispered.

I could see a reflection of the garden in his sunglasses—the two tables pushed together, the bottles of wine, a pyramid of glasses on either side of them. I could see Jin Mei's feast, distorted on Brody's dark lenses: small dumplings and dipping sauces, tiny bite-sized egg rolls, a cold chicken salad with water chestnuts and snow peas, and little round fish cakes with swirls of red bean paste on top.

"How is Mary Margaret doing?"

Even in all this heat, he had his jacket on, an ugly print tie, maybe a Christmas present from a brother or a cousin who'd received it the year before, a blue shirt that had been washed a few dozen times too many.

"Typical," I said.

"What?"

"You expect me to answer your questions but you never answer mine."

"I called to tell you about Elizabeth Bowles, didn't I?"

"You did," I said. "Now tell me something else. Confession is good for the soul."

"That's if you confess to a priest."

"Don't get technical," I told him, the line my mother had used when she was caught in a mistake.

He shifted his weight and cleared his throat.

"Anything?"

"Anything."

"Okay. The keys Parker claimed he lost—"

"The keys to Tim's apartment?"

He nodded. "They were there, at Ms. Bowles's place."

"Then why did he enter by the window?"

"Probably forgot to bring them with him. If criminals were smart, we'd never close a case."

He might have left them in the apartment when Tim caught him partying with his buddies, I thought, but I didn't share what I was thinking with Brody. Maybe after he got in through the window, he picked them up from the little table near the front door or from Tim's desk, wherever he'd dropped them after letting his friends in. Maybe he'd made a point to find them for a possible return visit.

Maggie was on the west side of the garden, talking to Jin Mei, both of them animated, as if this were a garden party instead of a memorial. I saw Maggie check her watch and frown. It was twenty minutes after four, but Dennis hadn't yet arrived and we were waiting. Netty was sitting in O'Fallon's kitchen so that someone would be there to buzz him in, but there was still no sign of him. As for the others, Irwin and his weird assortment of unsavories, no one knew if they were actually coming at all, so once Dennis showed up, the proceedings would begin.

"Maggie arrived when we were on the phone," I said to Brody. "I turned my back, hoping she wouldn't hear me, and when I turned around, she was gone."

"The bathroom?"

I nodded. "That's when I hung up on you. I figured for sure she was going to blow, that it was going to be Mount Etna at last. But it wasn't. She started to pack up the things she wants to keep, mostly family photographs and some of the books, and telling family stories."

"That's good. You're doing a good job."

"How so?"

"You make people comfortable. You're easy to talk to."

"Yeah? So talk to me, Brody. Tell me about the bone."

"Would you like a glass of wine? Something to eat?"

I shook my head. Half the people were eating, the other half waiting. Helene Castle was feeding her husband tiny egg rolls while baby Emma slept on his shoulder, her face red and crunched with concern. When I'd first come outside, Helene had introduced herself and David to me and Maggie, then asked if she could have her keys back. She said Tim had a set, in case Netty got herself locked out. Kevin, drink in hand, had introduced me to Rob and we'd talked about Tim for a minute and then about Rob's plans for fall plantings, how he wanted to keep things blooming in the garden until it was covered with snow, and about the pergola he wanted to build next year. He was thinking he'd put in a grapevine. Jin Mei had said she knew how to make grape jelly. Kevin thought it wouldn't be too hard to make wine if they had a good crop. Rob asked if I'd found his keys, by any chance. I said I had found some keys and I'd bring them out later on.

I checked my watch, worried that Brody would have to leave before the memorial got started. He shook his head, as if he knew what I was thinking.

"Let it go. These things never start on time."

The door opened and Irwin appeared in the doorway. I had the sudden image of him on stage, tossing back one side of a long silk cape, taking off a top hat and pulling a rabbit out, then letting it hop about the garden. I guess it was the way he stood there, not entering the garden until he had everyone's attention. But it wasn't that at all. There was a step down into the garden and that step made the garden not inaccessible but difficult for him. I watched as he held on to the doorframe, steeled himself and jumped, losing his footing for just a moment, regaining that and his dignity a moment later.

"Good to see you, doll." He bowed from the waist, one hand behind his back, the other covering his belt. "And Sergeant Brody, good to see you as well."

Brody smiled, excused himself and went over to talk to Maggie. I saw her look up, her brow wrinkled as he explained who he was. Then she was nodding, taking his hand, leaning closer to say something.

I took a step closer to Irwin. "I doubt one of your friends will be attending today," I said.

He looked up. "I read the paper, doll. He always did have poor impulse control. I tried to tell Tim that, but he wouldn't listen to me."

"What was it, a Messiah complex?" I asked. "He had to save—"

Irwin gave me a look that made me shut my mouth. But not for long.

"What?"

"Just something he felt compelled to do. We all have our little compulsions, don't we? What would you say yours were? You can tell me anything, doll, anything at all."

"So have you heard from him lately?"

"Who are we talking about, doll?"

"Parker."

Irwin smiled. "You mean they don't have him under lock and key?" He began to laugh. "New York's finest," he said. "Some joke."

"They'll get him," I said, not so sure of it myself. Like any other predator, Parker studied his prey. When he found someone weak, he knew just how to play it. He might already be using another name, living with another sympathetic citizen with an overpowering need to save the world one drifter at a time, or with some lonely man or woman who thought Parker was not only willing but actually capable of offering them whatever it was they so sorely needed. Of course, he'd failed to get what he wanted from me, but he hadn't selected me. He'd gotten stuck with me, and despite the fact that I was a poor candidate, he'd given it a try. He wanted his stuff and I was the key.

I wondered about Tim again, about Tim and Parker. I still didn't know what that was all about. I wondered if I ever would.

"We'll miss Parker at the game," Irwin said. "He was a steady loser. By the way, did you happen to find—"

"Your keys? Yeah. I'll bring them out later."

Irwin frowned.

"It was . . ."

"I know. For emergencies. And who better to trust with your keys than a cop?"

He lifted one hand and I noticed again how short his arms were. Unless he used a step stool, reaching the light switches without some sort of extension stick would be impossible.

"So, did you have *his* keys?" I asked. "Was it a swap?"

But before he had the chance to answer me, I heard the buzzer that opened the front door. I wondered if I'd know Dennis when I saw him, if he'd look faded and worn, the way his brother had, or too carefully put together, like his sister. But it wasn't a stranger at the door this time. It was Ape and Bill. They'd taken Irwin seriously and come to pay their respects. Or have a drink on O'Fallon, one last time. Ricky wasn't with them. Nor was Andy. Nor Parker. But no one was expecting Parker to show.

"I see you got the mutt with you again," Ape said to me. "He's going to say a few words about the dearly departed, too?"

"I doubt it," I told him. "He tends to play it pretty close to the vest. It's a pit-bull thing," I said, "not telegraphing what's on your mind."

"Yeah," he said. "Whatever."

Irwin snapped his fingers and pointed toward the table. "And don't forget one for the lady." Without another word, Bill went to get the wine. "He'll probably trip and spill the first round, that clown."

Bill was coming toward us with three cups of wine. For a moment, when he was stepping onto the flagstone path, I thought Irwin's prediction might come true. Bill took a step that seemed too big, his hands with the cups of wine flying up, about to spill, but he quickly righted himself. He looked puzzled as he continued heading our way. But when he handed me the plastic cup he was grinning, and once I had the cup in my hand and Irwin had his, Bill, too, took a bow. I wondered if all of Irwin's friends were circus people, drifters before, perhaps, drifters again now.

"Rachel says our pal Parker is a suspected felon now," Irwin said, gesturing toward me with his cup of wine.

"Say what?" Bill asked.

"They think he solved the New York housing shortage by offing his aunt."

"He wouldn't do that," Ape said, his hands awkwardly at his sides.

I could see him as the strong man, gone to seed of late. He was wearing a jacket and tie, but I noticed some food stains on his shirt, and his shoes hadn't been polished since he'd bought them. Bill just had a sweater on, red at that. Perhaps he'd done that so that the wine he spilled on himself would be less likely to show. Had Irwin meant he'd *actually* been a clown?

"He wouldn't hurt a fly," Ape said, glaring across the yard at Brody. "He'd say he was your best buddy while he was robbing you blind, but he wouldn't never lay a hand on you. Cops," he said, indicating Brody with his chin, "they never think you're telling the truth, even when you are. I ain't paying respects to no cop, even if he is dead." He turned and headed for the door.

"We'll get started now," Jin Mei announced.

I looked at Maggie, who was looking down, not at the door. Perhaps she knew all along that Dennis wouldn't come. I went back inside and asked Netty to come out and join us, but she said she was going home, that Helene and David had said that would be okay. I thanked her, locked O'Fallon's door, glanced once more down the hall, toward the front door, before stepping back outside.

People had shifted around, everyone with a drink of wine, all facing Jin Mei. Brody was standing near the door with Dashiell at his side. I stood next to them and waited.

"We're here today because we all cared for Timothy O'Fallon," Jin Mei began. "He suffered many hardships, but he always treated his neighbors and friends with kindness. Today, we've come together to talk about this. I'll go first. When I first moved here, Tim was already living here. If I'd been here first, I would have brought him long-cooked rice, oranges, shrimp dumplings. I would have welcomed him with food. Tim didn't do that. He knocked on the door but he didn't come in. He said he was my next-door neighbor, that there was only a wall between us. He said if I needed anything, I could come to him and he would help me. This was a better gift than long-cooked rice, oranges, even than shrimp dumplings. He was always kind. He was a sad man, but always kind."

When Jin Mei stopped, Kevin started, as if it had been scripted. But it wasn't. I could see that some of the mourners looked uncomfortable. Perhaps they were wondering what they could say about this man they barely knew.

"He was a stand-up guy. There was never a better listener. He was okay by me." He swiped at his eyes and backed away, closer to Rob.

"He didn't have a lot of time, but he always supported the garden," Rob said. "One year he said he remembered the tomatoes a neighbor of his used to grow and I bought some tomato plants. They're a lot of work, but we had a fantastic crop. Remember?" He looked at Kevin, at David and Helene, at Jin Mei. "But he never took any. I don't think he cooked." There was some laughter then. "I saw a lot of pizza boxes in the trash." More laughter. "But he thanked me anyway. He said just seeing the tomatoes reminded him of home."

"We live across the hall from Tim, as most of you know." David was bouncing Emma on his shoulder as he spoke. "Helene and I both work and we're very busy. We didn't know Tim well, but we'd see him in the hall and he always said hello, and after Emma was born, he'd always ask about her. He seemed like a very nice man."

"He chased me out of his house a few times," Bill said. There was an uncomfortable silence this time. "Hell, he had every right. You could never say he wasn't fair. He could've done worse."

There were three people there I hadn't seen before. The way they'd nodded when Rob talked about the tomatoes, I assumed they lived on the upper floors of the two buildings that shared the garden. Only one of them spoke, a mousy woman in her late forties. Even when she was talking, she didn't look at anyone.

"He had my keys, in case I got locked out. I was hoping he'd use them one day. I was hoping he'd come up and visit me." With that, her face turned the color of the clematis climbing up the back wall of the garden. "I thought he was very good-looking. Sometimes I'd sit in the garden, hoping he'd come out. But that never happened." She covered her face with a handkerchief and began to cry.

I looked down at Dashiell and found he wasn't where I'd last seen him. When I looked around, the mousy lady was kneeling next to him, her face against his back. He stood steady for her, his tail wagging.

"I always looked up to my brother. And I loved him very much." Maggie took a deep breath, gathering her strength. "But I'm sure I didn't tell him that nearly often enough, and I'll always regret that."

"He knew you loved him," Jin Mei said, her arm around Maggie's shoulders. "He knew we all loved him. Now let's eat some food, drink some wine and celebrate his life."

I went inside and brought out the little pot with all the keys, letting everyone pick their own. Jin Mei hesitated. "Now if I'm locked out, I'll have to call a locksmith."

"I know a good one," I told her. "I'll give you his number."

"It's not that," she said.

I nodded. "I know."

"It's the end of something good."

I nodded again, out of words for the moment.

"Did you keep his keys as well?"

"He didn't need keys to get in." She mimed picking a lock.

I started to smile at her joke, but Jin Mei was dead serious. I thanked her for all the work she'd done and went to join Maggie.

"I'm so glad you came today."

"So am I."

"Can you stay a while longer? I thought I'd run out now and get some more boxes and then we can have some supper before you drive home."

"I'd like that, Rachel. Do you want to ask Tim's partner to join us?"

I turned around too quickly so that she wouldn't see the expression on my face. Someone had put a box in front of the tables for Irwin, who was filling a plastic plate with Jin Mei's treats. Kevin and Rob appeared to be arguing at the far end of the garden. Bill was talking to Helene, who was now holding Emma. Jin Mei was standing all by herself, looking very small and lost. I looked for Brody, but he was gone.

CHAPTER 21

I borrowed a stepladder from Irwin so that Maggie could take down the books from the top shelves. I put out two rolls of paper towels so that she could dust the books she wanted to take and handed her the extra set of keys, but that made her shake her head, as if I'd handed her something too hot to hold. She put them on Tim's desk and I was pretty sure they'd be there after she left for home.

I remembered the pretty beaded purse then, wondering why it had been on the floor of Parker's closet. Had he been about to steal it when Tim had come home earlier than expected, or when the cops arrived? I took it out of the drawer and put it on the daybed with the things Maggie had gathered to pack and take home. There wasn't much there—a dozen or so framed photos that had been hung around the room. With the walls empty and the rectangles of paler paint exposed, the room looked really depressing. No wonder Maggie didn't want a key. I was starting to wish I didn't have to come back again either.

She was up on the ladder when I was ready to leave. I thought I'd head the other way, toward Greenwich Street, then over to D'Agostino's. Large grocery stores that delivered orders to their customers always had boxes lying around and they usually let people take a few if they needed them. I thought three more would do the trick, and three would be all I could manage with Dashiell along. I grabbed the leash and told Maggie I'd be back soon. Up on the ladder, a book open in one hand, she was reading something. She didn't turn around. She only waved her free hand.

The moment we were out of the house, Dashiell began searching the tree pits again. I was about to tell him to knock it off when I realized how bored he must have been, spending the day surrounded by grief with no way to work it off. After a pet-therapy session, I'd always take him for a long hike or play ball with him. I weighed the disappointment he might feel at not making a find against the search itself and let him continue. It wasn't a bad idea for him to understand that not every search would be successful. It was one of the many realities he'd have to deal with eventually.

He checked each pit, putting his nose between the plants and sniffing the earth below deeply. Each time he decided there was nothing there to warrant his attention, he went quickly to the next one, on and on toward the sidewalk bridge surrounding the corner town house. There was a hole cut into the bridge for the tree next to the house, but the tree pit had been covered with plastic. Someone probably thought they were being kind, protecting the tree from construction dust, but they were also protecting it from getting water. It was anyone's guess whether or not the tree would survive the amount of construction dirt on top of the bridge and the lack of sunlight below.

It was still light out. It wouldn't get dark until after eight this time of the year. The air had started to cool off a little, but the temperature must have still been in the high eighties. Under the bridge, it was permanently evening. The opaque plastic meant to protect the lower-floor windows made the house look haunted instead of temporarily vacated, and the plastic sheets that hung down from the sidewalk bridge made the sidewalk into a gritty tunnel for the length of the house.

Dashiell was finishing the last planted tree pit before the construction. I waited, wishing I had those teeth in my pocket so that I could give him a successful find for his trouble. But when we walked under the bridge, everything changed.

Dashiell stopped at the side of the huge Dumpster and froze, his head up, his tail out and rigid like a rudder, the muscles in his back tense beneath his short white fur. There was a sound next, not the single bark he used to signal a find. This was something Dashiell did when he felt it was imperative to get my attention, something he did when my mind was elsewhere, when I wasn't getting it. It was a song of sorts from deep in his chest, halfway between a moan and a bark. When I looked at him, he held my eyes, then turned to look at the top of the Dumpster, then back at me again.

It might have been anything, I thought. After all, I hadn't asked him to search. I'd only assumed he was doing what we'd just done the other day on this very block. There might have been the remains of the workers' lunches in the Dumpster—leftover pizza, chicken bones. People tossed all kinds of things into the Dumpsters, sometimes trash that was too big to put out for normal collection, furniture they no longer wanted or an old shopping cart with a missing wheel. People parked and cleaned up their cars, tossing everything in with the construction debris. Or they tossed in the dirty diaper they had been carrying in the pocket of their stroller since leaving the playground, having waited for just such a golden opportunity.

There might have been, in fact, rodents in the huge bin. It was a construction site and this was New York City. I listened for their sound but heard nothing. Still Dashiell was insistent. He approached the Dumpster now, smelling along the seam nearest us, then along the side, the sound of his breathing audible and strong. When he sneezed, he was so close to the Dumpster I could see dust blossom out in front of him. He stood on his hind legs, his front paws against the Dumpster, head up, mouth open, eating the air. He was totally absorbed, but I had left Maggie alone, promising I wouldn't be long. I was just about to ask him to move along when he sat, turned to look at me and barked.

I know I shouldn't have, but I tugged the leash and called him to come along. Dashiell wouldn't budge. Again, he looked at the Dumpster, his nose in the air, pointing toward the top of it and he barked once more, his front legs coming off the ground, the sound thundering down the deserted street.

The last thing I wanted to do was to climb up on something and peer inside. And then what? If there were rodents in there, or sandwiches, they wouldn't be sitting neatly on top. In order to be a good trainer, would I have to go Dumpster-diving, the way the homeless did? On the other hand, I didn't want to mess up Dash's training. I looked around, wanting to make sure no one was nearby, figuring I could stand on the bumper of the car parked behind the Dumpster and take a look inside. But Dashiell moved first. From a standstill, he landed on the hood of the car, but he didn't stay there. He barely glanced it and then he was in the Dumpster. I could see his back rounded, his shoulders moving. He was digging. Then he looked over the edge, his brow crushed with concern, and he began to whine, not stopping until I'd grabbed the end of the Dumpster and stood on the bumper of the car behind it so that I, too, could see what had gotten him so excited.

And a moment later I did. Dashiell's digging had bunched up a piece of the plastic sheeting, pulling it from what it had been covering. He was sitting close to the feet of a well-dressed man in his forties whose head was at an unfortunate angle and whose chest was no longer moving. I was about to hoist myself up to the Dumpster to see if there was any identification in his pockets when that became no longer necessary. As I reached for the edge of the Dumpster, I noticed something across the street that made me change my mind.

Then I noticed something else. Lying next to the body, there was a key ring. That was odd, I thought, because there were only three keys on it, none of them a car key.

I stepped back down to the sidewalk and called Dashiell. He put his front paws on the edge of the Dumpster and jumped down to the sidewalk. I took his face in my hands and looked into his eyes. "You're the greatest," I wanted to tell him, but when I tried to speak, the words wouldn't come. I sat on the curb, my arm around my dog, until I was able to swallow again. Then I stood, pulled out my cell phone and dialed Brody's.

"Where are you?" I asked.

"Rachel?"

"Where are you?"

"I'm at the house," he said. "What's wrong?"

"I'm on the corner of Horatio and Greenwich Street," I said. "Dashiell just found a body in the Dumpster next to the corner building."

"I'll be right there."

"Michael."

"Yes?"

I looked back at the car parked directly across the street. It was hard to miss, a brand-new, shiny gold Lexus with dealer's plates.

"It's Dennis O'Fallon."

CHAPTER 22

Is that you, Rachel?" she called from the kitchen.

"Yes, it's me." I unhooked Dashiell's leash and dropped it onto the little table right near the door.

"Did you have trouble? You were gone a long time."

I walked back to where the voice and the smell of Soft Scrub were coming from. The cabinet doors were all ajar to let their spotless shelves dry. You could have eaten off the counters. Maggie was on the floor, on her hands and knees, a small bucket with soapy water next to her. She was wearing a pair of rubber gloves and working on a particularly stubborn scuff mark.

"Almost finished," she said. "I didn't want to leave all this hard work to you. You said you hardly knew Tim. It just doesn't seem fair."

Dashiell started toward Maggie. Anything, or anyone, on the floor belongs to the dog, and having just worked his heart out, he was ready to press his cheek against Maggie's and get a little ear scratch for his troubles. I stopped him with a hand signal, watching Maggie trying to scrub away her grief, thinking about how we all did that, one way or another, thinking mostly of what I was about to tell her.

"There," she said, looking up for the first time, her face damp and flushed with pleasure. "That's much better now." She sat back on her heels. There was a dish towel tucked into her waistband, another under her knees to keep her slacks clean. "Did you get the boxes?"

"No, I didn't, Maggie. I never got to the store."

She pulled off the gloves and stood, picking up the pail as she got up. She turned and walked into the bathroom, dumped the rest of the water in the toilet and flushed. Then she put the pail down and came back out, pushing some tendrils of wet hair off one cheek.

"I don't understand."

But looking at her face, watching her watch me, I had the sinking feeling she did.

"Let's go in the living room and sit down," I said, holding out a hand for her to take.

"No," she said. "I don't care to sit down. There's work to do here." She turned toward the sink now, hoping for a miracle, a pile of dirty dishes to wash, a pot to scour, some way she could exchange her sweat for the truth to come.

"It's Dennis," I told her. "He did come for the memorial. We found his car across the street."

She faced me now. "What do you mean, you found his car?"

"Dashiell alerted near the corner. There's construction going on there and—"

"Alerted? What does that mean?"

"It means he indicated that he'd found something." I bit my lip, unable to deliver the next blow.

"He found Dennis? You mean he's hurt? Something fell on him?" Maggie pulled the dish towel from her waistband and without looking tossed it onto the counter, wiping both cheeks with her hand as soon as it was free. "Where is he? Is he in the hospital?"

I shook my head. "I'm so sorry, Maggie. He's dead. It wasn't an accident. Someone killed him."

She opened her mouth and roared, not a human sound at all. Her hands flew into her hair, tearing at it. I closed the distance between us with one step, putting my arms around her, squeezing her close, feeling her body shudder and convulse. "No," she cried, "it can't be. It can't be."

I got Maggie into the living room and sat her on the couch, going back to the kitchen to get her a glass of water. But when I offered her the water, she knocked my hand away, the water spewing out onto the carpet, the glass flying from my hand and bouncing twice before it hit the daybed. I sat with my arms around her while she sobbed. I don't know that I'd ever seen a person cry like that, decades of grief and pain pouring out of her, her body trembling, hot at first, then cold, then hot again.

After a long time, her head on my lap as if she were a child, my hand stroking her back, Maggie fell asleep. I sat there without moving. Night was coming in the windows now, blue-gray light, and I could hear the sounds changing, too. The birds were no longer singing and traffic had picked up, people coming to the Village for dinner or to go to a club were cruising around looking for a place to park. I heard a motorcycle pass and then, for a long while, the only sound was Maggie's ragged breathing.

She awakened and sat up nearly an hour later, her face swollen, her eyes red and puffy. I got up to make some tea. When I got back to the couch, Maggie hadn't moved. I offered her the cup of tea but she didn't seem to see it. Or me. I put it on the desk and sat down on the other side of the couch, not quite sure what to do.

"It was the push," she said, staring toward the windows, "it's been killing off the lot of us."

"What are you saying?"

She took a deep breath and let it back out and then she turned to face me. "I lied to you. I've been lying all my life. It's the way my family functioned. Lying wasn't only encouraged. It was the only thing allowed."

There was a softness in her eyes, beyond what you see after people sob their hearts out. Without the false smile, the stiff upper lip, the squared shoulders, without her mind rewriting history even as it happened so that her real feelings would be buried and only pleasantries would emerge, she looked naked. She looked, in fact, as if she'd just been born. Mary Margaret O'Fallon was here in the world, at last.

"I did follow the boys up to the top of Clausland Mountain that day. That part is true."

"Twenty-nine years ago?"

She nodded. "And I did hide my bike behind

some bushes, farther up the road from the boys' bikes. Then I went into the woods and wandered around until I heard their voices. I bent low, following the sound. It got louder and louder— shouts, jeers, catcalls, the most cutting comments a boy could hear. 'Come on, you little pussy,' Dennis was shouting, hands at the sides of his cruel mouth. 'Jump, faggot.' He turned to Tim and whispered something I couldn't hear. Then they all started to shout. It was like that horrifying crowd mentality when people see some poor soul up on a ledge and those below start shouting the same thing, 'Jump, jump, jump.' I don't understand the human race. Honestly, I don't. I know they were only boys, but still, they should have known better."

I waited for the rest. I might have thought it was the teasing that sent Joey off those jagged rocks to meet his maker at the green age of twelve, except for what Maggie had said earlier. "It was the push," she'd said. And I didn't think, not now, that she meant the push of words, the push of contempt, the push of thoughtless cruelty. I had the awful feeling, the insistent feeling, that she meant a literal push.

"Who did it?" I asked. But as soon as I did, I no longer needed Maggie to answer me. I knew.

"I could have stopped it. I could have shown myself. I could have said I'd tell on them. I could have . . ." She buried her face in her hands and wept again, but there was no sound this time, just the shaking of her shoulders and the tears falling onto her slacks. I moved closer and put my arm around her shoulders. She looked up, shook her head, wiped her eyes with her fingers. "They were all still shouting up at Joey when he left. He went around the back way, through the trees. And then we could all see him, coming out on top of the rocks, right behind Joey. 'Give him a hand,' Liam shouted and then he began to laugh. And they all did. They were laughing when it happened."

"When Tim pushed him off?"

She nodded.

"Say it." I took her hand.

"When Tim pushed Joey off."

"Have you ever said it before?"

"Not until last week."

"What happened last week?"

"After the wake, I went to the priest. I told him what I saw. I told him that no one knew I'd been there, that I crouched there frozen while they waited for Joey to come up from the dark well. They were laughing at first, then silent, then terrified. I watched it, the fear coming over them like the shadow of the mountain when the sun drops behind it. It was gradual at first, just a little shadow spoiling their fun. And then it covered them, made their world pitch-black, made their souls ache. Was it too much time already? No one had a watch. No one knew. Tim came back down and he and Liam jumped in. I was there each time they came up, gasping for air, blue with cold, but without Joey. I saw them huddle together and whisper. They hadn't saved Joey. Now they had to save themselves. They needed a story. We always needed a story back then. We couldn't have survived without our stories.

"I waited, flat on the ground, until Francis ran for help. After he'd gone, I ran, too. I ran back to my bike and went home the long way, through Nyack, just in case any of them might be back out on the road, just to make sure no one saw me or knew what I'd seen. It took me an hour and a half to get home. And another hour and a half for everyone else to get back to the house with the news that they hadn't been able to find Joey, that he'd disappeared in that cold, black pit, that he was gone forever. That's when I heard the story, again and again and again, of how they'd begged him not to jump, of how he'd gone and done it anyway, that he'd been a foolhardy boy and that he'd paid the ultimate price. That he'd done it, he'd gone ahead and jumped off that high place with them begging him not to all along. That's what they all said. That's what my parents believed. And I never said a word to the contrary, nor told a soul what I had seen, not until I told Father Jack last week."

"Why now, after all these years?"

Maggie got up and walked over to the windows. She stood there for a while, not answering my question. I thought about the note she'd written Tim that night. After she'd spoken to the priest.

"I knew that if I confessed my sin to Father Jack, he'd tell me I should tell my mother what I'd seen, what really happened. I couldn't do that. I wouldn't have done that, so there was no point. But once she'd died, I had a burden I wanted to put down. Once she was gone, I thought it would be safe to do that. Now look at what I've gone and done."

I was behind her in a moment, turning her to face me. "No, don't say that. Don't do that to yourself. This wasn't your fault, not any of it."

"I could have stopped them."

"Maybe. Maybe you could have, that time. But that only would have postponed it. It would have happened another time at another place, somewhere you wouldn't know anything about."

"That's what he said."

"Father Jack?"

"He said it wasn't my fault." Maggie's lips turned into a thin line.

"And what else did he say?"

"That I had to tell Timothy that I'd been there, that I knew."

"Is that why you wrote him that note?"

Maggie nodded. "He said I had to tell him."

"Yes?"

"And that I had to forgive him." Her fists were clenched now, her face flushed. "He said he understood why I hadn't come to confession."

"Because you didn't want to tell your mother, because the truth would be so painful for her?"

She nodded, her face lined with concern.

"And because I didn't want God to forgive Tim. I was that angry at him."

"And when you wrote the note?"

She waved a hand in the air, dropping it limply back to her side.

"You'd worked it all out. You let it all go."

"I did. You have to believe me, Rachel, I only wanted my brother back. I only wanted to say how sorry I was for the anger I'd held in my heart all these years." The tears were streaming down

her face as she spoke and she reached for my
hand, holding it tightly in both of hers. "I was
that cold to him at the wake that he didn't ask for
anything of our mother's. He didn't feel at home
in his own house."

"But you gave him the photograph of your
mother, didn't you? You didn't send him away
empty-handed."

"I did give him the photograph, but not out of
generosity. I wanted to remind him of what he'd
failed to do."

"Meaning?"

"Never being there for her, leaving it all to me.
He should have helped me. He was her son. He
should have been there, too."

Except that he no longer felt at home, I thought.
He didn't feel welcome there.

"I barely spoke to him. But Father Jack made
me see that Timothy didn't mean the harm he
caused. He didn't know what would happen
then. Or after."

"After? You mean Liam's suicide?"

"And my father's."

"You're saying both were related to Joey's death?"
She nodded. "They were."

"Tell me, Maggie."

"Liam was going to become a priest. That was
his wish, since he was a small boy. And his parents' wish, to give their oldest son to God. But
that day, he'd been part of it, not just a by-
stander, the jeering first of all, and the lying afterward. How could he have become a priest
after that, with all that blackness staining his
soul?"

"And you think that's why he killed himself?"

"I do."

"And your father? You think his death had to do with grief over Joey's accident? Because you said he believed it was an accident, that he never knew the truth."

She got up and walked over to the daybed, looking down at the pictures. "What's this?" she asked, picking up the beaded purse.

"I found that here. I thought it had belonged to your mother and that you might want it."

She weighed the purse in her hand and walked back to give it to me. "Why would Tim have a purse of my mother's?"

I shrugged. "People keep all kinds of mementos. I just thought . . ."

"No, it wasn't hers. I've never seen this before."

I watched her walk around the room now, looking at books, at the pictures she'd put aside, then coming back to Tim's desk and picking up the statue of the horse.

"This was my father's," she said. "I didn't know Tim had it." She moved the horse from hand to hand.

"You'll want that then?"

But Maggie put it back on the desk. "No," she said, shaking her head. "There's too much there already."

"At home?"

She nodded, then turned away. I thought she must be exhausted. I hadn't seen her eat anything at the memorial and she hadn't had a bite of food before or since then either.

"Shall we order in something to eat? You're looking pale. You must be starving."

"I dream about it a lot," she said, "about what happened at Breyer's Landing. We're all there at the top of the mountain, at the swimming hole, my brothers, my cousins and me. It's so clear, as if it were real, Joey still alive. And then it all happens, just the way it did back then, except for one thing." She faced me now. She walked right up to me, took my hands in hers. "In the dream, it's me. It's not Tim, it's me. My hands are flat against Joey's narrow back, against his white skin. I can feel the wings of his shoulders, his ribs. And suddenly, I push him—hard—and he goes over the edge. He disappears. In the dream, I'm the one who steals his life, not my brother."

She pulled her hands away and rubbed them against each other before tucking one in each armpit.

"It's me," she said, tears falling again.

I shook my head and wiped her cheeks with my hands. "Come on," I said, "we're going to my house. We'll have some dinner and you can stay over. In the morning, after you've rested, we'll come back here and finish up."

She began to shake her head. "I don't want to be any trouble to you, Rachel. You've been so kind already."

"It's no trouble," I told her, picking up Dash's leash, wanting to get her fed and to bed as soon as I could. She would have had to get up early to have gotten here by ten. She'd gone through a dead brother's possessions, gone to a memorial for him and lost a second brother. On top of that, she'd told her family history, secrets that had been kept under cover at a too high price since she'd been a little girl. I had no idea how she was still standing.

I picked up the briefcase, then hesitated. If the purse hadn't belonged to Tim's mother, then whose was it? I hadn't opened it. The stiff beads made it feel empty, but now I wanted to look inside, to see if there was a price tag, to see if this was just something else Parker had boosted. I opened it and found it wasn't empty. There were two slim gold bangle bracelets inside. And a ring. I emptied the purse into my hand and that's when I saw it, engraving inside the ring: "For EB, love AQ." Yet another reason Parker needed to get back into Tim's apartment, to rescue his aunt's purse, her ring, get rid of more incriminating evidence. I put the bracelets and the ring back into the purse and put the purse into my briefcase, opening the door for Maggie and Dashiell, locking it behind us.

We left her car wherever she'd parked it and walked to Tenth Street. The air seemed to wake her up a bit. We decided to stop at Pepe Verde and pick up some pasta to go but when we got to my house and sat down to eat, Maggie barely touched her food before putting down her fork and pushing the plate away. I took her upstairs to my bedroom and went to run a hot bath for her. But when I went back to tell her the bath was ready, I could hear her even breathing as I approached the open door. She'd taken off her shoes, her knee-highs and her slacks and was lying on her side, on top of the covers, fast asleep. I looked at her legs, the skin tight and shiny, even though the scars were nearly as old as she was. Then I turned what was left of the light blanket back onto her, shut off the light and closed the door behind me.

CHAPTER 23

       Sitting outside in the garden, Dashiell rooting around in the ivy, I couldn't get the vision of those terrible scars out of my mind. According to the story Maggie had told me, and *story* is without a doubt the operative word, Freddy Baker had been the poor little kid whose legs were burned. But that couldn't have been the story they all told their parents, the cover story, not with Maggie's legs burned so badly.

In that story, the one invented to deflect parental rage, Freddy Baker couldn't have been the victim. He had to have been the culprit, the kid with the matches. Freddy Baker, a kid who didn't exist, had been invented to take the fall. A brilliant ploy, I had to admit. Since there was no Freddy Baker, he could never be found to confirm or deny, not even when the irate father looking for him was a cop, ready, I'd bet, to break both his legs for the harm he'd caused to his only daughter.

Not only that, instead of getting punished, the perpetrators became the heroes. With Freddy as the bad guy, they were the good guys. They drove him off and saved Maggie from even worse harm.

I wondered if they had omitted the last name, saying it was a kid named Freddy from Nyack, that that was all they knew. Or was Freddy Baker a name they only used among themselves, telling their parents that they didn't even know the first name of the kid who'd been so malicious, or so careless, whichever way they'd played it? Whatever the specific details of the original story were, clearly Freddy Baker was their code name for the bushy-haired stranger.

But why was Maggie still lying about the incident now, thirty years later, and to someone not a member of her family, someone whose opinions shouldn't even matter? Or was the question not why, but who? Whom was she covering for this time? Was it Tim again? Had it been his bright idea to capture Maggie, tie her to the tree and set the leaves on fire? She would have jumped at the chance to play with the boys. She would have agreed to anything. Anything, of course, short of the fire. Is that why she still told the story, to mask her own complicity, to hide her brother's guilt?

Something was nagging at me. Suppose it was Tim who had set the fire, even accidentally, carelessly tossing a cigarette too near the dried leaves. And a year later, it was Tim who had pushed Joey off the rocky cliff. That might explain why he had devoted himself to locking up the bad guys at work but trying to save them from themselves, one at a time, on his own. He spends his life trying to make up for his own mistakes by trying to set other people right. And then, at a low point in his life, overwhelmed by grief and disappointment, he kills himself. Given his family history, the recent circumstances and his easy access to a means, this shouldn't be difficult to buy.

The police bought it, didn't they? His own partner bought it.

And then, unrelated to the suicide, Parker, suddenly without someone to supply him with a home, food, money and even a little unwanted advice now and then, kills his aunt so that he can live at her apartment, if only until the next rent bill comes due.

And Dennis? He parks his Lexus across the street from his late brother's apartment and then what? A mugging gone wrong? Fine. Then why not take the car?

But the car was still there. I had the feeling that when the cops had shown up, a sea of blue around the faded Dumpster, Dennis's wallet was still in his back pant pocket, his watch still on his wrist.

I could stretch my imagination around the first two deaths, but not around the third. Things just didn't fit together properly. Something was still very wrong.

Not a mugging. Something else.

I could hear the cell phone ringing where I'd left it on the kitchen counter after feeding Dash. I could have sent him for it but I didn't. I waited. But it didn't beep afterward to let me know there was a message waiting. Then I heard the house phone ring. Someone was anxious to get me.

I walked inside and stood on the stairs, listening. The office door was open. I heard Dashiell's recorded bark, then the incoming message as the answering machine was recording it. It was Brody, back at the house, still working but checking in to see how things were going. He wanted to know how Maggie had taken the news that her last remaining brother was dead. He wanted to tell me, he said into the machine, that the keys I'd found next to Dennis weren't his, that they fit the lock to Elizabeth Bowles's apartment door.

I grabbed the downstairs phone, told him I was here and walked back into the garden, the lights off so as not to attract bugs. I stood under the night sky, the air cool now, listening to his voice.

"Maggie's here," I told him. "She's upstairs, asleep in my bed."

"How did it go?"

"It was pretty awful."

"Yeah," he said, "it would be. How are you?"

"Pretty awful."

"Sounds about right."

"I was going to call. I have something for you."

"What's that, Rachel?"

I told him about the beaded purse, the mistake I'd made thinking it had belonged to Tim's mother, and then what I'd found inside it.

"Is it okay if I stop by for it in about ten minutes?"

"Sure," I told him, "I'm not going anywhere."

I went inside and put up coffee. Then I went upstairs and washed my face. Maggie and Brody weren't the only ones who were tired, but weary as I was, I was wide-awake. Even with Brody's news, I couldn't write a story I was willing to buy. I couldn't get that tickle out of my mind, the feeling that something was terrifically off.

I heard the bell and Dash and I ran out to the gate before it rang again. I was hoping to let Maggie sleep.

"Have they found him yet?" I asked when he stepped into the tunnel between the town houses.

"Parker?" He shook his head, his eyes hooded, his mouth tight.

"Come on in."

He stopped at the stairs again and sat.

"Coffee?"

He looked surprised, then nodded.

"Black?"

He nodded again.

I went inside, poured the coffee and retrieved the beaded purse from O'Fallon's briefcase. When I closed the door behind me, we were in the dark. Brody reached for the cup. I sat next to him, the purse in my hand, thinking about what Maggie had told me, about the push, deciding to keep it where it belonged, to myself. I thought about the fire, too, but didn't think that was my story to tell either. So I just sat there, not knowing what to say, not saying anything.

Brody put down the coffee and took the purse, opening the latch and looking inside. He reached in and took out the gold ring, an antique piece with an oval of jade. He held it close to see the initials but it was too dark. I reached into his jacket pocket, took out his matches and lit one.

"I always heard that some criminals seem to want to be caught," I said, my voice heavy with sadness.

"You'd think so, the things they leave behind."

I looked over at the purse.

"He'd probably confess, too," Brody said.

Probably. "You mean if you caught him."

Looking at me, not smiling. "Yeah. If." He sounded cautiously pessimistic. It was a big city, an even bigger country. Parker could be anywhere.

"I wonder if Tim knew."

"Knew what?"

"That he was failing with Parker. That it was too late for him, that he was never going to be . . ." I could feel the tears coming, and though I tried to stop them, I felt first one, then another roll down my cheek. "I never saw anyone cry the way Maggie did," I told him.

"I know," he said. "It's the worst job on earth, what you were stuck with. I'm sorry I couldn't do it for you. I had to—"

"Don't. It's just the way it was. I didn't expect you to take care of it. It's just a lot of loss, all at once. A lot of death." Dashiell got up then, walking over to the stairs, lying down against the bottom step, leaning on my feet, his chin on one of Brody's thick-soled cop shoes. Two sad birds with a single stone.

"She'll have to identify the body."

I nodded, squeezing my eyes shut.

"I'm sorry. You never should have been involved in all this."

"Why is that?"

He reached for my arm, put his hand there, thought again and took it away. It's not easy comforting a stranger, but it was part of the job. I wonder how many of them thought about that before entering the academy.

"Because he wasn't my friend, my brother, my partner?"

Brody's expression didn't change.

"That doesn't matter now, does it? For whatever reason, I'm in it. It's too late to change that, way too late."

"And you'll see it through."

"I will." Thinking that I, too, was a product of my family history, like Timothy O'Fallon, like Maggie. "I can't believe what some people live through," I said, "what they live with. The whole family, every last one of them, it's been . . ."

That's when it happened, an oceanic force pulling at me, taking me where I didn't want to go, where it was too damn dangerous to go. I reached for him, putting my hands on his shoulders, leaning toward him until I was kissing his mouth, tasting the coffee he'd been drinking, taking in the heat of his body, the scent of his skin. He reached around me with both arms and pulled me closer, kissing me back. For a moment, everything else disappeared, all those people, all those questions. For a moment, death disappeared. Then I let go, pushed myself back, the sadness rushing back at me.

A cop. A secretive workaholic with an aversion to showing emotions. What the hell was I thinking?

But, of course, I hadn't been thinking. That had been the point. Hadn't it?

Brody slipped his foot out from beneath Dashiell's head so that he could get up. "I'm going to go now," he said.

I stood, too. "Because if you stay, we'll both regret it in the morning." More a statement to myself than a question directed at him.

"No," he said, surprised. "Not that." He reached for my face, gently wiping my eyes with his fingers. "Because someone's in your bed."

I thought he might start to laugh, but he didn't. He was dead serious.

What the hell was *he* thinking?

I began shaking my head. "Just like that? No dinner, no movie, no flowers?"

Brody smiled. We followed him to the gate. I unlocked it and held it open. But he didn't leave. He just stood there looking at me as if I were the hunk of cake I'd neglected to give him with his coffee. Then he put his warm hand on my cheek, bent to ruffle one of Dashiell's ears, turned and headed back toward Tim's house.

CHAPTER 24

After Brody left, I let the cold water out of the tub and ran another bath. Soaking in the hot water, I closed my eyes and must have fallen asleep because when I opened them again, the water was as cold as the water I'd let out of the tub what seemed like moments before. I opened the drain and turned on the hot water, sinking back into the tub as it got hot again, thinking about Brody, about the warmth of his hand against my face, the taste of his mouth. But just as quickly as that image came, it disappeared. Now I was thinking about someone else in a bathtub, the hot water running.

Only that time it was the shower running.

And that time the drain had been obstructed.

I was thinking about Timothy O'Fallon falling into the tub, the gun dropping from his hand, the washcloth and his foot stopping up enough of the drain so that the tub begins to fill. I thought about the gun lying on the bottom of the tub, soaking, as I was, in hot soapy water, and then I opened my eyes and looked at my hands, the fingertips puffy

and wrinkled from being in the water so long, not
even looking like my own hands anymore.

What would have happened to the trace evidence on O'Fallon's hand?

Gone.

And the prints on the gun?

Also gone.

Parker had messed with the scene as well, turning off the water, letting the tub drain. And
there'd been that rookie cop who threw up in the
bathroom, then scoured it in an attempt to cover
up his weakness.

The scene was a mess. Had it all been an accident, the work of a bumbling fool and a raw be-
ginner? Or not?

Suddenly, lying in all that hot, soapy water, I
was no longer tired. I was wide-awake. I was feeling the cold stab of truth.

What if the washcloth hadn't stopped up the
drain by accident? What if O'Fallon's foot had
landed somewhere else, to the side of the drain,
for example, or in front of it? What if the drain
had been stopped up on purpose, to destroy the
trace evidence? What if someone knew O'Fallon's
patterns, his habits, the way a dog knows his
master's? What if that person had waited for Tim
to take his morning shower, waited, in fact, for
him to be shampooing his hair, his eyes closed?
What if he had picked that exact time to ease the
shower curtain aside, place the gun against O'-
Fallon's temple and pull the trigger?

What if?

Timothy O'Fallon had been a survivor. That
was why he'd gone to the post-traumatic-stress

group where I'd met him. My guess is he had been doing things like that for much of his life, any support group in a storm, including that one, including AA, anything he could find that would help him live with his own history, not die because of it. Because if that was what he was going to do, die because of it, he would have done it decades earlier, after he'd pushed his brother to his death or seen his cousin tumble so far into depression that he killed himself, or after the suicide of his father. Not all these years later. Not when he'd spent his life atoning for that one terrible mistake.

Timothy O'Fallon hadn't killed himself. Someone had committed an almost perfect murder, someone who had been studying O'Fallon for a long time. Had he shot him and then left the house, gone to meet someone who inconveniently never showed? Had he started a conversation with someone else in order to have an alibi?

If not for that alibi, if not for that one thing, everything pointed to Parker. But he did have one. Jin Mei, out in the garden, near the bathroom window, had heard Tim crying. And that was during the time that Parker was seen waiting for a friend, then settling for a stranger, quintessential Parker.

Of course, Parker didn't really need an alibi, did he? There had been more than enough reason for the cops to close the case quickly: O'Fallon's grief at his mother's death, the stress of the job, the photograph on his desk, not to mention the lack of trace evidence to prove otherwise. The photograph. A nice touch. A flair for the dramatic. That sounded like Parker.

The real evidence, the hard evidence, that which would nail it one way or another, all washed away. But more than enough of the circumstantial kind.

That was what was getting to me, eating away at me just beneath the surface of my consciousness. There was too much evidence, too many fingers pointing at Parker. The one thing that didn't fit, the one thing that stood out like a sore thumb was that alibi.

But suppose he didn't have one.

Jin Mei knew Tim had been to his mother's wake the day before. Standing in the garden near his closed bathroom window, she *thought* she heard him crying. But Jin Mei was hard of hearing. Perhaps what she'd really heard had been the shower running, nothing more.

Suppose there was no alibi. Suppose instead of rushing to close the case, the police had investigated further, suspecting that Tim's death had not been a suicide. In that case, there might as well be a neon sign pointing to Parker. Discounting his fingerprints, because he had been living there, there was still ample reason to look at Parker. He'd had a fight with Tim the day before and Tim had kicked him out of the apartment. He'd been stealing from Tim, lying to him. Suppose all these things had finally caught up with him. Suppose Tim wasn't just throwing him out, but threatening to send him to jail.

And then Parker's aunt goes missing, just when he needs her to. He moves into her apartment, fills the closets with his things, gets rid of everything of hers he can't use. He claims there was a note inviting him to stay, but he doesn't save it, a document, as far as the cops were concerned, that would be considered more valuable than a lease.

But there was that cell phone message, the one that told him he couldn't live at his aunt's house, not then, not ever again. There was Elizabeth Bowles, an actress's actress, disappearing in the middle of the run of a play. Then found dead.

Who, if not Parker, had a motive? It had to be Parker. Anyone would have come to that conclusion.

And then Dennis turns up dead, the keys to the place where Parker is living, his aunt's apartment, found lying next to the body. Who could have dropped them there but Parker? Who might have left the little purse, his aunt's purse, hidden in Parker's closet. Who indeed? There was no end of evidence against Parker.

All his life he'd been a liar, a thief, a con artist. Why not assume he'd finally escalated to murder? I went over the list again—evidence everywhere, nothing ambiguous. A rookie could make the case against Parker.

That's when I sat bolt upright. Nobody could be that careless. Not even Parker. Especially not Parker.

Parker wasn't a careless man. He was thoughtful, meticulous in the way he figured out exactly how to reinvent himself whenever he had the need. His survival depended on his skill. No way was it Parker who killed the O'Fallon brothers and his aunt, leaving enough clues around that anyone at all, hearing the so-called facts, would finger him as the killer.

The keys next to the body. That was the last straw. I know it happened sometimes, a killer would drop his keys, even his wallet, at the crime scene. But not Parker. He made mistakes, for sure. But not that many of them. Not with something so important, so dangerous. Because like Tim, Parker was a survivor.

Someone else had dropped the keys near Dennis, left them there on purpose. Someone else had left the beaded purse in Parker's closet. Someone wanted to be sure that if the cops figured out that O'Fallon's death had not been a suicide, there'd be someone lined up to take the fall. There'd be a Freddy Baker in the wings. Only this time the bushy-haired stranger was a real person. This time his name was Parker Bowling.

CHAPTER 25

I didn't think I'd sleep, but I did. Sometime before dawn, thinking about the O'Fallon family with all their secrets, Dashiell lying tight against me on the office daybed, using my legs as a pillow, I fell asleep and stayed that way until I heard Maggie in the hall, coming back from the bathroom. The office door was open and I saw she'd put her slacks back on, that she'd covered her legs.

"Why?" I asked her. "After all these years, why tell *me* that ridiculous story about the kid from Nyack whose legs got burned?"

She came into the office and sat on the end of the daybed, not looking at me. "I was that ashamed," she said, her voice barely a whisper.

"That you let them tie you up?"

She shook her head. "No. Not that."

"Then what?"

She sat on the very edge of the bed, as far away from me as she could get. "When I look at my legs, I think: There it is, Mary Margaret, there's the proof."

"Of what?" I sat up, leaning toward her, too tired to be patient or diplomatic, just fed up and wanting to know. "The proof of what?" I said when she hesitated.

Maggie turned to look at me then. "That God doesn't love me."

"Oh, Maggie."

"Last week Father Jack told me it's not true, but I don't believe it. How could He love me?" she asked, tears tracking their way silently down her pale, swollen cheeks. When I reached for her, she put up one hand to stop me. "Father Jack says God loves us all, that he loved my harsh, unloving father, my timid, alcoholic mother, my brother Dennis, who worked such long hours that there was no time left for his wife, his children, his mother, his brother or his sister. He said that God loved Timothy, even though he murdered his kid brother." She was sobbing now, and talking too loud. "And that he loves me, who instead of honoring my parents, my flawed, human parents, dishonored them with a lifetime of lies. That's why I told you that a boy named Freddy Baker got burned, because I didn't want you to know. I didn't want you to hate me, too. You've been so kind. I didn't want . . ." She stopped, one hand momentarily in the air, then falling to her lap.

"But you did want me to know."

"What do you mean?" Eyes as round as a child's.

"Maggie, you took your slacks off."

Her mouth opened but no sound came out.

"You've carried the secrets long enough, haven't you?"

Maggie nodded. "I have. Too long. But it's all I know." She got up and took the box of tissues off the desk, sat on the bed again, blew her nose. "When I look in the mirror, Rachel, there's no one there. There is no Maggie O'Fallon. She doesn't exist."

"Like Freddie Baker?"

"Worse than that. He never had the chance. He wasn't real. But I was. And I've let a pack of lies destroy my life and keep me from the people I loved."

"In the story you told your parents about that day . . ."

"Freddy Baker was the boy who set the fire. We didn't call him by name in front of our parents, of course. That was just for ourselves. Somehow that was supposed to make it less tragic, that we were fooling them. In front of them, he was 'that boy.' And when my father pressed us, we said his name was Freddy, Freddy something, that he'd never said his last name. But among ourselves, he was always Freddy Baker. We joked about him all that year. For the five months my legs were healing, they'd come and tell me Freddy Baker stories, how he 'borrowed' Tim's bike and got it stolen, how he took ten dollars from my mother's purse or a bottle of gin from the liquor cabinet, then how he got drunk in the woods, how he let the air out of old Mrs. Wilderson's tires, whatever mischief any of them made, they'd tell me Freddy Baker had done it. Until Joey died. That was the end of it, of joking, of just about everything."

"No more good times?"

She shook her head. "Not a one." She wiped

her eyes with her fingers and stood. "And it only got worse."

"Liam?"

She nodded.

"And then your father?"

"Yes."

"Was that right after Liam's death?"

"No. It was about two months afterward."

"And what happened during those two months, Maggie? Did he seem depressed? What was it like at home?"

"I was just a kid," she said.

"And like any other kid, a sharp observer of your parents."

She hung her head, not speaking.

"Was he sullen, angry? Was it more difficult to talk to him?"

Maggie looked up and laughed. But it wasn't a funny laugh. Not at all.

"Talk to him? Did you have a father you could talk to, Rachel? I never did. Everything was the same. It was the same, do you understand? It was as if Joey had never lived, as if Liam had never lived. It wasn't the same for us, for the kids. But when my father came home from work, he still expected to hear good news about school and about friends and about everything. You couldn't say . . ."

She stopped and covered her face with both hands.

"That you were grieving?"

Maggie nodded. Then she put her hands back into her lap. "You couldn't say you missed your brother or your cousin. You couldn't say that you were scared. Not that you thought . . ."

"What did you think?"

"That I'd be next. That I deserved to be next. Even when I'd wake up screaming, and my mother would come to my room, even then. I'd say, 'Bad dream.' She'd say, 'Don't be silly. There's nothing to be afraid of. You're safe at home.' I remember how the light made her face shine, all that cream she'd slather on every night and the rollers in her hair, everything about appearances, nothing about . . ."

"Feelings?"

"She never asked what the dream had been about. She never wanted to know. That's how they were, both of them."

Dashiell turned around and put his head on Maggie's lap. For a while, she held her hands up, then gently lay one on his neck, the other on his broad, warm back.

"She never sat on the bed, but sometimes she'd sit on the rocking chair. She'd shut off the light and I'd see her face again just for a second when she lit her cigarette. I'd see the shine of that night cream, the kerchief on her head to cover the rollers. Then I'd smell her cigarette and long after she had left, thinking I was asleep, or not thinking about me at all, I'd smell the ashes in the ashtray, a kind of cold comfort telling me my mother had been there, not exactly there, but there in a way."

"Did your parents show any emotion about the death of your brother or your cousin?"

"My mother cried at the funerals."

"But not at home?"

"Not that I saw."

"And your father?"

"If anything, he became harder than he'd been before, more closed, more demanding."

"Do you remember right before he died?"

She nodded. "Locked up in his den all day long."

"He'd been home that day?"

She nodded, then stood. "I'd like to take a bath before we finish up at Tim's, if that's okay, Rachel."

"Of course it is."

I went to put up coffee while Maggie took a bath, thinking about Freddy Baker all the while. Freddy Baker, the fictitious bad guy. I wondered if Maggie's father had tried to find him, a boy without a last name, a boy who didn't exist.

I could hear the water running again, Maggie rinsing her hair. I opened the door and walked outside, sitting on the steps where, last night, I had kissed Detective Brody. Last night. It seemed so long ago.

The phone rang. It was Brody.

"Don't you ever go home?" I asked him.

"Once in a while. Is Maggie awake?"

"She's taking a bath."

"I want to pick her up and drive her uptown, for the identification. Have you mentioned it to her?"

"Not yet. But I will. Can you give us forty-five minutes?"

"Sure. That's fine."

"And, Michael?"

"Yes?"

"When you bring her back, would you bring her to Tim's apartment? That's where I'll be, getting the things she wants packed up so that she can go home."

He didn't say anything else. Neither did I. I held the phone a moment too long, waiting for him to hang up, then I hung up first.

I wondered what I should be doing next. I wondered if I should be telling Brody the things I'd learned. And the things I'd surmised. But then I thought, if O'Fallon had wanted Brody to know his family's secrets, he would have made *him* his executor instead of me. He hadn't done that. He'd chosen me. He must have known I wouldn't stop until I'd dug up everything. He must have wanted that, to shield Maggie. He didn't know what she knew. She hadn't told anyone. He wanted to keep things from Dennis, too. And to keep the truth from Brody. I could understand that. It wasn't pretty, what I'd heard.

But why me? What did he want me to do with what I'd found out? Because if I was right and he hadn't killed himself, it had nothing to do with his murder, his death. It had to do with his life.

Maggie came downstairs dressed, her hair still damp. She accepted a mug of coffee, but she said she didn't want any food. I didn't think what I had to tell her would increase her appetite either. We sat outside at the table. I told her that Brody would come for her in half an hour, that he'd drop her off at Tim's. I said I'd pick up boxes on my way there and pack up the rest of the things she was taking.

She reached for my hand.

"I can see why my brother liked you so much," she said.

I didn't have the heart to tell her again that I hadn't known her brother, that we'd been strangers. Besides, Dashiell was barking and running toward the gate. It was time for her to go.

I sat in the garden for a while longer after Brody and Maggie left, thinking about Timothy O'Fallon, wondering if I'd ever have the answers I was looking for. I thought back to the beginning, to that day at Breyer's Landing—Joey standing on top of the rocks, the cruel faces of his brothers and his cousins below. But the goading hadn't been enough. Suddenly, from behind, his big brother gave him the push that sent him from this world down into the next, a pitch-black world of ice-cold water and unforgiving rocks. And then the other boys waited, jeering and laughing. And then they waited quietly. They waited for Joey to come up from where he'd gone down, his fair skin blue from the cold. But the water was still where it had closed around Joey, closed as fast as it had opened to accept him.

How long had it taken for the panic to set in? How long before the horrible realization? How long to make up the story, the story that would become part of their family history?

At day's end, only one truth is known: that Joey is dead. And even when his limp body is brought out of that cold, black place, none of them break. No one confesses. And so they are believed. There is no punishment from without. But the punishment from within is relentless. Not only for Tim, for every last one of them.

CHAPTER 26

       I stopped at the Golden Rabbit on the way to Horatio Street. They had two small boxes they said I could take. I dropped those off at Tim's and went back to the little deli on the corner of Horatio and Washington streets. They had two more boxes for me. I wanted to be sure I could get everything packed before Maggie came and have an extra box or two in case she decided at the last minute to take something else.

Taking things after someone died often had little to do with the intrinsic value of the items. People often want things they don't need, even things they'll never touch or look at again. The stuff becomes a substitute for love, and because of that, I thought that at the last minute Maggie might have trouble letting her brother's things go, that she might need things to make up for the love she hadn't gotten. And didn't we all fall into that trap at one time or another?

After I'd packed the pictures and the books that Maggie had set aside, I continued to work. I wouldn't have trouble letting go of the things in

Tim's apartment. I wanted to be finished, to go on to something I could understand better.

I decided to empty the desk, take the rest of the papers and records home and look at them there. I slipped the files into shopping bags, taking everything, even things I knew I'd toss later. Then I went back to the bookshelves and saw the little pot that had held everyone's keys. I turned it over into my hand: three sets left. Spreading them out on the desk, I could see right away that one of the sets was Tim's, spare keys to the apartment and the car. I put the car key with Maggie's things and tossed the now useless apartment keys. But then I reached into the wastebasket and held them in my hand. The little pot of keys hadn't been hidden. Anyone coming in here might have seen it. Parker certainly knew those keys were here. He could, in fact, have entered any of the other people's apartments and stolen from them, too.

As could any of the drifters he called his friends.

What else did they know, the men Parker hung out with, the men I had played poker with? If they hung out with Parker, they might have heard, at one time or another, big and little details about Tim's life, his schedule, his habits. They surely knew his work schedule because it was when he was at work that Parker would let them in, feed them Tim's food, offer them free access to the contents of his liquor cabinet.

They'd know about Parker's Aunt Elizabeth. Perhaps they'd been in her apartment, too.

Had they met her? Was there any way one of them could have called her and arranged a meeting? I tried to imagine this, one of Parker's friends calling Elizabeth and saying he was hurt. She was sick of him, fed up with him. But he was still family. She wouldn't have gone somewhere if he was broke. Broke? That was his middle name. But if he were hurt? Hurt was a different story. Hurt might have gotten her to the waterfront, to one more chance to bail out her nephew. Only it wasn't her nephew who was there waiting for her. It was someone else. A bushy-haired stranger. Freddy Baker. Was that when the purse was nabbed? Had good old reliable Freddy taken her money? Had he taken her keys, thinking they'd be worth having, all the easier to implicate Parker in yet another crime, should that become necessary? Had he left the jewelry she'd forgotten to put back on after the show, something to indicate whose purse it was? Was that how it had happened?

And did Parker's buddies know about Tim's family as well, pictures of them all around the room until yesterday? Did Parker ask who those kids were? And once he knew, did he tell his friends, "This is Dennis, Tim's brother. He's a Lexus dealer but his brother drives a piece of crap Toyota. This one's Maggie, his kid sister, the one who got stuck nursing his sick mother.

And if O'Fallon had been miserable enough to leak the truth one night, or if Parker had found the articles I'd found and, shrewd observer of human nature that he was, had put two and two together and figured out exactly what his benefactor was atoning for and why he'd gotten the leeway he did from a cop, of all people, if this had happened, might Parker have also said, "This little one here, this one's Joey, the one Tim pushed off the cliff"? Did anyone ask what the hell *he* was doing telling Parker how to live his life when all Parker had done was rob a few people who had more than they needed and would never miss it anyway and Tim had killed someone? Did anyone see the irony of that?

I dumped the keys back into the wastebasket and started to clean out the cabinets below the bookshelves, stacking the things for Housing Works on one side, the things I planned to take home on the other, a couple of books on crime detection and Tim's notebooks. I thought Brody might want them, but I planned on reading them first.

I'd only emptied one of the cabinets when I began to think about the poker game again and the motley crew that met at Irwin's every week. What *did* they talk about?

Because if Tim hadn't killed himself and if whoever did kill him was doing a hell of a job of framing Parker, that would mean that that person not only knew enough about Tim to know his habits, but that he knew Parker well enough, too.

I checked the time. Brody had said they'd be at least two hours. I decided to be rude instead of calling first. I motioned to Dashiell, clipped on his leash at the door and we headed upstairs.

"Doll," he said. "To what do I owe the pleasure?"

"Nothing special," I told him. "I have to wait around for Tim's sister to show. I thought it might be more fun to wait around with you, if that's okay. It's kind of creepy down there, what with what happened last week." I shrugged. He stepped back. I stepped in.

There were cards on the poker table, a game of solitaire set out. I pulled out a chair and sat. Irwin stood near the door for a moment, then closed it and took the seat next to me, the one with the pillow on it. I noticed that he didn't look at me when he was struggling to do something I could take for granted. But once he was seated, he was all eyes.

"You think about Tim much?" I asked.

"I think about lots of things," he said. He leaned forward and pushed the cards away with enough force that some of them went all the way across the table. "What makes you ask?"

"I don't know, Irwin, but going through his things, I just don't get the impression of a man who would . . ."

"You never heard of surprises, doll? You never had a man you loved insanely walk out on you? You never got slapped by Fate, hit with bad luck, dealt a bad hand?"

"I have. And Tim had, too. Hell, anyone over five years old has had his share of bad luck."

"Some even before they get to be five." He was holding his hands apart, as if he were about to catch a ball. "Crap happens. Crap abounds."

"And some people seem to be able to function anyway. I remember this old lady I used to visit with Dashiell. We do pet-assisted therapy."

He nodded, either because he knew what I was talking about or he didn't but wanted me to get on with it.

"She was ninety-one and senile. That's why she was living in a home."

He raised his eyebrows, tilted his head.

"An institution. She didn't remember who I was from week to week, but since she was stuck somewhere in her own childhood and she enjoyed my visits, she figured me for a cousin, someone she liked and played with when she was a kid. She called me Viola."

"There's a point to this, doll?"

"Yeah, there is. Even in that shape, the woman ate like a horse. She was in a wheelchair, a tiny little bird of a woman, and she'd pack away her meals like there was no tomorrow. Survival. Some people just have the knack. No matter what hits them from behind, they find a way to go on. I think Tim was one of those people. I'm not saying adversity didn't touch him, didn't hurt him. But he got around it. Or he carried it with him and went forward."

"You're saying?"

What I had come to say to this man should have been obvious by now; it's where the conversation had been heading all along. But since it wasn't and I didn't have all day, I decided to spell it out.

"I don't think he killed himself," I said.

Irwin blinked. He bent his head and scratched his red hair. Then he looked back at me. "Me neither," he said. "I never did."

I nodded. Irwin bit his lower lip. For a moment, his eyes looked shinier than usual, not as hard as they often did, even when he was joking.

"So what's the plan, doll?"

I shrugged my shoulder, lifted one hand, let it fall back into my lap. "Hey, I'm only the executor. I'm not the cops. I didn't even know the man."

"So, what? This is just between you and me?"

"I just wanted to know I'm not crazy, that's all. But if you think the same thing . . ."

"We could both be crazy, doll. Did that ever occur to you?"

"It did," I said. "That's another possibility."

I thought he'd smile then, show me his choppers, make a little joke. But he didn't. He drummed his fingers on the table. Then he pulled over the ashtray and the little dish next to it that was full of matchbooks, picking one of them up, then hesitating. He didn't take out his smokes. He just sat there, turning that book of matches over and over in his hand.

"It's Parker, right?"

"Who did it?"

"Nah." He shook his head. "What I'm asking you, is it because of Parker you came to your conclusion?"

I didn't answer right away and Irwin went on.

"I'm thinking you figure that if Tim had this mission, this calling, that he'd stick around and keep going. That he wouldn't quit in the middle."

I nodded, interested to see where he'd go with this.

"Yeah, that's what I think, too. Of course, he'd failed with Parker. Parker doesn't believe in the work ethic."

"What does he believe in?"

"Miracles." He tossed the matches back into the little dish, "Parker's hopeless. Well, if not hopeless, he's surely not the best example of Tim's work. There was this guy Harold, two years back. I took my keys back while Harold was living downstairs. That was a piece of work if I ever saw one. But Tim got him squared away, got him a job. It wasn't brain surgery, but it did something for him, for Harold. He changed. It's hard to explain it, what happened to him, but the point is Tim, right? When you get a success, even if the next one doesn't work out, you don't quit. You keep trying to get another success. You know it can be done. You know you can do it. It hooks you."

"Random reinforcement," I said.

"Say what, doll?"

"If you feed a dog from the table, say, but just once in a while, not every meal, he'll beg even harder than the dog who always gets a taste of your dinner. He'll . . ."

"He'll know it's possible. That's a powerful narcotic, knowing that."

"Exactly."

"Still, people get depressed."

"They do."

"Then what makes you think Tim just didn't get depressed?"

"The way I met him."

"Which was?"

"After 9/11. There was a post-traumatic-stress group for men at the church on West Eleventh Street. I was there with Dashiell, to help the men loosen up."

"And Tim?"

"Was there. But didn't."

"And you conclude what from this?"

"He wasn't there because of 9/11. He hadn't lost anyone, had he?"

"Not that I know of."

"That's what I thought. Of course, you didn't have to. There were other reasons to be there. Lots of people were scared and stressed and needed some kind of help after the attack—counseling, or anti-anxiety medication. He had every right to be there."

"And?"

"I think he was there, I think he did things like this, whatever he could, to help himself . . ." I stopped to search for the right word.

"Survive," he said. "That's your theory?"

I nodded.

He banged the table with one hand. "It's a good one, doll. I like the way you think."

I checked my watch. There was still plenty of time, and time with Irwin was what I wanted. It was what I believed would get me what I was after.

"Let's suppose you're right," he said. "And let's suppose I'm right."

"Meaning?"

"Meaning Tim didn't kill himself. Someone else did. But not Parker. Then the question is who?"

"A better question might be why."

"Because if we knew why . . ."

"We'd know who."

Irwin scooted back on his chair, reaching into his shirt pocket for a cigarette.

"Allow me," I said, sliding the dish with the matchbooks closer. I remembered all the matchbooks I'd pulled out of Parker's pockets, one from every place he'd been, I thought. If something was free, why not take it. If it wasn't free, why not steal it. I looked down at the dish, at the matchbooks. One from Hell. One from the White Horse. Matches from the Cubby Hole, the Blind Tiger, Hogs and Heifers. Six or seven others. One more interesting than the rest. I picked that one up, bent back the cover, took a match and lit it. I leaned toward Irwin, holding the flame to the tip of his cigarette.

"You're not going to tell me I'll stunt my growth, are you?"

Holding the matchbook in my hand, I smiled at him, the big one, the toothy one, the one I hoped would keep him talking. He smiled back, inhaling deeply, blowing the smoke up toward the ceiling.

"Could have been anyone, you know," he said. "You make the mistake of talking to Parker in a bar, you're going to hear his life story."

"You're saying he's friendly?"

"I'm saying he never knows when to shut up. He has no idea what's appropriate and what isn't. He has no sense of other people's privacy. That's what I'm saying. If anyone would listen, he'd tell them everything he knew about Tim. He'd invite them over for free drinks. It made him a hero, a big shot. He liked that."

"Where do you think he is now?"

"With the cops looking for him? Not anywhere near here. He's gone. He had some money. Whatever his aunt had lying around, pfft."

"Cash?"

"That's a no-brainer."

"Jewelry?"

"Gone. She had a lot of jewelry, too. Some really good stuff. He could be in California now. Or Florida. It's off-season, cheap fares. He could be snorkeling in the Keys, looking for a sucker in that bar where Hemingway supposedly hung out."

"Wouldn't the cops be checking with the airlines?"

"The cops!" He snorted. "Under what name? These guys"—he swirled one hand in a circle, indicating the seats around his poker table—"they've got no end of names, ID to go with them. They change names like other people change underwear."

"Why do you hang out with them, Irwin?"

It was a rude question. I knew it as I asked. There was so much more to him than to someone like Parker. So much less, too. Before he spoke, I had the feeling I knew just what he was going to say, not the details, maybe, but the crux of it. I could have said it for him.

He pushed himself away from the table and jumped down to the floor. The pillow slid off the chair and landed somewhere next to him.

"There's a convention once a year," he said, "the Little People of America. If that was my thing, I could go, hang around with people my own height, maybe meet a nice short girl who wouldn't mind going out with me." He shook his head. "The circus was good that way. We were all freaks in our own way. Ella used to say that." He began to walk around the table. "She was a good egg. A terrific cook. You cook, doll?"

I figured it was rhetorical. I didn't respond.

"Nah. You get taken out to dinner. You don't have to cook. People like Ella, they can't go out to dinner. They get a night off, they're on the road. They get a break, they wouldn't fit in the chairs at most restaurants. Maybe a booth would do it. She could have done that, taken a seat meant for two people. Or three. But then everyone would have been staring at her. That's no way to eat." He tapped his stomach. "Bad for the digestion. People like Ella have to cook. People like me . . ." He stopped at the side of my chair now, the side opposite the one where Dashiell lay, the matchbook I'd dropped between his paws. "People like me, we take what we can get."

"What about people like Tim?"

"Now here's the interesting thing, doll. Someone like Tim, you'd think he'd have a wife, a bunch of cute kids, Thanksgiving dinner with his family, all the nieces and nephews around. But that wasn't his life."

"Because?" But once again, I already knew the truth.

"Because he did the same as everyone, Rachel. He did the best he could. And it didn't include the wife and the kids. He couldn't go that route. So he . . ."

"Took what he could get?"

He nodded.

"Parker."

"That's right, doll. Same as I do. How about you?" he asked, the cigarette in his mouth, squinting past the smoke. He didn't wait for an answer. "Same, doll, am I right? And it's not always enough." He held his hands out, as if he were showing me the size of a fish he'd caught. "That's life, doll. Lonely people can't afford to be fussy. They get someone's ear, they blab too much. They never know when they're going to get another chance. You know what I'm saying, doll?"

"I do."

"And if you're lonely, if no one looks at you when you're out, as if you weren't even there, as if you didn't exist, and some bums want to hang out with you because you've got beer in the refrigerator and air-conditioning, what are you going to say? No? Most of the time, doll, you're not even aware you're settling for second- or third-best. After a while, your expectations adjust. Am I right?"

I thought about Colm O'Fallon, Tim's father, expecting nothing but sorrow from his life, getting exactly what he expected.

"I've got to go," I told him. "Maggie will be here soon."

I bent to pick up Dashiell's leash. Irwin headed for the door.

"Don't forget. I'm counting on you." I tapped my head with one finger.

Irwin nodded. "Sane," he said. "Both of us. I'm sure of it."

I bent down and kissed him on the cheek, then headed quickly down the stairs. I *was* counting on him, but not for confirmation of my sanity. I was counting on something else, on a lonely man's need to talk.

CHAPTER 27

I heard a car door close out front. Dashiell barked once. I waited a moment, then hit the buzzer to open the inner door. When I opened O'Fallon's door, Maggie was standing there, her face pale, her eyes red, Brody right behind her, seeing her home, in a way.

Was he worried she might not be safe? Because I was. I would have been a fool not to be. One death, Tim's, doesn't create a pattern. And Elizabeth Bowles had nothing to do with Maggie. With Dennis's murder, everything changed. It wasn't a big leap to think that the last remaining O'Fallon could be in danger.

Maggie didn't speak. She put a hand to her mouth. Her eyes welled up. She headed for the bathroom, half walking, half running.

Brody waited until we heard the door close, the water running.

"His neck was broken," he said.

"Just like Elizabeth Bowles."

"And both times, an opportunistic hiding place. Whatever's at hand."

Whatever's obvious, I thought. In neither case
was the body meant to remain undiscovered for
long. At this point, I didn't think whoever killed
Elizabeth Bowles had tied a sloppy knot. The poorly
tied knot had been intentional. The Dumpster offered the same advantage—easy discovery. More
evidence piling up against Parker. I looked at Brody.
The more things changed, the more they remained
the same. Neither of us was telling the other what
we knew, each of us for his own good reasons.

"I have to get back to the house," he said.

I reached out and put my hand on his arm. "Is
she safe?" I asked him.

"I've alerted the Piermont police. They'll drive
by, look in on her, make sure she's okay."

A lot of good that will do, I thought. I glanced
toward O'Fallon's kitchen. No sign of Maggie yet.

"Thank you for bringing her to the door," I
said, knowing what I had to do now, knowing I
had no choice in the matter.

My hand was still on his arm. He took it in his,
held it for a moment, then turned to leave. I
closed the door and stayed in the living room,
giving Maggie all the privacy she might need.
When she came back out, she'd washed her face
and combed her hair.

"The man who was living here with Tim . . ."

"Parker Bowling."

"Yes. Wasn't that the way his aunt was murdered, a broken neck?"

"Yes. That was what I was told."

Maggie was looking across the room, toward
the windows and the half-open shutter, the light
coming in over the top.

"Do they think that this person, the man Tim was helping, might have killed them both?"

"I don't know," I said.

"But they're looking for him, aren't they?"

"Yes, I was told they are."

"For questioning?"

"Yes," was all I said, not knowing where she was going, where I should go with this.

"And Tim?"

I felt my breath catch up in my throat.

"Do you think he killed Tim, too?"

"Would it make a difference, Maggie, if he hadn't done it himself, if someone else . . ."

Maggie took a deep breath, thinking before answering my question. "Yes. I know it seems odd. Either way, he's gone and I'll never see him again. Either way, it's a terrible tragedy. But I can't bear the thought that he was that unhappy." She put a hand to her lips and shook her head. "Detective Brody said they were looking for Parker for the other two murders. He didn't mention Tim. Of course, when there's been suicide in the family, it's not supposed to come as a surprise when it happens again. But it always does. It's the same with any death. Someone could be mortally wounded or terribly sick or frail and ancient, but the family always acts as if the death was the last thing on earth they expected. They act as if keeping a vigil at the ICU had nothing to do with anyone actually dying.

"I had a patient last year who was in her nineties and fading very quickly. The family was there a lot—her children, her grandchildren, even a second cousin. They came every day for three days. When she finally died, very peacefully while they were in the cafeteria taking a break, they seemed devastated when they returned."

"Because they hadn't been there when she died?"

"No. That would have made some sense. What they said to the doctor was, 'You didn't say it would be today.' "

"As if he should know that."

"Do you think Parker did this, Rachel?"

"No," I said. "I don't think Parker killed anyone."

Maggie's mouth opened, then closed again. She got up and walked over to the windows, unlatching the shutters and opening them wide. For a moment, she just stood there, her back to me, looking out at the street or lost in thought.

"Then who?"

"I don't know," I said.

"No thoughts? No theories? Then why all those questions?"

"What would be the point of speculating, maybe this happened, maybe that happened? It would only create more sorrow."

"What was the point of any of this—of Tim killing himself, of that poor Elizabeth Bowles getting murdered, and of someone killing Dennis? On top of everything else, why Dennis?"

"I don't know. I wish I did."

For a while, neither of us spoke.

"You must be so tired," I said at last.

"I am, yes."

"I have everything ready. All the things you set aside are packed up."

She nodded. "You've been so kind. You've been especially good to me. What you said about my burns, about wanting you to know, I've been thinking about that."

"And?"

"And about the no-talk rule, the way we grew up, about how it cripples you. The odd thing is, you take pride in what you're doing. You take pride in being a good liar, in doing the best job possible of keeping everything looking nice on the surface. And look where it leads, Rachel. Look where it leads."

"The day of the fire . . ."

"I know what you're going to ask, Rachel. I do. It wasn't anyone's fault. That's the truth."

"Then how did the fire start?"

"They'd stolen cigarettes. They were smoking, all of them. Someone dropped a match," she said, "or a cigarette. It fell into the dried leaves they'd put around the base of the tree, around me."

"You don't know who?"

"It doesn't matter, does it? No one did it on purpose."

"And once the fire got going, it was Francis who untied you?"

"Yes."

"And what did the other boys do?"

"At first, they were sort of yelling and running around, not doing anything . . ."

"Useful?"

"Yes. But then they began to kick snow onto the burning leaves and put out the fire. I didn't get to see that. Once Francis untied me, he wrapped his jacket around my legs, rolled me in the snow and then picked me up and began running toward home."

"He must have been a very brave boy," I said. But that's not what I was thinking. I was thinking that Francis was a twelve-year-old kid. He couldn't have picked her up and carried her all the way home. That wouldn't have been possible. I looked at Maggie, over at Tim's desk now, picking up the little statue of the horse, tracing the graceful arch of its neck with one finger. She was still doing it, still trying to glue the past back together with storytelling. Whom was she trying to kid this time, I wondered, me or herself?

"I meant to give this to Detective Brody," she said.

"I can do that for you if you like."

"You've already done so much, Rachel."

"It's okay," I said.

She put the horse back on the desk. "Then I guess I'm ready to go."

"There's one more thing I need to do for you, something urgent."

"What's that, Rachel?"

"I'm sending Dashiell home with you."

"Why? What do you mean? I don't understand."

"I don't want to alarm you, Maggie, but I have no choice."

"Rachel?" She took my hands in hers, holding on for dear life. "It's because of Dennis, isn't it?"

"Yes. I don't think you're in danger, Maggie, but you might be. Detective Brody has notified your local police and they're going to be watching your house and stopping by to make sure you're okay. Here's what I need you to do. Are you listening?"

"Yes, I am." Her professional voice now. She had spent her adult life taking care of crises. I knew she could do this.

"When you get home, if everything looks normal, and I'm pretty sure it will, unlock your door and send Dashiell in first. Tell him, 'Find it.' He'll check every inch of the house. If anyone's there, he'll take care of it. If you hear barking, go back to your car and drive to the police station. Do you understand?"

"I do."

"If Dashiell comes back to you, wagging his tail, you're safe and you can go inside. Lock the doors."

"I always do."

"Good. No one can get in without Dashiell warning you. He'll take care of you. You're not going to work for the next few days?"

"No, I'm not."

I nodded. "If everything's cool two days from now . . ."

"I'll bring him home."

"I'll come and get him."

"But you need . . ."

"Shhh. This isn't up for discussion, Maggie. I'm still not sure why Tim asked me to take care of things for him, but I am sure that it had to do with you, perhaps with protecting you from the secrets you already knew. He loved you very much, Maggie. You do know that, don't you?"

"I didn't."

"But now you do."

She nodded.

"So I'm just doing my job. I'm protecting you as best I can, with Dashiell's help."

"You're sure?"

"I'm sure. Why don't you bring the car around. I can take the things outside and wait for you, help you put them in the trunk."

"But what about his food and—"

"Feed him whatever you're eating. He'll be fine. And when you walk him, go out in front where people can see you. For his night walk, just let him out in the back. And keep him in your room when you go to bed."

"Where will he . . ."

"Not to worry. He'll figure it out."

When the car was loaded, I opened the back door and told Dashiell to hop in. I took off the leash and put it on the front seat, next to Maggie. Then I leaned into the back seat and put my arms around my dog's thick neck, pushing my face into his fur. He was looking out the back window as she drove away, his forehead creased with concern, but I knew he'd take care of her. Though I felt unimaginably empty watching them leave, I knew I'd done what I had to do.

I went back inside and closed the shutters. Then I picked up the little bronze horse, slipped it into the briefcase, locked up and left. I thought I'd head home then, but I changed my mind as soon as I was outside. I headed west, stopping for a little while in the park between Horatio and Jane Street. The waterfall was running. I sat there for a few moments watching a Border collie retrieve a ball, snorting in delight each time he'd snagged it.

After a few minutes, I headed out on the Jane Street side, turning left toward the Hotel Riverview on the corner. I still had the matchbook I'd taken from Irwin's house in my pocket. I crossed the street and looked up at the old brick building, gone to seed twice over.

Which one of those drifters lived there? I wondered. Which one had a tiny, depressing room with a view of the mighty Hudson, just a stone's throw from Timothy O'Fallon's apartment? It might be just a coincidence that one of Parker's buddies lived here. But coincidences always gave me a funny taste in my mouth, and one way or another, I wanted to know more. I pulled out my cell phone to dial the number on the matchbook, but then I stopped and put the phone away. Whom would I have asked for when the desk clerk answered? Except for Parker, if any of the men I'd met at Irwin's had last names, it was news to me.

I walked over to West Twelfth Street, crossing over to walk along the river, wishing Dashiell were with me to enjoy his favorite place, thinking about the question Maggie had asked me, how angry she had looked asking it. What *was* the point? I wondered now. Was the whole thing a way of getting at Parker, framing him for two murders, maybe three? But that made no sense. If someone was willing and able to murder three people, why not just murder Parker instead?

Was Tim the point? That made more sense. Suppose the crimes had been planned and executed by someone he'd sent to jail, someone who'd carried a major grudge and stewed about it for years and years. I thought about Ape walking out on the memorial. He'd been in Tim's apartment. He knew enough about Tim's life, and Parker's, to have pulled this off. The same could be said for any of the poker players, with the exception of Irwin. He could have shot Tim. All he would have had to do was to carry a step stool into the bathroom. But no matter how strong he was, no way could he have broken Elizabeth Bowles's or Dennis O'Fallon's neck without their complete cooperation and I never knew anyone that cooperative.

But it could have been any of the others. I wouldn't have been surprised to learn that any of them had been in jail. Is it possible that that was the connection to Tim? And if so, how would I find out who had been in jail, where they had been arrested and by whom? I wondered if I could get last names from Irwin. I wondered if he even knew them. If someone had three aliases, or four, or five, maybe they had another dozen they'd used before or might use again.

I sat on a bench facing the river and thought it all through again, each event, each story, each of the men I'd met or seen. Then I took out the phone again. This time I called Brody. The answer to my question would be another first name. At least that's all he said he knew. But it might be a significant one. It might be the first name of the person who set Parker up for a fall, just possibly the first name of the person who murdered Elizabeth Bowles, Dennis O'-Fallon and Timothy O'Fallon, and while this was not, I was sure, why Tim had left this job in my hands, knowing the whole story, knowing the truth was the only way I could really protect Maggie. So once again, I had no choice. There was no way I could let go until I knew who and why. I was in it until the bitter end.

CHAPTER 28

Brody didn't answer his cell phone and when I called the precinct, I was told he was unavailable. I walked back to West Twelfth Street, crossed the highway and headed north a block, back to Jane Street. There was an outdoor parking lot across the street from the hotel's entrance, the lot where O'Fallon's car had been parked. For a moment, I was sorry Tim's car was no longer there. But even if it were, this was a lot where the attendant parked the cars. I doubt I could have asked for the car to be parked on the north side of the lot and then have sat in it without the attendant thinking I was very peculiar. Unless, of course, I gave him an obscene tip.

I suppose I could have done that anyway, asking him to let me sit in someone else's car. But what would he say if the person came to pick up their car? There was no tip large enough to make him risk losing his job. And standing on the sidewalk at the side of the lot in broad daylight, I'd be completely exposed. Even without Dashiell, I could be easily recognized. I'd have to think of something else.

I thought about Irwin again, wondering if he knew the last names of the men he played poker with, if the names they used were their real names in the first place. But if I asked Irwin, wouldn't he just repeat what I'd said at the next game?

Whoever I was looking for had killed three times already. He might already be hunting for me in order to protect himself, because of what I'd told Irwin. But knowing I didn't think Tim had killed himself and knowing I was looking for him as the doer were two different things. Making him nervous was one thing. Making him feel his survival was at stake was another. Asking for names would rev up the hunt and the risk. There wasn't a doubt in the world that he would kill again if he thought his identity was about to be revealed. The question was whether or not I could find him before he found me. And in order to find him, I needed a name.

I headed back toward Horatio Street, let myself in and walked up the flight of stairs to Irwin's door.

"I knew it," he said, smiling. "You can't keep away from me."

"True."

"Like a bear to honey." Grinning.

"Speaking of which . . ."

"What, doll? Name it, it's yours."

"A cup of tea?"

"Yours, doll."

"A spoonful of honey."

He nodded, pleased to have the company.

"Got lemons?"

"I do."

"Real ones? Not that awful stuff that comes in a little plastic lemon-shaped container."

"Everything here's the real thing," arms out to the side, looking himself up and down as he did. "Care to check it out?"

"Not at the moment," I said. "But I would like a squeeze of lemon in the tea, then drop the wedge into the cup."

"Aren't we the little princess," he said. "You figure this for a full-service joint, doll?"

He didn't bother to wait for an answer. If he suspected it was all busywork, he didn't say so. I didn't have time to worry about that. I turned around and looked for the phone. It sat on a small cabinet near the daybed, two small drawers and an open space beneath where he kept his phone books. But I wanted the other kind, the personal kind.

"Mallomars or sugar cookies with your tea?" he asked, standing in the space between the rooms, a small plate in one hand. "I have both."

"Surprise me," I said. I waited until I heard him drag the step stool across the kitchen floor. Then I walked over to the daybed and opened the top drawer. His address book was there, as I thought it would be, some condoms that looked as if they had been manufactured sometime between the great wars, a hairbrush with red hair in it, a nail clipper, pain pills, more pain pills, and more pain pills. I felt a twinge of guilt as I lifted the phone book and slid it into the back of my jeans, under my T-shirt. I turned around, half expecting to be caught, to see Irwin standing near the partition that divided the living quarters from the kitchen area, irate. But then I heard him. He was humming. The refrigerator door opened and closed. The kettle began to whistle. I smiled at my own cleverness. I'd figured out a way to keep Irwin busy long enough for me to get what I'd come for.

I hadn't figured out how I'd return the address book. I could ask to use his bathroom, check it there, drop it anywhere in the apartment in the hope he'd think he'd left it out. Or I could take it home, worry about returning it another time.

We sat at a small table in the kitchen, the sun streaming in the window over the sink. I took a sip of tea, told him it was delicious and tried not to lean back onto the phone book, hoping it wouldn't slip out.

"Have you been thinking about my offer?"

I took a sugar cookie, broke it in half, put one half into my mouth, buying time.

"The dog," he said. "Even if he doesn't know that much, you could teach him. He's smart. And I'd give you a percent of whatever I got. Where is he, by the way? First time I've seen you without him."

"He's getting groomed," I said. "Bath, cream rinse, nails, the works."

He frowned again. "That is why you came, isn't it?"

"What is?"

"The dog. The deal I proposed the other day, help a little guy earn a living, make a buck for yourself at the same time."

I nodded, happy not to have to invent a cover story myself.

"Or was it something else?"

"What do you mean?"

"Whatever you slipped into the back of your jeans, doll. My address book, is it?"

"Shit."

"And the reason you took it is?"

"I need the last names of"—tilting my head toward the poker table—"your buddies."

"You ever thinking of asking, doll?"

"No, actually, I didn't." I pushed the cup away, reached my hand behind me, pulled out the address book and put it down on the table. "That's not true. I did think of asking."

"And?"

"I was afraid you'd mention it to the wrong person."

"And which person would that be, doll?" He pulled a cigarette out of the pack in his shirt pocket, began patting his pant pockets looking for matches.

I took the Hotel Riverview matches out of my pocket and lit one, holding it near the tip of his cigarette.

"I don't know which person that would be, Irwin. That's the problem."

He hopped down from the chair, walked over to where I was sitting, put his hands on the edge of the table. "But you're thinking that whoever it is . . ."

"I am."

He pointed toward the phone book. "Be my guest, doll."

He walked out of the kitchen. I opened his address book to the beginning and began paging through it. None of the names I wanted were there, not even the first names. I got up, carried the book into the living room and put it on the poker table.

"I'm disappointed in you," he said. "That you'd think so little of me. I'm short, doll, not stupid."

"How did you know?"

He walked back toward the kitchen, pointed up to a mirror in the corner of the room, near the ceiling, the kind you see in stores so that the clerk at the register can see who's in the aisles, and what they're doing.

"Do you think I'd let those deadbeats into my home if I couldn't keep an eye on them?"

"I feel so foolish," I said. "I should have been honest with you."

"Always the best policy," he said. "But you can make it up to me."

I didn't ask how. I wasn't *that* foolish. He decided to tell me anyway.

"You could go to bed with me, doll. That would square things." Smiling now.

"I could," I told him. "But the minute you were finished you'd be telling me you're out of clean socks. Next you'd tell me I could stand to lose ten pounds. You'd start telling me what I could and couldn't do, what I should think, who I should vote for, as if any of that was any of your fucking business. Makes me think it's not the best idea in the world."

"Too much caffeine today, doll?" He tossed his cigarette into the sink, where it made a hissing sound. "So now what?"

I shrugged.

"You're giving up?"

"Yeah, I am. I'll leave it where it belongs."

"With the cops?" He snorted, shook his head from side to side. "Bull."

"No, really. I'll finish up with Tim's apartment in the next couple of days, sign whatever paperwork the lawyer sends me and look for some respectable work."

His hand came up, the palm toward me. "Don't try to kid a kidder, doll. It never works."

"You got mirrors somewhere else, too?" I asked. "You think you can see into my mind now?"

"More than that, doll, more than that."

For a moment we just stood there, glaring at each other. When I walked to the door, he walked back to the kitchen. I didn't say good-bye. Neither did he.

I was tired and hungry and needed to get the sour taste of failure out of my mouth. As I passed the building on the corner, I noticed that the Dumpster was gone, hauled away, I guessed, by the police to check every piece of debris in it.

It was one of those steamy afternoons when the air is thick and still, not enough breeze to get the sweat to evaporate off your skin. I headed for Hudson Street, trying to keep in the shade as much as possible. When I was a block from home, my cell phone rang.

"You called?" he said.

"Yeah, I was wondering if there's any news about Parker."

"Not yet. These things take time."

I had always been under the impression that most of the successful work after a homicide happened within the first forty-eight hours. Time was the enemy in a case like this, but once again, I didn't say what I was thinking.

"I was just sort of going over things in my mind," I said.

"And?"

"Well, I was thinking about that guy Parker said he was supposed to meet the morning Tim died."

"Fred?"

I inhaled so loud he asked if anything was wrong. I told him no, I was crossing the street, I said, and I hadn't noticed a car coming. He told me to go home, get some rest. I said I would. I could hear someone yelling in the background, someone totally out of control.

"Fred?" I said. "You're sure that's the name he gave you?"

"That's what he said. 'I went out to meet this guy Freddy, but he never showed.' That's a quote."

I felt a little prickle at the back of my neck and on my arms.

"Rachel?"

"Oh, yeah, sorry. You're right. I think it's all catching up with me. I'm on my way home to get some sleep. I can't think straight anymore."

"We're taking care of this, Rachel. Do you understand?"

"I was just thinking, that's all," I said into the phone, remembering Irwin telling me, "Don't try to kid a kidder, doll." The line was still open. "I'll talk to you later," I said, taking the phone away from my ear and pressing *end* before Brody had the chance to respond.

The phone still in my hand, I dialed a number I knew by heart now, waiting for the desk clerk to pick up.

"Freddy Baker, please."

"Hold on," he said, "I'll ring him."

I hung up without waiting for an answer. I no longer needed the names I'd hoped to get from Irwin's address book. There was something much more urgent now. I headed home, crossing against the lights, not a minute to lose.

CHAPTER 29

Standing across the street from the Hotel Riverview, I waited for someone familiar to exit. I didn't know which of the men I'd met it would be, or even if the person calling himself Freddy Baker was someone I'd ever seen. Anyone in New York City might have heard any of Parker's stories, meaning any of Tim's as well.

Even if Tim had never said a word about the incident at Breyer's Landing, why not tell the Freddy Baker stories? "Look," he might have said, "I used to lie and steal and do stupid, hurtful things and I straightened myself out. It can be done," thinking they'd be grist for the mill, that they might inspire Parker to change.

And how might Parker have reinterpreted what he'd heard? As comedy, no doubt, how this guy he lived with and his brothers and cousins had successfully hoodwinked their parents; his father a cop, too. That must have been the best part, putting one over on a cop, making him believe a terrible accident was the work of a kid who didn't even exist, for God's sake. It was an unbeatable story, one someone like Parker would not have been able to resist telling anytime he got the chance. And then there was the kicker: how this guy, the one he lived with, was a cop himself, and how he, Parker, kept putting one over on him. Priceless.

And what about the rest of it? Lying in the dark, one of those terrible nights when Tim couldn't sleep for remembering, had he hinted that he'd done worse, far worse than lying and stealing? Parker might have said, "Hey, man, who didn't? I could tell you some stories of my own." And then what? Did Tim say, "No, you don't understand," thinking no one could, least of all Parker, ending the conversation right there. He might have told the Freddy Baker stories, that made sense, but he never would have told Parker what was keeping him up in the first place. He never would have told him about what really happened at Breyer's Landing.

How often, I wondered, had Parker told the Freddy Baker stories, perhaps mixing in some details of his own invention, entertaining his fellow miscreants in bars, at the poker game, sitting and shooting the bull in Abingdon Square Park, where he'd talked to me, confiding, confessing, getting the attention he needed with someone else's pain. Didn't we all do that at one time or another? Wasn't that what we called gossip, not all of it harmless?

The sky was overcast and it was as dark as it gets in New York City, not very. But there was light under the canopy of the Hotel Riverview and none across the street where, behind the row of cars parked on the south side of Jane Street, I was leaning against the chain-link fence of the parking lot, not knowing if I'd recognize anyone, hoping no one would recognize me.

Of course, since Parker had probably told Tim's stories to dozens of people I'd never met or seen, chances were good that no one would recognize anyone. That aside, my whole damn theory could be wrongheaded. One foot behind me, slouching so that I could see under the canopy, I watched the throngs of people heading up the stone steps to see *Debbie Does Dallas* at the Jane Street Theater, people who wouldn't ordinarily be in the neighborhood, hanging on to each other for dear life. I switched legs and waited some more. An old black man came out, walked slowly down the stairs and sat in a little niche to the right, taking in the cool evening air. A woman with a small teddy bear sticking out of her backpack came down next, heading toward Washington Street, sipping out of a bottle that she kept in a paper bag. A golden retriever, a bottle of Poland Spring water in his mouth, passed, his owner glancing at me, then looking away quickly, as if I might be one of the hookers who hung out on street corners two blocks north of where I stood. I waited some more, not knowing if this would get me anything, wanting answers and not knowing what else to do.

The people coming from Washington Street were in a big hurry. I checked my watch. It was nearly show time. And when I looked back at the hotel, there he was at the top of the stairs. Like nearly everyone else who had exited the hotel, he stopped partway down the steps and looked around. He stood in the light, his shoulders hunched, his hands in his pockets. I didn't think he'd recognize me, especially without Dashiell. I was just someone he'd passed on the stairs one day. Andy was looking down, pulling a pack of cigarettes out of his pocket.

I pushed off the fence, crossed the street and joined the latecomers, as if I, too, were going into the theater. When I got to where he was standing, I stopped and fished around in my pockets, as if I were looking for my ticket, so that I could get a better look. And that I did. A cigarette was dangling from his mouth now. He struck the match, holding it to the cigarette, cupping the flame with his other hand.

The hands gave him up, raw and shiny like Maggie's legs, even after all these years. As he shook the match, he glanced over at me, and for just a moment, I saw his eyes. The fire Maggie had described was long gone. His eyes, now that he was a grown man, were as cold and black and uncaring as the swimming hole that had swallowed his closest friend, the swimming hole that had become the beginning of the end for all of them. Standing on the steps, latecomers brushing by, I didn't have a doubt in the world that I was a foot away from Francis Connor, a foot away from the man who had killed Timothy O'Fallon, Elizabeth Bowles and Dennis O'Fallon. And knowing who, I knew why.

CHAPTER 30

I didn't know if Francis Connor had recognized me. The first time I'd seen him, he'd never looked up. But I wasn't about to take a chance. Instead of turning around and heading home, which is what I would have liked to do, I kept on walking, following the crowd. That way, even if he realized he'd seen me before, he might assume seeing me now was mere coincidence, that, like everyone else coming up the stairs, I was going to the play. Besides, there was safety in numbers. Once inside, I looked around, found the nearest ladies' room, pulled out my cell phone and called Maggie, listening to the ringing, wondering where she was.

Monk, my ass, I thought, leaning against the inside of the bathroom door. Why had I thought that only the children were lying, making up acceptable stories to cover homely, painful truths? Where had the children learned it from?

And where had Francis really been all these years? Reform school? Jail? A psychiatric hospital? Or had he been with the circus? Who would notice one more freak?

Maggie still hadn't picked up. I was about to give up when she answered. "Did I wake you?"

"Rachel?"

"Yes, it's me."

"No. I slept a little when I got home, but now I'm up. I had to feed Dashiell and take him for a walk. Rachel?"

"Yes?"

"I feel so safe with him here. I can't begin to thank you. I know you must miss him terribly."

I didn't want to think about that, about how it felt not to have Dashiell with me or waiting for me at home. But now, with what I had just seen, it wouldn't be long. If I acted quickly, if I had just a little bit of luck, it was possible I could get him back in the morning. But if I was going to tell my story to Brody, I wanted all the answers, and there was a piece missing I thought Maggie could help me with.

"I hope I can get back to sleep. I'm really tired. But I can't stop thinking."

"Me, neither."

"What are you thinking about?"

"Your father," I said. "About that last day, locked up in his study."

"I wish someone had known what *he* had been thinking that day."

"But no one did."

"No. He never said a word."

"He was alone all day?"

"Yes, all day. Tim knocked once. I was two rooms away and heard my father's voice, it was that loud."

"Saying what?"

She hesitated. Old habits die hard. "Telling him to go away."

"That's it? What exactly did he say?"

"Get the hell away from the door."

"Was that all?"

"No."

"What else did he say?"

There was another silence on the line.

"Maggie? It's important. Was there something else? Did he say something else?"

"There was one other thing."

"Which was?"

I heard her put the phone down on a counter or a table. Then I could hear her sobbing. There was a little table with a mirror over it, a chair in front of it. I pulled out the chair and sat, looking back at the door, half expecting Francis to open it, half thinking he might have figured out that seeing me here wasn't just a coincidence. But the door remained closed, no other ladies needing to use the facilities, no obsessed murderer coming in to do whatever was necessary in order to keep his secret, in order to survive.

I heard a scrape as Maggie picked up the phone again.

"He said, 'Haven't you done enough already?'"

"Had he been angry at Tim the day before?"

"No. In fact, they were working together in the front yard. My mother had gotten some shrubs and Tim was helping my father plant them." There was a pause again. Maggie blew her nose. "And then Francis came by."

I glanced at the door again, as if the mention of

his name would make him appear. But the door remained closed. I was all alone.

"And then what?" I asked.

"Well, they stopped planting. Tim came inside."

"And Francis helped your father with the shrubs?"

"No. They went into the study. No one planted the rest of the shrubs. They'd planted one, an azalea. But it died. It was the wrong season. They're supposed to go in the ground in the spring."

"So the shrubs sat on the lawn and Francis and your father went into your father's study, and what?"

"Why, they shut the door."

"Wasn't that unusual, Maggie?"

"No, I don't think so. Francis adored my parents. And he looked up to my father. In some ways, he was closer to them than to his own folks. He might have come for some advice."

Or to put down the secret he was carrying, to confess his lie, put the blame where it belonged, on his uncle's oldest son.

I thought about asking Maggie for her aunt and uncle's phone number, but then I thought it was probably in Tim's address book. And what would be the point in calling them? I already knew their son had not given his life to God. Quite the opposite, as far as I could tell.

"And after Francis left, then what?"

"I don't know. It got very late and I'd gone to bed."

"And the next day?"

"I never saw my father again after that. The next day was the day he was in his study alone, the day he shot himself."

"Was anyone home at the time? Did anyone hear the shot?"

"No one was home. Tim and Dennis had things after school and they came home late. I was at a girlfriend's house. But my mother heard the shot. She was getting out of her car, just home from her rosary group. She ran inside but the study was locked. She called 911, the way we were all taught to do in case of an emergency, but she didn't wait. She went outside and smashed the study window with the shovel that had been left out on the lawn the evening before. But of course it was too late to do anything."

"How awful for her."

"I should have told her. I should have told my mother."

"What?"

"That he was so angry at Tim."

"It can't have been the only time."

"No. But . . ."

"He was angry often, wasn't he?"

"Yes, but it was just because he loved us and wanted . . ." Maggie stopped.

"Try to get some rest," I said. "I'll call you in the morning."

I sat in the ladies' room for a few more minutes, the phone still in my hand. What was his explanation for his poor burned hands, I wondered, that he'd been a cook perhaps and there'd been a grease fire? Is that where Parker got the notion to say he'd worked as a cook, from Francis? Or, if he'd been with the circus, he might have said there'd been a tent fire, fast and furious, a match dropped in straw, that he'd gotten burned saving the sword swallower or the big cats. He might have been a hero in the story. Why not? What else did he have but his stories?

Francis Connor had come from a family of storytellers. The skill, the art of storytelling was his birthright. I bet they all told good stories, every last one of them. But the best ones, the most compelling ones might have been the ones Francis told, especially the ones he told himself.

The lobby was empty when I left the ladies' room and headed home. All the pieces fit now. In its own horrible way, it all made sense.

I thought of walking over to the precinct but went home instead. It would be easier to talk to Brody in the garden. I was ready, I was thinking as I unlocked the gate, to make what I'd told Irwin the truth. I had the answers I'd been looking for, even, I thought, why O'Fallon had chosen me for the job that no one wants. I was ready to put it down, to leave it to the cops. I sat on the top step, looking up at the cloudy, dark sky, and dialed Brody's cell phone. Listening to the phone ring, I wondered how I'd tell him what I knew. I wondered where to begin.

CHAPTER 31

Where's your better half?" he asked, standing at the gate and looking down the tunnel toward the garden.

"He's with Maggie."

Brody frowned.

"It's just until . . . I thought she might be in danger. That's what I wanted to talk to you about, about Parker's friend Andy and—"

"Andrew Chase. We know all about him," he said. "Parker told us that it was Andy who got him out of the house the morning Tim died, that he'd gotten one of his buddies to pretend his name was Freddy, claim they'd met before."

"But—"

"Parker couldn't possibly remember every guy he got drunk with, every piece of garbage he bullshitted in the past six months."

"Then you have him? You have Parker?"

Brody nodded.

"I just saw him," I said, the things I had to say coming out backward, not the way I'd planned.

"Who? Parker?" Scowling.

"No. Andy. At the Hotel Riverview. That's why I called you."

He didn't seem to be listening. He walked past me into the dark tunnel. I locked the gate and began to follow him, but he turned so suddenly, I nearly walked right into him.

"But that's not his real name."

Brody frowned again.

"Andrew Chase." I stopped. A chase, I thought. His life's work. Waiting for his aunt to die, then coming after Tim.

"Not now, Rachel," Brody said, his voice hoarse, a man who hadn't slept in too long a time. "We know all about Andy. We're taking care of everything."

I wanted to tell him that Tim hadn't committed suicide, that Parker hadn't killed anyone. "You don't understand," I wanted to say. But I didn't. I didn't say another word. I thought he probably did understand, that that was why his eyes looked so old and sad, that that was why he was reaching out, putting his hands on my shoulders, why he was pulling me toward him, because it was all over now, because everything was okay.

I could feel my shirt clinging to me, the evening so warm, barely a breeze anywhere. It was even hotter in the tunnel, all closed-in the way it was, no air moving at all, Brody standing so close I could feel his breath on my skin.

So I didn't say that when I'd waited across the street from the Hotel Riverview to see who had registered there as Freddy Baker that I'd seen Francis Connor, that I'd seen his hands, that finally everything made sense. I didn't say that Tim was the point of it all, that Elizabeth was killed to set up Parker and that poor Dennis was in the wrong place at the wrong time, that Francis had seen that flash of recognition in his eyes, and that that's why he was dead now, too.

Brody slid his hands down my arms, taking my hands in his, stepping even closer.

They were taking care of it, he'd said. Maybe they'd been at the hotel when I was there, waiting outside or following him out, not wanting to arrest him in the middle of the theater crowd. Is that what Michael was trying to tell me, that they had him already? Surely there was nothing I could tell them they didn't already know. Or, if there was some small detail I knew that they didn't, well then, it could wait. It had waited for twenty-nine years, it could wait another few hours.

I pushed my face into Brody's neck, breathing in the smell of his skin. When I looked up into his face, he bent to kiss me. We stood together in the tunnel a long time, holding on to each other with everything we had. Then we went inside and up the stairs. He removed the .357 magnum from his holster, emptied the cylinder into his hand, placed the unloaded gun and the bullets on top of the dresser. Without a word, we stood in the dark undressing ourselves and each other, inhabiting a world apart from the one that had obsessed us both for so long.

For over a year, I had been sharing my bed with my dog and only with my dog, feeling wounded and unready to risk getting hurt again. Now desire changed all that. I reached for Brody and pulled him close, wanting nothing other than to

lose myself completely in this man and this moment. We made love again and again, holding on
to each other as if for dear life. When Brody finally fell asleep, I couldn't. My hand on his chest
rising and falling with the rhythm of his breathing, my breathing in harmony with his, I felt as I
did when I lay close to Dashiell—that we were
separate, but we were one.

I might have dozed off. I didn't hear the downstairs door open. I heard it close.

I sat up, the sheet coming with me. Brody
sighed, rolled over, taking the sheet as he did,
now covered from head to toe.

Another step. Another sound, the old boards
groaning under the weight of a man. He was on
the wooden steps now, coming slowly, trying
hard not to make noise.

I rolled off the bed, stood, grabbed Brody's gun
and the bullets, crouching as low as I could at the
side of the bed away from the door. There was another sound, in the hall this time. I grabbed the
pillow, loaded the gun, folding the pillow around
the gun to muffle the sound of the cylinder snap-
ping into place, my breathing sounding as loud as
a respirator in the quiet, dark room.

He appeared in the doorway, standing still for
a moment. Then he raised both arms, one hand
cupping the gun, the other ready to pull the trigger, pointing it toward the bed, toward the figure
covered by the sheet. There was no time to think,
to weigh options. There were no options. I
pointed Brody's gun at the intruder's chest and
fired, the gun flying up, the concussion feeling
like an explosion in my face, the sound seeming

to crush everything else out of the small room, even the air. And then there was silence. I saw Francis Connor crumple to the floor. I saw Brody leap up. I saw his lips moving, but I couldn't hear what he was saying.

Brody came around the bed, took the gun from my hand and wiped it on the sheet. Then he held the gun straight out in front of him and fired once into the frame of the door.

He pulled me up. I saw his lips moving again.

"Wash your hands," he was saying, "and put on a robe." He reached for the phone, balling up the sheet he'd used to wipe the gun as he did.

CHAPTER 32

Brody stayed after all the others had left, Francis carried out in a body bag, his mission over at last. We sat in the garden, on the front steps, neither of us speaking. Brody was deep in thought, not sharing what he was thinking, not a man who wasted words. He hadn't wasted words when the cops arrived, either—uniforms, detectives, the whole damn station house squeezed into my little bedroom or standing in the hallway, an explosion of blood and bone on the wall behind them.

He'd heard a noise, he'd told them. He'd rolled out of bed, grabbed and loaded his gun. When Francis had appeared in the doorway, when he'd lifted his gun and pointed it at the sleeping figure in the bed—that would be me in this story—Brody had fired twice, missing him once, firing again and hitting him fatally in the chest.

"It doesn't seem right, Dashiell not here," he said after a while.

"No, it doesn't."

"He would have heard Francis when he broke the lock on your gate."

"He would have."

"He would have barked," he said. "We would have had some warning."

"Correct."

"Without him . . ." He stopped and looked at me. "If not for you . . ."

I waved a hand at him, telling him to stop.

He took the hand in both of his. "You saved my life."

"Guys always say that after sex," I said. I got up and stretched my back.

"Tell me something," he said, standing too.

"What?"

"Tell me about Tim in the group where you met him. Tell me every detail, everything he said."

"There isn't much to tell," I said, describing what had happened, and, more important, what hadn't happened, repeating what Tim had said to me that last day.

The sky had started to lighten. It was time to go get Dashiell. Brody told me I could use his car. He said he'd take care of the lock on the gate, that it would be replaced by the time I got back, and that he'd get someone in to take care of the upstairs.

"Michael, when this first happened, did it make any kind of sense to you? Did you think of Tim as the kind of man who would . . ."

He shook his head. "Nobody's that smart, Rachel. Nobody knows what's going on in someone else's head, in their heart."

"He didn't talk to you about any of this?"

He shook his head, looking over toward the oak tree, the muscles in his cheeks jumping.

"But you knew about it?"

"Some of it. I knew he'd lost his kid brother."

"But not how."

"An accident."

We walked out onto West Tenth Street. A uniform was standing outside the gate. Brody pointed to his car and handed me the keys.

"I'll call you when I'm on the way back," I said.

When we got to the curb, I stopped and turned toward him.

"Michael, I did what I had to do," I whispered. "I did what you would have done. There's no need to discuss it."

"Are you okay?"

I shrugged. "I will be," I said, "in time."

He touched my arm, then headed across the street toward the station house. I stayed where I was for a moment, watching him go.

CHAPTER 33

I still don't understand," Maggie said. "How did Francis find Tim after all those years?"

"Internet search, perhaps. I tried it. Tim's name showed up twenty-seven times in newspaper articles. There are also national phone directories. Tim had a driver's license, so the Department of Motor Vehicles had a record of his whereabouts. But my guess is that he found out from his parents."

"Simple as that?"

I nodded.

We were sitting in the backyard, Dashiell lying across my foot, not taking any chances that I might leave when he wasn't paying attention.

"I think he stayed in touch with your aunt and uncle all along. He was too hung up on family not to have done that. But since they had said he'd become a monk, they wouldn't be telling anyone anything to the contrary—that he'd been in jail, perhaps, or that he was living as a drifter with occasional jobs washing dishes or delivering takeout."

"Is that what he's been doing?"

"I don't know what he's been doing. I only know what he did."

"But why did he wait so long? I understand he couldn't do anything when he was twelve, but why wait twenty-nine long years, hold all that hatred in your heart and act on it after all that time?"

"Because of what happened with your father. I don't believe his intent was to hurt your father. My guess is he was horrified at what happened."

"What was his intent? To get Tim into trouble? To hurt him back?"

"That's what I thought at first. But that might not have been the case. He was still a kid, a very, very troubled kid. He'd lost the two people he was closest to in all the world, his best friend and his brother. His life had been turned upside down. Worse than that, it seemed to be destroyed. I think in talking to your father he was trying to alleviate some of the pain he was feeling."

"How? I don't understand the point of telling my father what really happened. Didn't he see that . . ."

I shook my head. "The point was confession. No one could fix the sorrow he felt. But maybe talking to his uncle could help with the guilt."

"Over Joey's death?"

I nodded. "And more. When someone you're close to commits suicide, there's always the feeling that . . ."

"If only you'd known, you could have done something. You could have prevented it."

I nodded.

"I know that well."

"I know you do, Maggie. It was a heavy burden to grow up with."

"So Francis was only trying to help himself to feel better. He thought my father would be able to help him live with it," she said. "But it didn't turn out the way he expected it to."

"No, it didn't."

"Once my father knew what had truly happened that day, *he* couldn't find a way to live with it, to live with himself."

"That's what I think, too."

"Because if one of his sons killed the other, what kind of a father could he have been?"

And what kind of a man? I thought. When he learned he'd failed to protect those who needed him most, his own children, how could he have lived with himself another day?

"And after your father's suicide," I said, "no way was Francis going to take the chance of being the cause of your mother's death, too."

"By killing Tim while she was alive."

"Exactly. My guess is that when his parents told him that your mother was sick, that's when he began to stalk Tim in earnest. That's when he moved close by and began watching the apartment, when he befriended Parker, when he readied himself for what he would do once your mother was gone."

Dashiell had gotten up and put his chin on Maggie's lap. Absentmindedly, she stroked his head.

"And all those years, while he was waiting, the hatred he felt never diminished."

"No. It festered."

She turned away, then swiped at her cheeks

with the palms of her hands. When she turned back, her face was determined, her lips tight.

"Why didn't he just leave, after he'd killed Timothy? Why stay around? Wasn't that risky? Wasn't it stupid?"

"Rage was the only thing that made him feel good. It was the only thing that empowered him. It was all he had by then. It was his life."

"So he stayed to keep the rage alive."

I nodded.

"He stayed for the pleasure it gave him, the only pleasure he had. And he stayed because if he left, he'd be starting over from scratch. Perhaps he didn't have the imagination or the courage to do that, to start a whole new life."

"Because he'd finished the old one."

"Yes. He had."

When I got up to go, she walked me to the car. Neither of us could speak. I put my arms around her and she held me tight. Then she bent and whispered something in Dashiell's ear. She was still standing there when we drove away.

I thought about the place where it all started, up on top of the Palisades, just a bunch of kids fooling around. And then one careless accident, one push destroyed two families.

I thought about O'Fallon, too, about how he had hidden his grief along with a lifetime of secrets. He'd carried the weight of it alone. Until now.

I pulled into the gas station right before the bridge to fill the gas tank and call Brody.

"I think I know the answer to that question now," I said.

"What question?"

"What Tim wanted me to do for him, why he chose me for this."

He waited.

"When it was all over, whenever that was going to be, he wanted someone to understand."

"What he'd done?"

"And how he'd tried to make up for it by taking in men who might have been his brother, had his brother lived. I think he was hoping that someone, that one other human being, would know it all and then forgive him," I said. "Because he was never able to do that himself."

They'd tried, each of them, in their own way, to find a way to live despite what had happened at Breyer's Landing, and only Maggie was left now. I wondered if she was strong enough to let it go, to decide to live in spite of it.

Driving across the George Washington Bridge, I could see the Palisades in the rearview mirror, harsh and rocky, rising up from the Hudson. Toward my right the river, flowing toward the ocean, looked calm, the sun painting the ripples of water with quick, graceful strokes of silver. And beyond, the city, tall and strong against the bright summer sky, tapering toward downtown, where in the year that Joey O'Fallon was pushed to his death by his own brother, the World Trade Center had been completed.

Acknowledgments

For the generous sharing of information about cadaver dog training, I thank Bill McGlynn of the Rochester NYPD; Carla Collins, K9 training director of Search One Rescue Team of Texas; and retired bloodhound handler Gina Lyn Hayes. For being a constant resource about police work, my gratitude to Lieutenant Detective Commander, NYPD, Peter C. Fenty.

I would also like to thank Anita LaTorre, Philip Levy, Stephen Solomita, Barbara Jaye Wilson, JoAnn Fleming, Victoria Joubert, Beth Adelman, Wayde Vickrey and my sweetheart, Stephen Lennard, for information, advice and general shoring up.

No book is as good as it could be without an eagle-eyed editor. I thank Trish Grader for this and for her generosity. This story wouldn't have become a book without my agent, Gail Hochman, miracle worker. I thank their able assistants as well, Erin Richnow at Morrow and Joanne Brownstein at Brandt and Hochman.

With special thanks to G.D., who showed me that the dead do tell tales. And to Dexter and Flash—no words can begin to cover what I owe you.

Turn the page for a glimpse of
WITHOUT A WORD,
the next suspenseful
Rachel Alexander Mystery
from
Carol Lea Benjamin

One

Leon Spector had dead written all over him, not the kind where they put you in a box, say a few words and toss the earth back over you, not the ashes to ashes kind of dead, but the kind that lets the world know that whatever the battle was, you lost, the kind that says that some-time, a long time ago, you were beaten into the ground by circumstances beyond your control. I didn't know what those circumstances were in Leon's case, but on a particularly sunny after-noon at the Washington Square Park dog run the month I turned forty and my pit bull, Dashiell, turned five, Leon apparently planned to tell me.

He met me as I was closing the inner gate, a wide, multicolored camera strap slung around his neck, his Leica hanging low on his chest. I'd seen him at the run before, not with a dog but with his camera, and I'd seen him taking pictures on other occasions as well, the opening of the new park along the river, the annual outdoor art show, the gay pride parade. Someone said he was a free-lance photographer. Someone else said he was working on a book. Until that afternoon, that was all I knew about Leon, but not why he carried not only a camera everywhere he went but also the weight of the world. You could see it pulling him toward the ground, as if the gravity under Leon was working overtime.

"I've been looking all over for you," he said as I bent to unhook Dashiell's leash. "I couldn't call you because . . ."

I looked up. Leon stopped and fiddled with the strap of his camera.

"Because I'm not listed?" I asked.

Leon shook his head. "I never got that far," he said. "The person who told me about you, who said what I needed was a private investigator and that's what you . . ." He stopped and shrugged. "It is, isn't it?"

I nodded.

Leon nodded back. "She just said she'd seen you here and that your dog wore a red collar with his name on it and that you had," he made a spiral with his left pointer, "long, curly hair. She didn't know your last name."

I didn't know his last name either, at least not yet, but I didn't say so. Leon didn't look in the mood for small talk.

"What's the problem?" I asked.

Instead of answering me, Leon put the camera up to his face and looked through the viewfinder. I wondered if he had a deadline of some sort or if he was just one of those people who talked better if he was doing something else at the same time.

I heard the shutter click and looked in the direction Leon's camera was pointing. There was a little girl of about nine or ten sitting alone on a bench, watching the dogs. She was wearing dark glasses and a shirt that looked three sizes too big. Next to her, on the bench, there was a small, see-through plastic purse the shape of a lunch pail, with something colorful inside, but I was too far away to make out what it was.

I waited. Sometimes, doing something else or not, I let the other guy do the talking, see what comes out before adding my own two cents.

"I need you to find my wife," he said.

I guess that explained the sagging shoulders, the hangdog look. He'd been a good-looking man once, you could see that. But now he looked faded, used up, worn out. You could feel the effort it took for him to form sentences, as if he could barely muster the energy to speak.

"It's not for me," he said. "It's for my daughter. She's in trouble and she needs her mother."

Dashiell was busy digging a hole in the far corner of the run, a hole I'd have to fill in before I left. I turned to look at Leon now to see if his face might tell me what his words hadn't. But Leon's face wasn't talking either.

"Where is her mother?"

"That's the whole point. I don't know, not since she walked out on me and Madison."

I took out a small notepad and a pencil. I wrote down "Madison."

"Divorced you?" I asked.

He shook his head. "Nothing so . . ." He scratched at the dirt with the sole of his shoe. "Nothing as clear as that."

"Missing, you mean?"

Leon nodded. "I do," he said. "Every day."

I nodded. I knew what it was like to miss someone who was gone. I figured, one way or another, just about everyone did. But Leon had a bad case of it, not only being abandoned, but being abandoned with a kid.

"Come on," I said, "let's sit down."

We walked over to the closest bench.

"No clue as to why she left," I asked, "or where she went?"

"You ever notice the way things look one way, but they're not, they're another?"

"How did you think things were?"

"Permanent," he said.

I felt that little stab that sometimes comes along with an unexpected truth, simply stated.

Leon lifted the camera to his face again. But this time I didn't hear the shutter click. I wrote down, "How long is wife missing? How old is Madison?"

"After the initial shock of it, the police investigation, all of that," he moved the camera away from his face and turned to look at me, "everything just a dead end, I managed okay." He tilted his head left, then right, as if he were arguing with himself. "At least that's what I thought. Not perfect. Far from perfect. But okay. Considering." He shrugged. "But now." He shook his head. "I don't know how to handle this."

If his daughter was pregnant, I wondered if there might be some female relative who could help. Or a neighbor they were close to. Was this just an excuse to try to find his missing wife again? I was about to ask when Leon started talking again. Perhaps he was finally on a roll.

"She went out one night and never came back," he said, covering his face with the camera. He was pointing it at the southern end of the run where a Weimaraner had dropped his ball into the water bucket and was trying to fish it out with his front paws, but I had the feeling Leon wasn't actually looking through the lens this time.

"Your wife?"

Leon moved the camera away and nodded. He hadn't taken a picture this time either. "Just like that," he said. "Went for a walk. Didn't take a thing with her."

"No money, no passport, not even a change of clothes?"

"Just a change of heart, I guess. And Roy."

"That was the man she ran off with?" I asked quietly, sympathetically, finally getting it.

Leon shook his head. "That I could understand, if that's what she had done."

"But it wasn't, is that what you're saying?" Wanting to shake him by now. "Spit it out, Leon. I'm going to be a member of AARP before you get to the point."

"Roy was the dog," he said.

"The dog?"

Leon nodded, though it was sort of a rhetorical question. "See, what I don't get is that Sally never wanted him in the first place. She said, 'No matter what you say now, Leon, I'm going to be the one taking care of it. I already have more than I can handle with the kid, going to school at night and you, Leon. What the hell do I need a dog for?' Leon shrugged again. "Guess I was the one who needed a dog. Guess that's what she was saying.

So I said I'd take care of him. I figured that would take care of the problem, you know what I mean?"

"But it didn't?"

"One night she says, 'I think Roy needs a walk. I think he needs to go.' So I get up to take him out, but she flaps her hand at me, picks up the leash and walks out the door. That was the last time I saw either one of them." He scratched the side of his nose with his thumb. "I guess she was the one who had to go, not Roy."

"The police . . ."

He shook his head.

"What about Roy? Did he . . ." I stopped to consider how to word what I wanted to say. But was there anything I could say that Leon hadn't thought of a thousand times over? "Did he ever turn up?" I asked.

Leon shook his head again. For a while, we just sat there. Leon didn't say anything and neither did I.

"That's why I was looking for you," he finally said, "to ask if you could find her for us."

"How long has she been gone?"

"Five years, two months, eleven days." He looked at his watch but he didn't report back to me.

"That long?"

Leon nodded.

"Without a word?"

He nodded again.

"How do you know she's still alive?"

"I don't," he said.

"There was no credit card activity that night? Or afterwards?"

"She didn't have it with her." He shrugged. "She'd just gone out to walk Roy."

"Did she have a driver's license?"

"We didn't have a car." As if that answered the question.

"What about social security payments made under her name? Did the police follow up on that?" I asked, thinking she could have a new name, a new social security card, a new life.

Or not.

"They didn't come up with anything," he said. "No sign of . . ."

I nodded.

He was probably in his forties, but he could have easily passed for sixty, the hair sticking out from under his baseball cap a steely gray, his skin the color of honeysuckle, that yellowish white that looks great on a plant and really lousy on a person. But it was mostly his eyes that made him look so old, his sad, dead eyes.

"Look, someone gone that long," I shook my head from side to side, "Leon, if your daughter's pregnant and that's, that's a problem, there are only a few choices that can be made. Why go through all this . . ."

"Pregnant? Wouldn't that be . . ." For a moment I thought he was going to laugh, but then he looked as if he was about to cry. "Madison's not pregnant," he said. "She's suspected of murder."

"Murder?" Why was he talking to me? His daughter didn't need her mother, she needed a good lawyer.

"They say she killed her doctor in a fit of rage. She gets them sometimes."

"Fits of rage?"

Leon nodded.

"And did she?"

Leon looked shocked. Then his old, sad eyes looked even older and sadder. "I don't think so."

"But you don't know?"

Leon shook his head.

"Did you ask her?"

"I did."

"Well, what did she say?"

"She didn't say anything. Madison doesn't speak. She stopped talking three days after her mother disappeared." He glanced around the run, as if to assess whether or not anyone might be listening, but there wasn't a soul near enough and besides, a Jack Russell had spotted a squirrel on a branch and was barking his fool head off. "I was hoping if you could find Sally for us," he whispered, "maybe Madison would start to talk again. Maybe she'd say what happened that day instead of letting people who weren't there say what was in her heart and what she did."

"Does she respond at all? Does she write things down? Does she nod for yes, shake her head for no?"

"Sometimes she draws pictures but even then, you can't always know for sure what she's thinking. There was a picture on the doctor's desk, a heart with a scraggly line going into it."

"Stabbing it?"

"It could look that way."

"And was she angry with her doctor?"

Leon nodded. "She has these tics and he was

treating her with Botox, to paralyze the muscles so that she'd . . ."

"Look more normal?"

" 'Pass for normal' is what he said. Can you imagine saying that to a patient? To a kid?"

Pass for normal, I thought. Isn't that what we all tried to do?

"But the last shot he gave her, he screwed up." Leon looked straight at me. "He said it would go away, that it would wear off, but meanwhile it made one eyelid droop and she was really freaked out by it."

"So was the picture an expression of her anger, maybe a threat, is that what the thinking is?"

He nodded. "She was his last patient of the afternoon. The receptionist was there when Madison showed up but not when she left. When she went back to the office, she found him, Dr. Bechman, dead."

"Stabbed in the heart?"

"With the Botox injection that Madison had refused."

That did it for me. No way could I turn down the case now.

"Alexander," I said. "It's Rachel Alexander." I gave him a card with my land line and my cell phone numbers.

It took him a while to find his card. It was in the third pocket he checked. I explained my fees and the advance I required. I said there might be some expenses in a case like this and that he'd have to cover those, too. And finally I told him I couldn't guarantee I'd find Sally after all these years, that there was only the slimmest chance of that, but if he still wanted me to try, I would. He said he did.

As for Madison, I hoped there'd be some other way to prove her innocence, if she were innocent, because even if I found her mother and even if the kid started talking again, told the cops what happened on that terrible day, said the blame wasn't hers, who says anyone would believe her?

Leon and I shook hands. Looking at his sad face, I wasn't sure who needed Sally more, the father or the daughter. And I had no idea at the time what I was committing myself to and how it would change my life.

"So the receptionist found the doctor when she got to work in the morning?" I asked, wondering why no one had called earlier to say he hadn't arrived home. "That must have been a shock."

"It wasn't in the morning. She went back that night."

"Why would she do that?"

Leon shrugged.

"You think maybe his wife called the receptionist—if he had a wife?"

"He did. He kept her picture on the desk. They all do that for some reason."

"So maybe she called the receptionist at home to ask where he was, if there was some meeting or conference or business dinner he'd neglected to mention?" Why call nine one one, I thought, when it might just be miscommunication, or a lack of communication?

"I wasn't told why she went back, just that she did."

"And the doctor was there, dead?"

"That's correct."

"What about Madison? Was she there?"

"No. Madison was at home. She came home right after her appointment."

"And did she seem upset?"

Leon didn't answer my question.

"Were you there when she arrived home, Leon?"

"What I say to you, what you say to me, it's confidential, right?"

"It is as far as I'm concerned."

He nodded. "Well, then," he said, "I wasn't at home when she got there, at least not right at that exact moment. I got home about an hour later."

"How do you know she was home an hour if she doesn't speak, if she doesn't communicate with you?"

"She always came straight home from . . ." Leon stopped and looked at me.

"So when you got home that day, did she seem upset? Was anything different, anything off?"

Leon shrugged.

"Not that you noticed?"

"No."

"And when did the police show up?"

"Late. After Madison had gone to bed."

"Were you asleep as well?"

"No."

"And when they came, they told you what had happened?"

"Yes."

"And they showed you the drawing?"

"No. They described it to me."

"And what else did they say?"

"That no one else was there, just Madison and Dr. Bechman. And then they said that the receptionist had gone back and that she'd found him."

"But they didn't tell you why? They didn't say she'd been called, nothing like that?"

"I never thought about it, about why she went back. They were saying that Madison was the only one there and that Dr. Bechman was dead. That's what was on my mind."

"What else did they say?" Wondering if they'd gone beyond implying to accusing.

"One detective said they'd been told that Madison had a history of violence and that she'd been very angry at Dr. Bechman for the perceived harm he'd done to her. Can you imagine? 'The perceived harm.' Then the second detective, he said they were told the doctor had ruined her eye. You see how it was going?"

I nodded, wondering what the cops thought about Leon that night, first his wife had gone missing and now this, the man getting agitated just telling me about it.

"What happened next?" I asked him.

Leon rubbed the back of his neck, looking away, looking anywhere but at me.

"Leon? I'm on your side. Speak up."

"I kind of . . . I got angry. She's my daughter and . . ."

"So you said what?"

"That they should be ashamed of themselves implying that a child with a disability had committed murder."

"Good. That's good you said that. And what was their . . . ?"

"I was yelling—well, yelling softly, if you know what I mean. I didn't want to wake Madison. But they remained calm. Cool. It was almost spooky. They asked if I was there. You know how they do that? They knew I wasn't. Trying to trip me up, to make me out to be a liar, the way they did when Sally disappeared." Leon's lips tight for a moment, his hands balled into fists. "I told them I hadn't been there. So then they asked what time Madison got home." He stopped again, looking at me, then looking away.

"Confidential, Leon, straight down the line."

"I said she'd come straight home, that she was home by 5:45. Then they asked if she'd been upset when she'd gotten home, if anything was out of the ordinary and I said no," talking faster now, "that she was fine, that she did her homework before dinner, watched TV afterwards, went to bed on time, everything as usual."

"But you weren't home."

"No, I wasn't." Looking me in the eye now, letting me know he'd do anything to protect his kid.

PERENNIAL DARK ALLEY

Be Cool: Elmore Leonard takes Chili Palmer into the world of rock stars, pop divas, and hip-hop gangsters—all the stuff that makes big box office.
0-06-077706-0

Eye of the Needle: For the first time in trade paperback, comes one of legendary suspense author **Ken Follett**'s most compelling classics.
0-06-074815-X

More Than They Could Chew: **Rob Roberge** tells the story of Nick Ray, a man whose addictions (alcohol, kinky sex, questionable friends) might only be cured by weaning him from oxygen.
0-06-074280-1

Men from Boys: A short story collection featuring some of the true masters of crime fiction, including Dennis Lehane, Lawrence Block, and Michael Connelly. These stories examine what it means to be a man amid cardsharks, revolvers, and shallow graves.
0-06-076285-3

Fender Benders: From **Bill Fitzhugh** comes the story of three people planning on making a "killing" on Nashville's music row.
0-06-081523-X

Cross Dressing: It'll take nothing short of a miracle to get Dan Steele, counterfeit cleric, out of a sinfully funny jam in this wickedly good tale from **Bill Fitzhugh.**
0-06-081524-8

The Fix: Debut crime novelist **Anthony Lee** tells the story of a young gangster who finds himself caught between honor and necessity.
0-06-059534-5

PERENNIAL
DARK ALLEY

An Imprint of HarperCollins*Publishers*
www.harpercollins.com

DKA 0405

**Sign up for the FREE
HarperCollins monthly
mystery newsletter,**

The Scene of the Crime,

**and get to know your favorite authors,
win free books, and be the first to learn
about the best new mysteries going on sale.**

To register, simply go to www.HarperCollins.com, visit our mystery channel page, and at the bottom of the page, enter your email address where it states "Sign up for our mystery newsletter." Then you can tap into monthly Hot Reads, check out our award nominees, sneak a peek at upcoming titles, and discover the best whodunits each and every month.

*Get to know the magnificent mystery authors
of HarperCollins and sign up today!*